TWO TRIBES

CHRIS BECKETT
TWO TRIBES

CORVUS

Published in hardback in Great Britain in 2020 by Corvus, an imprint of Atlantic Books Ltd.

This paperback edition published in 2021.

10 9 8 7 6 5 4 3 2 1

A CIP catalogue record for this book is available from the British Library.

Paperback ISBN: 978 1 78649 933 2
E-book ISBN: 978 1 78649 934 9

Printed and bound by CPI Group (UK) Ltd, Croydon, CR0 4YY

Corvus
An imprint of Atlantic Books Ltd
Ormond House
26–27 Boswell Street
London
WC1N 3JZ

www.corvus-books.co.uk

For Aphra, hoping you'll find out
that other futures are available.

ONE

Harry Roberts describes a shallow valley, like an indentation in a quilt, with green pastures and trees on either side. A pair of crows cross the sky ahead of him, three women outside a bus shelter turn to watch him pass.

I managed to obtain a permit to visit the area. The shallow valley is still there, of course, but in place of pasture there are sunflowers and maize growing out of bare brown earth. There are shacks by the roadside and on the low ridge to the south stands an automated watchtower built during the Chinese Protectorate and still in use, a steep cone of stained concrete the height of a ten-storey building rising out of the sunflowers to bring forth its own strange flowers in the form of satellite dishes, cameras and remote-controlled cannons. Beside the road is an old sign, so rusty as to be almost completely unreadable apart from the initial letter W, and pierced by multiple bullet holes from the time of the Warring Factions. (Give guns to a bunch of barely trained young men and they tend to want to play with them.) What we now call the Eastern Prefecture was then a stronghold of the Patriotic League.

I feel the holes with my fingertips: Thomas testing the wounds of Christ. The past is so tenuous, so small and far away, that it always seems slightly miraculous to me that pieces of it are still around us. Driving through that soft green quilted landscape two and a half centuries ago, Harry passed the very same sign that I saw and touched. 'Welcome to Suffolk', it read and he reached it at half past six. He doesn't mention bullet holes. The Warring Factions were still in the future and, though he thought of the time he lived in as a troubled one, the idea that British politics might degenerate into civil war would have seemed to him far-fetched.

I look back across the old county boundary into Essex and towards London and close my eyes to make the fields green again, with big green billowy trees, and crows high up in the cool blue sky. And I imagine his car approaching from the Essex side, billowing out its invisible fumes. It was a fairly small red car, somewhat old and scratched, and, though it had four seats, Harry Roberts was the only person inside it. He was forty-six years old. It was 26 August 2016, 250 years ago, before the Protectorate, before the Warring Factions and, I suppose, before the Catastrophe, though 2014, 2015 and 2016 had each in turn been the hottest year ever yet recorded and far off in the Arctic regions, the ice was already breaking up.

Something shifted when Harry crossed into Suffolk.

The way he puts it in his diary is that he'd been experiencing life as 'hollow', like the toy food that was made at the time for children to play with: hollow oranges and apples and hamburgers, moulded from coloured plastic. And yet as he crossed the county boundary, he suddenly noticed the world had become nourishing once more:

the trees, the fields, the winding road, the women chatting at the bus stop in the evening sun . . . It was sufficient again, somehow. He was savouring the feeling of being alive.

Harry was an architect. Janet, his wife of many years, had left him eight months previously. They had no children, their only son Danny having died five years previously of meningitis at the age of two. Harry was driving himself, as people often did then, in a metal car with an internal combustion engine that consumed a litre of refined oil every ten minutes, to the weekend retreat of a couple called Karina and Richard. Karina was what was called a 'food writer' – strange as it now seems, she made a living by describing the food in restaurants – and Richard ran his own 'actuarial consultancy' in London, which was at that time a global centre for lending and borrowing money. They were friends of Harry's twin sister and only sibling, Ellie. Ellie and her husband were also going to be there, and it had been Ellie's idea that Harry should join them. 'You spend much too much time moping around on your own, bro.'

Crawling his way out of London, whose streets at that time of day were packed with several hundred thousand crawling lumps of metal (each one of them burning a litre or so of fuel every ten minutes, and emitting the acrid residue into the air), Harry had been resenting Ellie's interference, her attempts to organize him and make him conform to her idea of what a person in his situation ought to be doing. Why on earth would he want to waste a whole weekend with her friends, he'd been thinking, when after all he had friends of his own? But now, he had to admit, he was looking forward to it.

*

Karina and Ellie came out to meet Harry as he pulled up into the drive of the half-timbered cottage. Karina was tall and imposing, dark-haired and dark-eyed, and wearing white; Ellie was a short, lively woman in a pretty red dress, who observed her twin brother with her characteristic combination of affection, pride and exasperation. She'd worried about him a great deal during the months after Janet left, and he knew she found his passivity irritating. There were things a person could do to move on from a setback like that, and Harry seemed to her to stubbornly refuse to do any of them.

Karina led them through the house. In the living room Richard, Karina's husband, and Phil, Harry's brother-in-law, stood up to greet him from one of three elegant grey sofas. While Karina was very good-looking in a dark-haired Mediterranean way, Richard, with his untidy red hair, short legs and slight pot belly, could almost be described as ugly if it were not for a smouldering energy which was apparent as soon as you met him. Phil, who'd been a friend of Harry's even before he'd got together with Ellie, was a tall thin man, rather intense, with large hands and a pointed head that he kept completely shaved.

The room was beautifully laid out, thought Harry, looking about him with a professional eye. Modern design had been cleverly married with many of the original features of the three separate workmen's cottages that this had once been: the black wooden beams, the uneven floor.

There was a pleasing smell that mingled wood polish and old woodsmoke with the warm scented fat of a lamb dish cooking in the kitchen.

*

The two largest bedrooms, each with its own bathroom, had been allocated to the couples, but there were two smaller bedrooms, and Harry had been given one of these, at the back, which had a bathroom right next to it. (This all seemed quite opulent to Harry, given that this was Richard and Karina's second home, but it wouldn't have seemed as luxurious to him as it does to us now, for this was a time when almost all English homes had at least one bathroom with hot and cold running water.) He unpacked his bag, laid the notebook he used as a diary on the bedside table and checked his hair in a mirror that hung over a chest of drawers. He had a pleasant, nicely proportioned face, open and friendly even in repose or sadness. Harry smiled at his own reflection. Outside the bedroom window, the pleasantly rolling Suffolk fields glowed in the evening sun.

Downstairs the others were talking about their teenaged children but tactfully stopped when he came to join them. (Harry had learnt from his sister that the two couples had become friends because of their children: Ellie and Phil's older son, Nathan, played in the same rock band as Richard and Karina's son Greg.) Karina asked him about his work and where he lived. She was a very attentive host. Having put a question to him, she would compose herself into the optimal posture for conveying attention. Richard, on the other hand, rapped out his questions, one after another, absorbing the answers with a slight frown, as if continually puzzled by Harry's reasoning.

When the evening meal was ready, Richard sat at the end of the table, with Ellie and Phil on one side and Harry on the other. By the time Karina brought out the lamb dish – her being a food writer, it was of course exquisite – they were talking about 'Brexit'.

Britain was in those days a member of a supranational body called the European Union, which, while not a federal state, had acquired many of the characteristics of such a state – a currency, a parliament, a court, a legal system, a president, free movement within its borders and so on – and it was unpopular with a substantial section of the population for that and other reasons. Strange as it seems to us now, this was a time in which virtually the entire adult population of the country was entitled to choose the government. Very occasionally other more specific matters were also put to the public in a kind of vote known as a *referendum*. Recently, and against the advice of almost all of the major British institutions that embodied authority and expertise, the country had voted in such a referendum to leave the European Union. British Exit. Brexit.

From our perspective, when the European Union and the British state no longer exist, this all seems pretty trivial stuff by comparison with what was to come, but it was a big thing then, and the five of them round that table were members of a class in shock. They'd been unhappy about political developments before, of course, but this was completely different. It felt personal somehow, as if they themselves were under attack. And so they grieved and raged, obsessively itemizing, over and over again, all the precious things that would be destroyed by this reckless vote, all the reasons why the vote should not have happened, all the ways in which it had been unfair.

Phil and Richard, in particular, were very agitated. In fact, they were almost shouting. Everyone in the room had some version of the received pronunciation accent, 'RP', characteristic of the professional middle class at the time, which lacked the marked regional variations found in the speech of less educated people.

(It was the rough equivalent, I suppose, of the somewhat Sinified English pronunciation of our own more educated classes.) In the earlier conversation, before they got on to Brexit, all five of them had to varying degrees slightly softened this RP speech, as they habitually did, by making small concessions to the demotic speech of London and the south-east – 'a glottal stop here,' as Harry puts it, 'a nasal twang there' – but now, in their anger, Richard and Phil had ramped up their accents to the register with the highest possible social status. It made Harry think of frightened animals fluffing up their fur to look as big and fearsome as possible.

'If Parliament had any guts it would simply disregard the result of the referendum,' Phil boomed, and Richard roared that it had been ridiculous to ask the general public to make a decision on a matter as complex as this. Ellie observed more quietly that, since many blatant lies had been told by the 'Leave' side, the referendum result was surely invalid.

'Absolutely!' her husband bellowed. 'Absolutely! And a question of this complexity can't be reduced to—'

'And what about Scotland, for God's sake?' Richard butted in. 'There's no mandate for Brexit there, or in Northern Ireland, or in London, or in—'

'Or in pretty much any city with a reasonably high concentration of educated people,' interrupted Phil, for they kept interrupting one another, not to disagree but because their need to agree was so vehement. 'We shouldn't beat around the bush here; this is a victory for ignorance and stupidity!'

'Ignorance, stupidity *and* racism,' Karina amended. She was worried for Sofija, her lovely Lithuanian cleaner. There'd been an ugly upsurge of verbal attacks on foreigners by strangers on the streets and on public transport, and Sofija had been told to 'fuck off back to whatever shithole you come from' by a total stranger at a bus stop.

Harry wondered whether this had happened to Luiza, the Polish cleaner who he'd recently let go. Luiza actually *wasn't* particularly lovely, and he'd decided he'd had enough when, thinking to be humorous, she'd referred to her black neighbours as 'dirty monkeys'.

'Yes, and we *need* those people here,' Richard growled. 'The economy needs them. Hospitals, service industries, farms, the care sector: they all depend on immigrant workers.'

'Apart from anything else,' Karina said, 'where are we going to find a decent plumber? Most of the British ones are either incompetent or crooks. And that's assuming you can even get hold of one.'

The group shared stories for a while about various impressive services they'd received from bright, courteous, hard-working migrants from Eastern Europe until Richard moved the conversation on again by suggesting there may have been some Russian interference in the election: a relatively new theme, but one that was to become more prominent and better substantiated in the months ahead.

Then they returned, as if to the chorus of some long and tragic folk song, to a lament that the vote had happened at all. Why, why, why had a decision of such great importance been entrusted to people who were simply not qualified to understand its complexities?

They were still at the early stage, this little group, still reeling, still trying to construct a shared narrative about what had gone wrong. But they were also, though they were not aware of it, constructing a new story about themselves and their relationship to the world.

*

Harry felt oddly detached. Their aggrieved, frightened mood was out of kilter with the contentment that had come over him so unexpectedly somewhere between London and the Suffolk border. For a while he zoned out completely and instead contemplated this exciting new feeling of being reconciled with the way his life had turned out. There were new possibilities now, there was no longer a wall holding him back.

'This country's reputation is in tatters,' Richard was pronouncing when Harry next paid attention. 'We've made ourselves an utter laughing stock.'

'Perhaps you could clear the plates, Rich,' Karina suggested, and, without answering her or breaking the flow of his tirade even for a moment, Richard duly gathered up the crockery with his powerful, hairy hands. (There was a particular way, Harry thought, in which very bright, very driven, very focused people stacked plates.)

'The smart money's already looking elsewhere,' Richard went on. 'But these people don't seem to either know or care just how much damage that's going to do the British economy . . . '

'I've made a summer pudding,' Karina said, 'but shall we have a fifteen-minute break before I fetch it out?'

Harry took the opportunity to go outside for a cigarette.

These days the small road that goes past the cottage is a cul-de-sac ending in a marsh just half a kilometre further on, but the cottage still stands. It's three dwellings again now, each one inhabited by a three- or four-generation family. Behind it is a yard with vegetable plots, chicken runs and various sheds, backing on to a field.

Maize is grown in that field now – this is a crowded country, too poor to import food – but back then it was pasture, and a row of mature chestnut trees divided it from Karina and Richard's garden, with a bench beneath them where Harry went to sit and smoke. I close my eyes and do my best to imagine Harry there under those big, dark, rustling trees that no longer exist: a handsome, muscly, solidly built man – he played rugby football in his school days – with thick, curly brown hair. He liked to dress well, and I picture him in a light grey summer jacket, nicely pressed trousers and fashionable shoes. Like his sister he has interested, lively eyes. He was about the same age then as I am now.

Harry drew in a treacly cloud of smoke. It was a habit of his youth that he'd given up for many years but had taken up again in the aftermath of his separation from Janet. He'd stop soon, he decided. He didn't like the clogged lungs in the morning, and he no longer really needed the primitive comfort of something warm to suck on, sorry as he'd be to give up this simple pleasure.

He exhaled slowly. How good that smoke tasted! The light was fading, the leaves were jostling about above him in the evening breeze and, even through the smoke, he caught the earthy aroma rising from the cooling ground. A car passed on the road in front of the house and a cow flicked and snuffled in the field behind him. He leant back and wriggled his shoulders into a more comfortable position. Several small bats were working the air above the garden. Mysterious creatures, he thought, and, as he smoked, he watched them make a long series of zigzag passes between him and the cottage, sometimes one at a time, sometimes two or three all at once.

Presently Ellie came down to join him.

'You okay, bro?'

'I'm fine.'

Birds squawked and fluttered in the tree above their heads in a dispute over the ownership of a roost, and a single feather came drifting down on to the lawn.

'I wish you'd stop smoking,' Ellie said as she sat down beside him. 'I don't want to lose you before I have to.'

'I know. I really should. I'll tell you what: I'll make this my last packet.'

'That would be good.'

They sat in silence for a while, these forty-six-year-old twins, watching the aerobatics of the little bats. Then Ellie looked round at her brother. 'Jesus, Richard is a bit bloody full-on, isn't he, when he gets a bee in his bonnet? And he *always* gets Phil going too.'

Harry took in another delicious draught of smoke. 'To be fair, Ellie, Phil's always been quite capable of having a good rant without anyone's help. And there are a *lot* of people ranting about Brexit just now.'

'Not surprisingly.'

'No, of course not. I don't think we've seen anything like it in our lifetimes.'

'I guess it gets a bit wearing, though, when you've got other things on your mind.'

'It doesn't bother me at all. It's not as if I don't agree. I just thought a little break would be nice. It's one of the best things about smoking, actually. You've got a reason to go off by yourself from time to time and take a break from human company, without it seeming standoffish or rude. A non-smoker couldn't just say, "I'm going to go and sit by myself for ten minutes."'

'You need to start moving forward now, Harry. Come back into the world. It's been a good many months, and I know I keep saying this but things really weren't great between you and Janet for a very long time.'

He smiled. 'I really am fine, Ellie.' Drawing one last tarry lungful, he stamped out his cigarette and turned to face her. 'I'm not just saying that! In fact, I'm more than fine. I feel absolutely great.'

This took her by surprise. 'Seriously? Do you honestly mean that?'

He laughed at her bewilderment. 'I really do. Janet was, of course, absolutely right to leave. Absolutely right! Things *weren't* good between us at all. In fact, we'd had an absolutely *miserable* marriage, ever since . . . well, ever since, you know . . . ' He flagged momentarily under that old weight of grief but managed to shrug it away. 'And you're quite right, even *before* that, it wasn't great. We'd wasted more than enough time on it. It just so happens that Janet had the courage to face that before I did, and that was hurtful to my pride. But she was right and I ought to be grateful to her. I'm finally looking forward to the future.'

Ellie took his hand. 'That's amazing, Harry. I'm so pleased. I've been really worried for you.'

'You know how it is when there's been a persistent noise going on in the background and suddenly you notice that it isn't there any more? It was like that driving over here. I started out every bit as miserable as usual and then, along the way, I suddenly noticed that the misery had gone! I'm sure it will come back. In fact, I think it's quite likely that tomorrow I'll be as miserable as ever – there's so much to do still, so much to rebuild, so many things to grieve over – but this is a start, isn't it? This is my head telling me it doesn't always have to be grim. Remind me about it, won't you, if I seem to forget?'

'I certainly will. I'm very happy for you, Harry, very happy, and very relieved.'

'You go back to the others, dear sis.' He kissed her on the cheek. 'I'll be along in a minute.'

*

The others were *still* talking about Brexit when he rejoined them, obsessively going over and over what had happened like (as Harry puts it) 'the dazed victims of a car crash'. Richard was holding forth about the contempt for experts that had been evident in the 'Leave' campaign. This had become a major strand in the emerging narrative being constructed by the 'Remain' half of the population and it was something that troubled Harry too: he had written in his diary only a couple of days before about 'the sheer pig-headedness of climate change deniers who think they know better than people who've dedicated their whole lives to researching the subject'.

But now, as he settled himself back among them, he was struck by something quite different: everyone around the table *was* an expert. Karina was an expert on food (and also, incidentally, a qualified barrister). Phil was an international authority on land tenure in late medieval Europe. Ellie had trained for seven years to work as a GP. Richard had a Ph.D. in probability theory and advised financial institutions in the City of London on their actuarial strategies. And Harry himself was an architect, which had also taken seven years of training, even if all he seemed to do nowadays was to design people's kitchen extensions. And *that* was what made this so personal. Comfortably off as they might be, none of these people were barons or oligarchs, living off the rents from accumulated assets. They earned their living by knowing things, and they were dependent on people listening to them. There had been a rising tide of irrationality around the world – religious fundamentalists, flat-earthers, anti-vaxxers – and Brexit was part of this strange new assault on what lay at the core of their standing in society.

'You're very quiet, Harry,' observed Richard.

Harry shrugged. 'Well, I'm sad about it all, obviously. I've always been very pro-EU. That little circle of stars on my number plate has felt very reassuring somehow: a collection of countries working together in a big bad world. In fact, I like the EU so much I'd have been happy for it to become a single state.'

'Not sure I'd go *that* far,' Richard muttered.

'But I will just say,' Harry said, 'that I can *sort of* understand why people might be sceptical about economic experts, or even experts in general, after what happened to the financial system in 2008. That was a fairly major failure on the part of experts, wasn't it?'

For a moment, they all glared at him. It wasn't that they couldn't see his point. What jarred was that Harry had unilaterally changed the rules of the conversation. Up to now this had been a collaborative endeavour, an exercise in mutual reinforcement, but he had turned it into a debate. They were reasonable people, though, and quickly swallowed their irritation, conceding in various ways that there was some truth in what he said.

'No, that's a fair point,' Karina said, standing up to go and fetch the dessert. (A curious feature of early twenty-first-century British English was that people often said 'No' to signify agreement.) 'I'm sure a lot of people wanted to stick it to the system.'

'And the geography's interesting, I think,' Harry went on. 'It's almost like nationalists and unionists in Belfast. In one area it just seems obvious to most people that we belong in the EU. A few miles down the road it seems equally obvious to most people that we don't belong there at all. I mean, here in the east of England, for instance, Norwich and the area round Cambridge voted Remain, but everywhere else voted Leave, regardless of whether you're talking about Tory toytowns like Southwold or Saffron Walden, or rough working-class towns like Stevenage or Yarmouth.'

'But it's those working-class towns that are going to suffer the *most* if this—' Richard began.

'You were at Cambridge, weren't you, Harry?' interrupted Karina, who had returned with the pudding.

'I was indeed,' Harry said. 'And of course Ellie and I grew up in Norwich.'

The little group moved into the living room for coffee and tea and Karina's handmade chocolates, and then gradually made their way upstairs. The only one sleeping alone, Harry sat up in bed for what must have been at least an hour, meticulously writing up the day. The window was open. He could hear those big trees where he'd gone to smoke swaying and rustling in the darkness, and from time to time a night bird of some kind gave an odd tremulous cry from a wood beyond the pasture. A car came past at one point and, in his notebook, Harry imagines it out there in its own little pool of light as it moves through that gently undulating landscape, further and further away from him, until it's swallowed up by the quietness of the night.

I run my fingers over the page. I feel the indentations and the tiny tears in the paper that he made as he pressed down with his nib, and for a moment I can almost sense the coolness on my skin of the night air around the cottage as if I was actually there, and hear its silence, and smell its earthy smell.

TWO

The day after my return to London, I walk, as usual, the three miles from my watery home to the offices of the Cultural Institute where I am employed as a historian and archivist. In my small, stuffy cubicle with its yellow cardboard walls, boxes of old notebooks are stacked on the floor and the desk. They are a collection of old diaries from the early twenty-first century, assembled many years ago by another historian for a project he never completed. The entire collection was recently sold to the Institute by one of the historian's grandchildren, and I have the task of going through them and recording the dates they cover, the circumstances of the writer, a summary of their contents and an assessment of their authenticity. (It seems the historian paid quite generously for these old notebooks at a time when many people were struggling to find enough to eat, and there are a number of obvious forgeries among them.)

Needless to say, this cache is where I found Harry's diaries, the most comprehensive and articulate in the collection. But what has really captured my imagination is the discovery that, by an extraordinary stroke of luck, one of the other diaries actually overlaps with his, so that I have two accounts – both genuine, as far as I can tell – of some of the same events by two people with quite different backgrounds. My colleagues were very excited when I told them this, but they all lost interest when they learnt that neither of these diaries is a chronicle of major events and neither of the diarists could be described in any way as a significant player. For myself, though, I'm still excited.

I work hard from seven thirty in the morning till six in the evening, keen to prove that my trip to Suffolk has not affected my productivity, then I head downstairs and along a corridor to the cubicle of my friend Cally who works on the records of the Warring Factions period.

'Hello, Zoe!' She greets me with a kiss on the cheek. 'I didn't think you were back until tomorrow!'

'Well, here I am. I've been working on those diaries all day and I've had a brilliant idea. Fancy a glass of Shaoxing?'

We emerge into the intense heat of a London summer. The air is thick and treacly, with a strong whiff of drains and rotten fruit behind the cooking smells, and the street is a chaotic mass of barrows, bicycles, traders and beggars. Two militiamen ride by on an electric cart, both of them wearing shiny white helmets and those big hemispherical goggles that show them things that mere eyes would miss. (A black arrow jiggling up and down above a person's head indicates a criminal record, or so I've been told, a flashing red arrow that they aren't carrying valid ID, a blue arrow that they're currently under surveillance.) I wait for them to pass. It's said they have directional microphones inside those helmets that enable them to home in on conversations and my instinct is to let them know as little about me as possible, even if what I have to say is completely innocuous.

'So let me tell you my idea!' I say, as we launch out into the crowd. 'You know I told you about two of the diaries linking up?'

Across the road, on the wall of the old Borough Council offices, is one of those murals from the days of the Protectorate, faded and flaking now, but with the usual stencilled portraits of the Eleven Great Sages still just about visible: Confucius and Marx at one end and Hu Shuang, the Great Synthesizer, at the other. 'Support the work of our Guiding Body!' says the caption beneath the picture, in English and Hanzi characters. 'Study and apply the Nine Principles!'

'Yeah, of course. What a coincidence! When you think of how many people there were in England even back then, and what a small proportion of them would have kept diaries, and what a tiny proportion of those diaries would have survived long enough to be collected by that historian guy.'

'I know. It's absolutely amazing. On the way back from Suffolk I was thinking about how to make the best use of them. I've spent all these years on the news media and social media archives, and recently all this time on this cache of diaries, but what's the point of collecting information if we don't process it into something meaningful? And I thought, those two diaries might not deal with the kinds of events that historians normally talk about, but they do tell a story. Why don't I make them into a sort of . . . well, a historical novel, I suppose you could call it? Obviously I'll have to add stuff to fill in the gaps, but I could use the diaries as the basis of it, and draw on all the work I've done on the archives to provide an authentic background.'

We steer round a hawker who's sidled up to offer us black-market cheese.

'That's a bit deviant, though, isn't it, Zoe? A *novel*? That's definitely not what they pay us to do!'

'They pay us to reconstruct the past. And that's what I'd be doing, isn't it? A reconstruction, based on the diaries, but also drawing on all I've learnt, to create a kind of snapshot of that early period when things began to unravel.'

'But also drawing on your own imagination, which is not what we—'

'I'll need to flesh it out, yes. I'll fill out the dialogue a bit. I'll add some detail to the scenes. I might make up a story or two about minor characters to help the reader understand the historical context. But, you know, without imagination, history is nothing.'

(I really believe that, by the way. You get things wrong if you make guesses, but why collect these fragments of bone if not to try to imagine the living creature they came from?)

Cally laughs. 'That sounds *very* unorthodox, Zoe. You want to be careful. Our workscreens are their property, don't forget, and they can look at them whenever they like.'

Another pair of militiaman pass by, this time on foot, on the far side of the road. One of them looks in our direction. His goggle eyes make me think of those huge praying mantises I keep finding on my window ledge. It's impossible to tell if he's focusing on us or something else, let alone what arrows he sees above our heads, though I know that over both of us there hovers the modest white star that signifies a Level 3 Associate of the Guiding Body. (It confers a bit of status, but also makes us more visible.) In any case, he turns back to his colleague and they carry on.

'I thought the idea would appeal to you,' I say. 'Life is all about guesswork, isn't it? Everyday life, I mean, not just history. We create the world from fragments all the time. We get it wrong, of course, but if you're not prepared to make guesses, there's hardly a world left at all.'

THREE

On Monday morning, as Harry was getting ready to drive back to London, Charlie Higgins left his parents' house on the outskirts of the town of Breckham, and walked to the Heath Road to be picked up from his usual spot opposite the empty brick shell of the old suitcase factory. He was twenty-four, a kind young man, good with animals, loved by his little nephews and nieces, popular with elderly neighbours, but he wasn't particularly bright or good-looking and he had no special talents apart from being big and fairly strong.

He climbed into the minibus and it moved off again, burning up diesel oil inside its four cylinders at about five or six litres an hour. 'All right, Jake?' he called out to the driver. 'All right, everyone?'

'Morning, Charlie,' Jake said. The others grunted.

Ben, Brett, Tom and Mac were already on board, along with the two Polish guys, Clem and Alex. And today, as on every other day, Charlie braced himself for the teasing he would have to put up with on the six-mile journey, and for the things which he suspected were teases, but wasn't quite sure. He'd never been good at detecting irony.

It wouldn't be quite true to say that Charlie was picked on. A lot of teasing went on between the other men too – it was the main source of entertainment on this daily commute – and the two Poles in particular had to put up with a good deal of banter, but (at least from Charlie's perspective) everyone else, the Poles included, gave as good as they got, while he could never find the right tone, the right mixture of playfulness and aggression. His attempts at jokes usually fell flat, and even when he did get a laugh, he was uneasily aware that the others were probably laughing at him rather than with him. Yet if he abandoned altogether the exhausting many-layered game of male verbal jousting and tried to be straightforwardly friendly, that didn't quite work either.

'How was Thailand, Mac?' he asked one of the older men, who'd been away on holiday the previous week.

'Thailand was shit, mate,' Mac said. 'Or at least the bits of it I can remember. Can't speak for the rest.' Charlie thought that Mac was making some sort of joke, but he wasn't sure if he understood and had no idea how to follow through. It was as if Mac had deliberately made it impossible for Charlie to continue the conversation.

Charlie's biggest conversational successes were on the subject of Brexit. There were certain verities that you could express on that topic, without any irony, and still be sure that everyone would agree (or everyone except the Poles, who usually remained silent on the topic, though Alex would occasionally mutter at the Englishmen that they were all bloody idiots). 'Why can't they just get on with it?' Charlie would say, for instance, or 'Just fucking *leave!*' and nine times out of ten he would earn growls of assent, or even have the gratifying experience of having started a conversation.

So he tried it again this morning. 'What the fuck's happening with Brexit?' he said. 'It's doing my fucking head in. Why don't we just walk away?'

But it didn't work this time. The others liked to go over Brexit fairly regularly, rehearsing and refining the various articles of their steadily hardening tribal creed, but there were limits all the same and Charlie had said something quite similar on Friday.

'You just want us all to cheer you like we did last week, don't you, Charlie?' observed Ben the engineer, who was crueller and less patient than the other men. And for the rest of the journey, Charlie felt his shame prickling in the roots of his hair.

They didn't *dislike* him. He knew that. When he met them individually at the plant, they would be perfectly pleasant to him, even Ben, and some could be quite affectionate. Jake, who was also the oldest of them, could be positively paternal. But what saddened him was that all of them could see through him and knew him for what he was, which was to say, nothing special. He didn't dispute their judgement. It was how his dad and his brothers saw him too, all three of them more able and more worldly than Charlie. Still, it would be nice to find people who saw something else in him – and not just his mum and grandma, who doted on Charlie as the baby of the family, but were generally agreed to be nothing special either.

Charlie and the other men all worked in a small power station on the edge of a forest, where straw and other farm waste were incinerated to generate electricity. Some of the men had responsibility for various pieces of machinery, others for driving the fork-lift trucks that were used for unloading bales of straw from lorries and moving them about the plant. Charlie's job was mainly sweeping up and scrubbing down. He was heading across to the main building where he'd receive his instructions for the morning when Jake called him back. 'Don't take any notice of Ben, Charlie,' he said, patting him on the arm. 'He's a sarky sod. I think it's great the way you speak out for Brexit. You should be proud of yourself. You're standing up for your country. You're standing up for what the people voted for.'

FOUR

Harry emailed his wife Janet and asked to meet. Her response was wary: *What are we going to talk about that we haven't talked about before?* Harry had been extremely awkward over the past few months. He'd refused to accept a separation that he hadn't chosen and he still lived in what had been their home, hating it, but carrying on anyway, all by himself in the rooms of the tastefully renovated house which had, a hundred years ago, housed an entire Edwardian family.

I'm not going to be difficult any more, I promise, he told her. *I really do want to move things on.*

They met that evening in a pub in a part of London known then as Wood Green. (I've looked for the building but it no longer exists. The Wood Green area was badly damaged by street fighting during the Warring Factions.) Harry arrived at 6.50, determined not to irritate his wife by being late. Janet arrived at 7.10. She had a rather long face suited to seriousness – when they first met she'd reminded Harry of the twentieth-century author Virginia Woolf – and as she stood just inside the door, looking round for him in the big, shabby, wood-panelled room, her whole body seemed to him to be braced in anticipation of having to ward off unreasonable demands and unwelcome pressure. When he stood up and called out to her, she approached him uneasily and stood as stiffly as a statue as he greeted her with a kiss on the cheek. He'd already bought her a glass of Merlot and she eyed it without enthusiasm as she sat down. 'I can't stop very long,' she told him. She had grown up in Scotland and still had a trace of a soft middle-class Edinburgh accent.

'Of course,' he said. 'But I honestly don't think this needs to take much time.' He drew a breath. There were so many intense and contradictory emotions wrapped up in the simple fact of being in her presence.

She did that particular kind of shrug that means, 'I'm in your hands. I have no idea what this is about.' Harry felt as if he was standing on the bank of a cold river, steeling himself to dive in.

'Okay, well, I wanted to say first of all that you were quite right about all this, and you were very brave. And I was wrong and a coward.'

She studied his face for several seconds. 'I suppose you've met someone, have you?'

'No, I haven't. I haven't even tried yet.'

She seemed unsure whether to believe him or not. Their last communication had been an exchange of text messages only a couple of weeks ago, and he'd been as difficult and hostile as ever. She couldn't imagine what else could possibly have brought about such a sudden change of heart.

'But I'd like to meet someone else,' he said, 'and I know you would too. You're absolutely right. You've been right all along. We've wasted far too long over this. Danny would always have stood between us in one way or another.'

There were tears in her eyes now, and that brought tears into his.

'And another thing you've always been right about . . . ' he said. Here he had to pause to collect himself. 'Another thing you've been right about is that what happened to Danny is my fault.'

Harry's hands were shaking. He'd never conceded this before, never spoken it aloud to anyone at all. Janet had been a very anxious parent and Danny an exceptionally precious, almost miraculous child who'd arrived after many harrowing years of fertility treatment, just at the point when they were thinking of giving up. Janet had worried constantly about his health and often called the doctor. The locum GP who'd been on call that night had suggested that, unless his condition deteriorated, they leave it to the morning before getting Danny seen. Harry had been fine with this, but Janet became convinced that his condition had become worse and wanted to take Danny to a nearby hospital to be checked out. Harry had resisted this.

They could have been seen at the hospital completely free of charge – an extraordinary thing, of course, from our perspective, and pretty much unprecedented in human history – so that, unlike most parents these days, Janet and Harry weren't faced with the agonizing dilemma as to whether this was the moment to dip into the roll of yuan stowed under their bed, or whether they should hold their savings back for a still more serious emergency in the future. But it was ten past eleven at night, Harry was fed up with Janet's constant fretting, and he was very tired. He didn't fancy sitting up for hours, drinking nasty coffee out of cardboard cups under the cold white lights of a hospital waiting room. He told Janet she was being silly and that he'd had enough of these dramas. By the time it had become obvious that their son was very ill indeed, it was too late.

But now, quite unexpectedly, Janet reached out and put her hand over his. 'Well, the other nine times I insisted on having him checked out, you were right. So you were very unlucky that this was the occasion you finally took your stand. I had a part in this too, Harry. I'd cried wolf once too often. Plus, I'm a grown-up and if I really didn't agree with you, I could have taken him to the hospital myself.'

These had always been Harry's defences against the charge that he was to blame for his own son's death. Just as he'd never accepted responsibility, so she had always denied that her own behaviour had played a part.

Janet laughed. Her hand was still over his and she gave him a friendly squeeze. 'Look at the pair of us! Blubbing our eyes out together in the middle of a pub!'

Blubbing our eyes out was something of an exaggeration, Harry thought, but his eyes and hers were certainly moist. He took his hand from hers to put it round her shoulders and give her a kiss. She didn't feel like a statue this time, and she even kissed him back, though she withdrew as quickly as she could without actually being unfriendly.

'That's better,' he said. 'I hated us being enemies.'

She laughed. 'You insisted on us being enemies, Harry.'

'I know.'

'And yet you also insisted we shouldn't split up.'

'I know. It made no sense, did it?'

He studied her face. That sweet seriousness, that intensity. For the first time in many months, or even years, he remembered a time when her Scottish voice had sounded soft and caressing and not prim and taut. A single ember was still glowing even now under all that cold grey ash. Perhaps, after all, they—

'No, Harry,' she said, though he hadn't spoken his thought out loud. She squeezed his hand again. 'Bless you, but no. Let's go through with this, eh? Go through with it as friends, not as enemies. I mean, be honest, we were never that great together, even before Danny. I've always been too demanding for you. I've always made you feel controlled and overruled. And you're too pliant for me, and too gentle. I love you for it, don't misunderstand me, but it drives me nuts. It makes me feel I've nothing to kick against. We'd have made the best of it, if Danny had lived. Of course we would. And we wouldn't have done so badly, I'm sure. But we've got a second chance now. It's the one good thing our tragedy has given us: a chance to start over, now we're older and understand ourselves so much better than we did when we first met.'

He picked up his wine, turned the glass from side to side in his hand. He knew how often during their marriage he'd privately regretted that the two of them had ended up together, particularly during the miserable years when the programmes of fertility treatment, one after another, had become the focus of their lives and Janet's consuming obsession. And she was right: controlled and overruled had been exactly how he'd felt. He liked to think he could be assertive when he really needed to be, but should it really have to be such hard work just to hold your own against your life's partner?

'You're right,' he said finally. After all, this was what had come to him on that drive down to Suffolk, this was what had released him that evening from months of unhappiness: the realization that Janet was right and that the freedom he'd often fantasized about was now actually his. 'I'm dreadfully sad about it, but you're right.'

'I'm sad about it too.'

He took a gulp of wine. 'Okay. Let's sort out a divorce, in whatever way turns out to be simplest, and let's sell the house and split the money fifty-fifty. Do you agree? I'll find myself a flat, like you did. I hate living in that house anyway. It feels like a mausoleum. To be perfectly honest, I've only been hanging on in there out of spite.'

She laughed at that. 'Well, when you're ready, Harry, and if you're sure you're happy with that, it sounds like a plan. It's not like either of us needs to support the other financially.'

'You should take more than half of our savings,' Harry said, 'such as they are. Seeing as you earn more than me, and work way harder.'

Janet had been an architect too, but hadn't felt sufficiently challenged, so she'd built up a business that designed and ran large exhibitions and other public events.

'Just have a think and tell me how you think we should do it,' he said. 'I promise not to be obstructive. And the furniture and stuff . . . Well, apart from my books and the things that came from my parents, I'm happy for you to take whatever you think is fair and leave me the rest.'

She laughed again. 'There you go, Harry. Pliant. Gentle. You know that never in a million years would I agree to you taking whatever you want.'

He smiled and shrugged. 'Well, I've tried to be stubborn these last few months and look how obnoxious I became as a result. It just doesn't suit me, does it?'

Later, when he was at home again, Harry felt numb. He called his sister, and she congratulated him, and told him she was sure he'd done the right thing. This was reassuring but it left him even more numb afterwards, because telling her had made it more real.

Restless and hollow, he ate most of a tub of chocolate-chip ice cream, somehow unable to stop eating at the point of mild nausea and for several minutes afterwards. He tried to watch TV. He knew the numbness was dammed-up tears, but though he screwed up his face a few times and tried to force them out, he couldn't find the trigger to release them. He was briefly tempted to go out and buy cigarettes but managed to resist the impulse. Instead, sitting in front of the television without taking anything in, he began to play with his phone.

There he is, two and a half centuries ago, at one end of a large sofa in his living room. The heavy curtains are drawn, and the only light in the room is an electric lamp in the corner to the right of the window, and the large TV in front of him that makes the walls and ceiling flicker with its constantly fluctuating bluish glow. There are shelves of books behind him, framed pictures on all four walls, and on the mantelpiece, in a silver frame, stands a large black-and-white photograph of the cheerful little toddler who died five years ago. To the left of the window an elegant ceramic vase stands on its own small table, and above it hangs a little antique portrait, done in enamels, of a man in his middle years who is dressed, like a Jane Austen character, in the style of the late eighteenth or early nineteenth century: a black double-breasted coat, white cravat, sideburns and curly black hair. It is Harry's great-great-great-great-grandfather, Gideon Providence Roberts, the bright, energetic farm labourer who, by training as a lawyer and then marrying the daughter of his wealthy patron, had established the Roberts family in the ranks of the respectable classes. Harry has never been fond of the picture but his father gave it to him and he keeps it out of a vague sense of loyalty.

Gideon looks out at his descendant with an expression that is amused, complacent and a little contemptuous, but Harry isn't noticing him. His face is completely blank as he manipulates the smaller screen in his hand with his thumb, occasionally glancing up at the TV, and then turning back again to the phone: a perfect specimen of early Twenty-First-Century Man, absent from his own body, dislocated from physical space, engrossed instead in a kind of conceptual substitute for space that an electronic mechanism has assembled for him.

He's looking at Twitter, a 'social media platform' of the time. It provides him with a constant stream of little comments, short clips and images, collectively called 'tweets', that, on the basis of what it's learnt about Harry's interests and preferences, an algorithm has pulled together for him from the vast Niagara of tweets that pours constantly into the platform in scores of languages and from literally every continent on the planet. His *timeline,* this little stream is called, or, more expressively, his *feed.* Like chicken pellets, as Harry observes somewhere. Or pigswill.

And this strange construct allows him simultaneously to inhabit a cave of deep solitude as he's doing now – blank-faced, indifferent to his posture or body language, barely in the room at all – while at the same time participating in a conversation with a large number of fellow-creatures, many of whom have never physically met but who are now simultaneously cooperating in validating one another and competing against one another to be the most entertaining and up-to-date, and, from time to time, taking part in skirmishes with other, rival groups from which trophies are brought back for purposes of mockery or outrage. ('Can't believe that anyone is still saying this in 2016.' 'They call us snowflakes, and then they cry over this!')

But at the moment Harry's not thinking about any of this in a critical way. What Twitter is doing for him now is simply allowing him to forget his own corporeal existence. He's done this a lot over the last eight months. By his own reckoning he's been spending an average of two or three hours a day on it over that period, a total of between 480 and 720 hours, though he's confessed this to no one but the pages of his diary.

People on Twitter are talking about Brexit, of course. Almost all of those he follows are Remainers, and from them flows a steady stream of anger and distress about the dishonest campaign, the unnecessary vote, the mess that has ensued, the villainy of the politicians who made it happen, the spectacle that the country is making of itself, the saint-like patience of the European Union . . . The same litany, in other words, that was rehearsed around Richard and Karina's dinner table in Suffolk. Occasionally Leavers intrude. 'You lost, get over it!' they say, or, 'Why can't you get behind the country?' Often these interlopers display a union flag or a flag of St George and sometimes their language is very ugly: 'Traitors! Enemies of the People! . . . You ought to be strung up!' Invariably a spat breaks out. The Leavers point to the popular vote as the source of their legitimacy, the Remainers trot out, one by one, all the many very good reasons why this particular vote didn't count. Insults are thrown. Each side compares their opponents to the Nazis of seventy years ago. Then they each 'block' the other, so they won't have to hear from each other again, while the people who've been attacked are commiserated with and reassured that they've done brilliantly and are on the side of good.

Harry didn't join in. He didn't have the energy. But for forty-five minutes, neither did he have the energy to withdraw. When he finally brought the Twitter session to an end, he was only able to do it by throwing the phone across the sofa as if the object itself had been controlling him.

'We loved each other,' he told himself, turning off the TV and standing up. On the wall opposite the window hung a large round mirror. He walked over to it. 'We loved each other,' he repeated, looking into the dark eyes of his own dim reflection. 'We each thought the other was good and beautiful and fun to be with, and we got married, imagining a happy life together, and children. But our only child died, and now our marriage has died as well.'

And finally he wept. This made him feel a whole lot better. He took himself up to bed and, after writing his diary for perhaps half an hour, fell into a deep, comforting sleep.

FIVE

As he'd anticipated, Harry's moment of elation didn't last but, in spite of much private agonizing on his part, he and Janet pressed ahead with formalizing their separation. They spoke to solicitors about a divorce. They discussed the details of the carve-up of their possessions, and Harry mostly kept his promise to let Janet decide what was fair. They put their house on the market for a substantial sum, not far short of thirty times the average national wage at the time. It had been a wreck when they bought it, and the two of them – both architects, after all – had restored and extended it very elegantly together.

Harry found a rented flat, so as to give himself time to look around for somewhere to buy. He thought he'd take some time off work and contemplated reducing his working hours on a more permanent basis. He'd always said that what he really wanted to do was paint. In the years after Danny, Janet had immersed herself in her work, setting up the new business which, after only a year, was yielding a considerably higher income than Harry had ever earned. In that context, the idea of him cutting down on work so as to pursue what was, after all, only a hobby had always felt too

CHRIS BECKETT · 35

indulgent to seriously contemplate, even though he muttered to himself that they didn't *need* all that money and he would rather she slowed down and relaxed.

But that was in the past and no longer applied. He could suit himself from now on. In fact, why not take a few days away from London right now, go up to the Norfolk coast with his sketchpad and paints, and try to generate a few ideas? He booked himself a room in a pub in the village of Blakeney. It was an hour or so away from Norwich where he'd grown up, and, during their childhood, his parents had owned a small terraced house there as a second home, where he and Ellie had spent countless holidays and weekends.

I have been able to reconstruct his likely route from his home in the north of London to Blakeney via the then M11 motorway, and then the A11, the A14 and a number of smaller roads. The M11 still exists today – those old roads will be there for many thousands of years – but of course it's no longer used for its original purpose. In fact, for a considerable proportion of its length, the western side of the old M11 now forms the southern end of the No 5 China–England Friendship Radial Vactrain tube, while part of the eastern carriageway has become the straggling linear settlement known as Eleven Town, which explains its curious name.

But there's plenty of footage still accessible to a professional like myself of what these highways were like in Harry's day. And I've watched, almost hypnotized, as, second by second, torrents of metal and rubber hurtle past, three streams in one direction and three in the other, cars and trucks weaving back and forth, while all of them bullet forwards at 70 miles an hour, propelled by the fossil hydrocarbons that, in every single vehicle, are exploding thirty times a second in their rows of cylinders while the exhaust pipes drip incontinently and spurt out smoke. How many hundreds of thousands of litres of fuel must have been burnt on that road every day? But the cars hurtle on regardless.

The latter part of the journey took him off those big busy roads on to smaller, winding ones, passing through woods and farmland, villages and small towns, until the coast came into view. At that time, the village of Blakeney sat at the edge of the dry land, with a wide expanse of marsh between it and the sea. The marsh, with its grey-green vegetation and its labyrinthine creeks, was, as Harry saw it, neither land nor sea but another category again, a place where larks coexisted with crabs, and crumbling houseboats lay stranded in banks of flowers. Grey creeks wound through it and when the tide was out, millions of molluscs and worms waited beneath the soft grey mud for the water to wash back in, when they could extend once again their various siphons and tentacles and feathery limbs to graze on the fresh plankton that each tide delivered. And the molluscs and worms in turn were food for birds. Gulls, ducks, geese, egrets, oystercatchers, herons, curlews, terns in their thousands thronged the creeks, honking and squawking.

There is little left these days of that in-between realm. Storm erosion and rising seas have swept almost all of it away, leaving only a few mudflats that emerge when the tide is very low. Of the birds and shelled creatures Harry saw, many are now extinct, and the village has seen a similar decline. In Harry's day, delicatessens, restaurants, gift shops and art galleries served the prosperous visitors who came, as Harry's family had done, to sail or watch birds or play on the beaches, but when I visited the place, there were no holidaymakers, only rather wretched local people – many of them old-fashioned white people of the kind who burn in the sun until they look like boiled ham – trying to eke out a living from nothing very much at all. I only stayed about an hour before I felt the need to get away from the constant pestering of beggars, hawkers and would-be guides.

Harry had gone there to paint, but he didn't do much painting. His mood was too unsettled. Instead, he went on long, fast walks, along the marsh and across it, out on to the wide beaches, and back inland through the woods and villages. One day he got chatting to a woman about his own age on the marsh, an amateur artist like himself, with an easel and watercolours, trying, not very successfully, to capture some sense of that enormous and nearly featureless expanse on a little rectangle of cartridge paper. He sat down beside her and they talked about painting, and about the area, and had what Harry calls 'the now-standard groan about Brexit: *Never needed to happen . . . Colossal blunder . . . Internal problems in the Tory party . . . Referendums not suitable to questions of this kind . . . Public not qualified to decide . . . Lamentable lack of respect for evidence and expertise . . . Enlightenment values under threat . . . Rise of the populist right . . .* '

He learnt that she was an arts administrator whose home in London was only a mile or so away from his new flat. She was divorced and had a son – Alex, aged eleven – who was staying with his father while she came up here for a painting trip. He liked her. She was warm and lively, and it was delightfully easy to get a laugh out of her. She was pleasant to look at too, and rather clearly very much liked the look of him. (All the photos I've found in the social media archive confirm that Harry really was quite a good-looking man.) 'I'm Letty, by the way,' she told him, after they'd been talking for the better part of twenty minutes, and the conversation hovered around the possibility that one or other of them would suggest they meet up again for a drink or a meal. But something made Harry back away from this – he describes the feeling, a little oddly, as 'claustrophobia' – and I suppose she picked up on his reservations and held back herself because in the end he carried on his walk with a friendly but non-committal, 'Nice talking to you, Letty. Hope we'll run into each other again.'

Later, writing his diary in a pub after a meal he'd eaten alone, Harry considered what might have unfolded if he and Letty had spent an evening together. 'First there'd be the getting-to-know-each-other phase, and the best behaviour,' he writes. 'And then either the embarrassment of realizing you really don't have that much in common, or, if all is well (and probably more likely), the discovery that you indeed have lots, and all the silly elation that goes with that. (Silly because why wouldn't you have a lot in common? Human beings come in a finite number of varieties!) And if the latter applies, we'd no doubt have met again and then, all being well, in due course and probably quite soon, there'd be sex and so on. Whooey! How exciting! Getting naked with someone new!'

This really *was* an exciting prospect, actually, in spite of his efforts to make light of it. He'd not had sex with anyone for quite a while.

'But pretty soon the best-behaviour phase would be over,' he wrote, 'and then there'd be the phase of noticing irritating differences: the quirks and foibles, the idiosyncratic needs, the peculiar friends, the difficult relatives, the hang-ups about intimacy, the lack of synchronicity around sex, the different attitudes to money and standards of cleanliness and TV watching, the relationships with exes, all of which would have to be painfully negotiated and compromised over. Dear God, how daunting! How dull! I feel weary of the whole business before I even start.'

Yet he wondered why he was so resistant, given that he was quite sure he didn't want to remain single for ever. He wasn't quite ready, he decided. That was all. It was just too soon to be thinking about things like this.

Yet he couldn't *stop* thinking about it, and it struck him that, although having to negotiate differences all over again might feel wearisome, his biggest concern was almost the opposite. As he'd continued his walk after meeting Letty (who he had liked, after all, and whose company he'd enjoyed) he hadn't been able to rid himself for some time of a kind of distaste for the little self-affirming worlds that people with similar backgrounds constructed together around themselves. Relationships, friendships and friendship groups, tribes and classes: they were a shield against the void, of course, and yet they involved so many compromises. And it was the prospect of *likeness*, the idea of discovering things in common, that made him feel bored in anticipation. The reason an architect could meet an arts administrator on the marsh and immediately recite together a set of views that they shared was not the result of an extraordinary coincidence. It was because they were part of the same tribe, and had been socialized into that tribe, with its own particular set of manners, tastes, beliefs and priorities that both had learnt and internalized. For some reason he was weary of that tribe.

'But then again,' he concedes ruefully in his diary, 'if Letty walked in now and we had a few drinks and got talking, I would almost certainly have a *much* more pleasant evening than I'm actually going to have on my own, so I'm probably a fool.'

He was forty-six, he had no children. Much of his energy over the last ten years had gone into designing nice extensions for the already nice houses of reasonably prosperous people like himself. Whatever his fantasies about becoming a painter, deep down he doubted if he really had the drive or the patience, and he had serious doubts too, in spite of his technical competence, as to whether he really even had the talent. He had no other marketable skills other than designing buildings, so what choice did he have but to carry on living the life he already lived, among the kind of people who lived in the same sort of way?

He'd brought a book with him, a novel about people in a world much like his own, and he tried to read it but gave up after a page when he realized that his eyes were just scanning the words without taking in their meaning. He briefly considered buying some cigarettes, but managed to resist. Instead, he took out his phone and, connecting to the wireless link to the World Wide Web that the pub provided, he began to scroll through the stream of tweets which that algorithm had deemed suited to him. He plugged himself, in other words, into his *feed*.

That kept him going pretty much until he was too tired for anything but sleep.

SIX

Two days after meeting Letty on the marsh, towards the end of the afternoon, Harry headed back towards London. But outside the small south Norfolk town of Breckham, his car developed a fault – a problem with the 'alternator', as it turned out – and he had to pull over and call a roadside recovery service. By the time the repairman got to him, it was after six o'clock. The repairman couldn't fix the fault himself because he didn't have a replacement alternator of the appropriate type, so all he could do was tow Harry's car to a garage in Breckham, which would be closed until the morning. Harry walked into the centre of the town. In the market square there were one or two handsome Georgian buildings and some older houses faced with knapped flint in the traditional Norfolk style. There were small- and medium-sized branches of many of the various chain stores you'd find in a larger town. There was a tiny museum. The place looked slightly run-down. A couple of shops were boarded up. There was a Pound Shop, a desolate-looking bookmaker's. There had been more money here once than there was now.

He took out his phone. He needed to make a decision about his evening. He could get a train to London, be back at his flat by ten and come back in the morning to sort out the car, or he could check into a hotel. The first option didn't appeal to him. It would involve changing trains at Cambridge and again in London itself, meaning that, with the return journey, he'd spend maybe five hours or more sitting on trains and standing on station platforms just so that he could sleep in his own bed. The hotel option didn't appeal to him either: he'd always hated the kind of hotels you found in little towns like this, with their tired red carpets, their overcooked vegetables, and their pretensions to a kind of gentility that was already dated when Harry was born. Yet he was mildly interested in the town itself, one of the countless small towns of England, neither desperately poor nor particularly prosperous: a place with not much happening and nothing very much in its neighbourhood other than forestry plantations, the odd pig farm, a couple of American airbases and a bunch of other small towns of similar size and character: Thetford, Mildenhall, Brandon, Diss, Soham.

It was a town in which most people would have voted for Brexit. That was obvious. He would have known that just from the look of it, even if he hadn't recently reminded himself of the electoral map of the east of England and, when he tried to imagine living here, he immediately felt suffocated. Along the pedestrianized high street with its brick clock tower built to celebrate Queen Victoria's Diamond Jubilee, its wrought-iron bandstand, its heavy, woody, slightly run-down pubs, he noticed a shop that specialized in stocking food for Eastern European immigrants, something that had become common enough on British streets over the last decade for him to have learnt the Polish word for 'shop'.

He had an 'app' in his phone – a software tool – that allowed him to find local homeowners who let out rooms to visitors, and he found a house about half a mile from where he was. He called the number and a woman answered. She sounded as if she was in her thirties or forties and spoke with the twangy London-influenced accent of south-eastern England that was sometimes known as Estuary, as opposed to either the distinctive rustic-sounding accent of Norfolk or Harry's own RP. The room was available, she said, so, pausing to eat some fish and chips on the way, he walked over there.

The house was in an estate originally built by the local government to provide affordable homes for rent. Harry stood across the street from it for a few seconds. As an architect he was always interested in buildings, even when he was a little weary and discouraged, and he looked at the house and its identical neighbours and wondered what it would be like to live all your life in a place like this. Their plain rectangular design was almost wilfully unimaginative, the pale bricks were of the cheapest and least interesting kind, and the one small gesture towards decoration on every house, a sort of panel between the upper and lower windows that was filled with lapped brown tiles, was a tired cliché that surely could never have looked interesting even when it was first invented. It was true that there was no particular reason to think that these houses wouldn't be at least as comfortable inside as, say, his current flat, but as objects, as elements of the visual world, they offered no nourishment at all.

But did this matter, he wondered, as he crossed the road to ring the doorbell? Was it really a problem for most people that these buildings had nothing to say? And actually was it even true? Was what he saw a thing that people who lived here could see as well, or was it just that he'd been taught since childhood to think like this about these kinds of houses, so different from the large Edwardian semi-detached in Norwich in which he'd grown up?

He heard chimes inside the house. He could see the blue light of a TV flickering in the front room, and hear gusts of studio laughter. He noticed a 'Take Back Control!' sticker in a window of the house next door to the left, a small child's bicycle leaning on the wall beneath it. Then there was movement behind the frosted glass in front of him. A light went on in there, diffracted into stars by the pattern of the glass, and a fragmented approximation to a human form approached the far side of the door. He heard the latch being turned and stepped back a little to give the householder some space.

He wasn't an especially tall man, but Michelle was half a head shorter than him and very slender. Her hair was dark and straight with a fringe, divided in the middle. Her eyes were light grey and . . . well, Harry's initial word for them is 'flayed', which I found puzzling, but he mentions a kind of wariness that was apparent though she was not in any way unfriendly, and he speaks also of a certain nakedness in her gaze, as if some protective surface layer had been stripped away. She had a small gap between her two front teeth and a narrow but instantly noticeable scar, slightly paler than her otherwise quite brown skin, which started halfway along the right-hand side of her upper lip and extended about a third of the way to her nose. She was wearing jeans and a white, short-sleeved top. Her nails were painted shiny black, and she wore rings on all her fingers. Her smile was slightly asymmetrical, perhaps due to the scar, and, in a rather likeable way, it was also somehow conspiratorial, as if, just by coming face to face, she and Harry had shared some kind of secret. To his surprise (because he wasn't a teenager any more and not prone to such instant responses) he felt a small but distinct stab of desire.

'Hi. You must be Harry. Nice to meet you. Shall I show you the room?' In his diary Harry *again* notes her south-eastern accent. He doesn't like to talk about class, but he is very class conscious.

A Dalmatian dog lumbered out of the living room and stood there looking at Harry with large rheumy eyes, its mouth hanging open and its tongue lolling out.

'Oh yeah, this is Pongo,' she said. 'I hope you're okay with dogs? I did put it on the website that I've got him, but people don't always—'

'I'm absolutely fine with dogs,' Harry said. 'Hello, Pongo.'

The dog stared at him. 'He's a rescue dog,' she said. 'He's a bit weird.'

She led Harry upstairs to a small but comfortable bedroom. He told her it was fine and suggested they get the money sorted out. The unusual yellow and brown decor struck him as a bit loud and not entirely to his taste, but it was nicely done and showed some originality and imagination. It wasn't what he would have expected, and not what he imagined he'd find in the bedrooms of Michelle's neighbours, though admittedly he had very little experience on which to base this statement. She said she'd leave him to sort himself out and that she'd be in the front room downstairs.

He used her bathroom, and glanced into the two other bedrooms, one of which was very small and being used as a store. He had no sense that anyone other than her was living here. There were strong, bold colours in all three rooms, and a strong, if homespun, sense of design.

Michelle's living room was unusual too. It had black walls, with white skirting boards, a large round white-framed mirror and a white fluffy synthetic rug on a black-painted wooden floor. Like his bedroom, it didn't quite work in Harry's opinion – he especially hated the 'kitschy' rug – but she was clearly interested in creating her own effects, and he appreciated that. There was a photo of a little girl of about six on the mantelpiece: Michelle's now grown-up daughter, he thought, or maybe a niece, or the child of a friend, given that Michelle seemed to him to be barely old enough to have a daughter who'd left home. Curled up in a large white armchair, and with bare feet – her toenails were also painted glossy black – Michelle was watching a game show he didn't recognise, but she flipped the TV to silent as soon as he came in.

'Have you eaten?' she asked. Lying at her feet, the dog watched him anxiously. 'There's a pub just a street away that does okay food, but if you like I can rustle you up a sandwich or something.'

He said he was fine for food but that perhaps he'd go to the pub anyway, have a drink, catch up on some emails and then have an early night.

'Okay, but you're very welcome to sit here, if you'd prefer.' She saw him glance at the screen. 'I'll turn that off if you don't want it. I was just watching it to pass the time. I'd offer you a drink, but I'm not sure I've got much in. I'll go and have a look if you want.'

He thought about the pub, visualized the dull, nearly empty bar of an establishment owned by some large brewery with no more personality than the estate it served, and he imagined spending an hour there doing nothing but sipping at a tepid, sour beer he didn't really want while flipping without interest through his phone. So why not stay here and chat to Michelle for a bit, he asked himself? He could always turn in early if it became awkward or tedious.

'Okay, well, if you're sure. I've actually got a bottle of wine in my bag upstairs, if you fancy a glass? Took it with me to the coast but ended up sitting in the pub every night and never got round to drinking it.'

She turned off the TV. Her very slightly lopsided smile was friendly and humorous in spite of its wariness. 'Yeah, why not?' she said. 'That would be nice. I can probably scrape together a bowl of olives or some crisps or something.'

He asked her about herself. Pretty soon, he and Michelle were on to their second glass, and she had told him quite a lot of her early life story. She was thirty-eight. She came originally from Romford in Essex, just outside London, and was the youngest of three: her older sister, Jen, was fifty-two, and her brother Trevor fifty, so there was quite a gap between them and her: 'My mum refuses to admit it but I was *definitely* a mistake.' She was seen as the bright one of the three children, and her father, a bright man who felt he'd missed out on the opportunities that an education would have brought, had wanted her to go to university, but she never went.

'I was a big disappointment to him, I'm afraid.'

'Do you regret that now?'

Michelle considered this. 'Do you know what? I really don't. This is where I feel at home.'

She and her parents had moved to Breckham when she was fifteen, followed a little later by both her brother and her sister. They'd come to work in the factory of a local company called Kwalpak that made suitcases and bags. It had since closed down. Her father had been a very heavy smoker and had died of lung cancer five years ago but her mother, sister and brother were all still living in Breckham. Michelle had been a worry for her parents when they first moved here. Bitter about having to give up her friends in Romford, she'd been a surly, stubborn teenager, and she'd got involved with drugs and had some scrapes with the law. 'But that's in the past now,' she said, glancing at him with her sly smile, 'give or take the odd puff now and again.'

She'd trained as a hairdresser and beautician. She and her friend Cheryl – the first friend she'd made when she started at the Breckham comprehensive – rented a small shop just off the high street and called themselves Shear Perfection. Michelle had painted the sign and decorated the place, Cheryl was the businesswoman, always keen to expand the business and offer new services. 'I could do without the hassle myself,' was Michelle's view.

Harry had friends in London who had a similar background to Michelle – people who'd come from small towns, people whose parents were factory workers – but they'd all climbed up out of it and become very similar in tastes and outlook to Harry, though his family had been comfortably middle class for generations. Some of them liked to identify themselves as working class – apart from anything else there was a certain kudos in his circle that came with being able to identify with a disadvantaged group – but they all read the *Guardian* newspaper, went to art exhibitions and so forth, and were often scathingly dismissive of the worlds from which they'd come. Michelle hadn't done any of that. In spite of her father's hopes for her, she'd left school at sixteen and remained in this obscure corner of a county that itself was a byword for provincialism, and claimed to have no regrets about it. Harry couldn't conceive of how an intelligent and imaginative person could survive in a town like Breckham without becoming dull or bored or bitter, yet this didn't seem to have happened to her. She talked humorously and with affection about her customers, her family, her neighbours, her dog: Cheryl was so conscious of her appearance that she made herself up each morning 'as if she was going to be on national TV' . . . her brother was 'thick as shit, but thinks he's God's gift' . . . her mum had 'so many gnomes and crap in her garden, it's a job to find anywhere to sit down' . . . Pongo was the world's worst hunting dog and 'wouldn't notice a rabbit if it sat down right in front of his nose' . . .

Harry liked her. And he liked her sideways way of glancing quickly across at him when she smiled, and the shape her body made when she curled up in her chair, and the way she held her chunky IKEA wine goblet in her small, graceful fingers with their rings and their long black nails. She was a pretty woman, no doubt about that, but, odd though it was to say it about a white English woman in a former council house in a little provincial town, a lot of her appeal to him lay in her *exoticism*. She was very different from anyone he knew.

'Anyway, tell me about you!' she said. 'I've been going on about me for ages!'

He told her he was an architect and lived in London. His father had been a consultant in the Norwich and Norfolk hospital, his mother a professional artist. He'd been to private schools and Cambridge University. His twin sister was a GP.

She was impressed. 'Christ! I feel embarrassed now. My life must seem pretty boring compared with yours.'

'Why should you be embarrassed?' Harry protested. 'It's really interesting hearing about your life. Why wouldn't it be?' and then, more tentatively: 'I notice you speak about your mum and your siblings, but you don't speak about a family of your own . . . ?'

'Yeah, well.' She chewed at her left forefinger. 'That side of my life is a fucking disaster, to be honest.'

'Ha. Same. But don't feel you have to talk about it if you'd rather not.'

She shrugged, offered him more wine, filled up their glasses. 'I'll tell you if you want to hear.'

She'd married at eighteen a man she referred to as Fudge, who was seven years older than her and a heavy user of cannabis. He'd rarely been in work, was serially unfaithful, and sometimes hit her. She'd left him when she was twenty-three. After a couple of other relationships, she'd met her second husband, Mick, when she was twenty-seven. He was the assistant manager of the local Tesco supermarket at the time, and was now the manager. They'd had a daughter, Caitlin – Michelle pointed to the photo on the mantelpiece – but four years ago, when Caitlin was six, she'd lost control of her tricycle when Michelle was walking her back from school, swerving on to a road to be crushed by a passing truck and killed instantly. She and Mick had been unable to cope with the aftermath of that together, and after two miserable years they'd split up.

In the course of telling Harry about this, Michelle had knocked back another glass and a half of wine, and there was now none left in the bottle. 'I could use another drink,' she said before he could comment further on her story. 'You too? I *might* have a bottle somewhere. Let me go and have a look.' She went out and clattered noisily about in the kitchen. Pongo lumbered stiffly to the door and waited there for her. Harry walked over to look at the little girl on the mantelpiece.

'It happened to me too,' he told her when she came back in. 'I lost my only child, my little boy Danny. And my wife and I have not long split up, just like you and Mick did.'

'Oh, no way!' She put the bottle she'd found on the small side table between the chairs and the TV and came to stand beside him, touching his arm. Pongo the dog came over to them, awkwardly, as if he imagined that something was expected of him but didn't know what, and then lay down again. 'You should have said, before I went on and on about Caitlin!'

He looked down into her raw, grey eyes, then back at the photo on the mantelpiece. 'It feels impossible to bear, doesn't it? A lovely cheerful little person, full of optimism, full of enthusiasm for life, and then . . . '

'Don't!' she begged. 'Don't!' And suddenly she put her arms round him and hugged him against her, seeking comfort, perhaps, but more than anything trying to stop him speaking.

They stood like that for a few seconds. And then, without speaking, she stepped back from him to open the second bottle of wine and fill their glasses.

They drank all of that second bottle and talked for another hour about what it was to lose a child. The very same calamity that had broken up both of their marriages had the opposite effect of making the two of them feel close. They talked about the sheer physical weight of grief pressing down on them and the way that, even now, they still found themselves rehearsing every day the things they could have done to prevent the blow from falling. When Caitlin swerved on to the road, Michelle had been distracted for a few seconds by a text from her sister, just long enough for the little girl to be beyond her reach by the time she realized what was happening. She'd never dared to admit this to Caitlin's father. In fact, she said she'd never admitted it to anyone at all until now, the worst part being that the text hadn't been urgent in the least. She could have left it to reply to later – it would have made no difference to her sister – and, if she had done, Caitlin would still be alive.

The dog wandered through to the kitchen and began to whine and bark, so Michelle went to let it out into the garden. 'I'll tell you the truth,' she said when she came back. 'I didn't notice my little girl was getting too far away from me because I was looking at my stupid fucking phone and trying to decide whether I wanted to go to the pictures with my sister on Saturday.'

They were both silent for a few seconds. 'Well, I failed to notice my son was dangerously ill,' Harry said, 'because I was more interested in how pissed off I was with my wife than I was in wondering whether my child had meningitis. All I had to do to save him was set my annoyance on one side, just for a few minutes, and look at him, really look at him, without thinking about anything else but how he was. And the stupidest thing about it was that we were going to have a sleepless night anyway, with Janet fretting and worrying, so we might just as well have taken him to the hospital.'

Michelle nodded. 'You might as well have done, but you didn't. I go over and over it. It's like some dumb part of me thinks that, if I think hard enough about what I could have done differently, I'll be able to put the clock back and actually do it. Every fucking day I think about that text coming through, and I think about how all I need to do is leave it to look at later when we're safely home, and I'm actually thinking to myself, "Yeah, I'll just wait till I get home", when I remember it's too late now. I *did* look at that stupid text. It's done and I can't take it back. It makes no difference what I'd do about it if I had my time again. I've had my chance, and now my baby's gone.'

'But of course that's unbearable,' Harry said, 'so off you go again, thinking about what you could do to prevent it, and half-persuading yourself that you still really can. And so on and so on, round and round, for days and weeks and months.'

'And years,' she said.

'Yes, and years.'

In one of his many reflections on that evening, Harry observes that intimacy between two people doesn't just come from being alike. 'If I could be cloned,' he writes, 'and could meet an exact copy of me who shared every memory and every feeling that I had ever had, that wouldn't feel like intimacy. I can't imagine what it would be like but it would be another thing entirely. Intimacy comes from being quite obviously *different* from another person and yet still finding a point of contact.'

Eventually Harry looked at his watch and said he ought to get to bed. He needed to sort his car out as early as possible, and then get back up to London for a meeting with his two partners about his involvement with the firm in the longer term. He stood up.

'It's been lovely talking to you,' he told Michelle quite truthfully, 'and you wouldn't *believe* how much nicer this evening has been than I imagined when I found out I wasn't going to be able to drive home. Much nicer than it would have been if I *had* got home, come to that.'

She stood up too. She came towards him, touched his arm for a moment, and then seemed to make a sudden decision because she took hold of both his arms and reached up to very lightly kiss him on the mouth. It was completely unexpected and the electric sweetness of it was extraordinarily intense. 'It was a *lovely* evening,' she said.

She still hadn't let go of him. 'Listen,' she said after a moment, 'I promise you I've never even thought about saying this to any of my guests before, but . . . I mean, it's probably a stupid thing to say, but we're both single, aren't we, and . . . well, do you want to . . . ?'

Seeing him flinch, she instantly went on the defensive. 'Oh shit, I'm an idiot. Ignore me. I've had too much wine. Just forget I said it, eh?'

She'd let go of him but he took her by the hands. 'No, please don't be embarrassed. It's a lovely offer and I'm very flattered, but do you really think it's a good idea? I mean, we've both drunk a fair amount. Don't you think you'd regret it in the morning?'

She examined his face. 'If you want an honest answer to that, no, I won't regret it. Not as long as you won't. I want us to have sex, Harry, if you would like that.'

'I do too, to be honest. I want it very much indeed. But it's important we both . . . '

There was a momentary flash of anger in her eyes. 'Important that we both know there are no strings attached? Of course. You come from a completely different world to me. Of *course* I don't think it's going to lead to anything. I just think it would be . . . well, comforting.' She laughed. 'I'd certainly *sleep* better, anyway.'

He managed to fight a silly and dishonest impulse to reassure her that coming from different worlds had nothing to do with it. 'Well . . . if you're sure, I'd love that.'

So they kissed again, more slowly. He was already very aroused.

'To be honest,' he said, 'it's a very long time since I slept with anyone. You'll have to forgive me if I'm a little—'

She interrupted him with a laugh. 'It's a long time since I've slept with anyone who wasn't a total arsehole.'

*

Obviously Harry didn't write a diary that night but he makes several attempts later to describe how it had felt when he and Michelle lay down together. 'Sex is hard to write about,' he concludes. 'It's partly a kind of prudery that holds me back, I suppose, but the main problem is that the right words just don't seem to exist. One set of words sounds like porn, the other like a medical textbook, and there's nothing in between. I mean, for instance, there isn't a way of describing the moment she took me inside her that feels like I'm saying what I actually want to say, and that includes the words I've just written, which sound sort of coy and cringey.'

He gives up trying and speaks in general terms: 'But kissing, touching . . . Such implausibly delicious pleasure. Such heaven. Being naked with another person who wants to be touched and wants to touch, and doesn't say no, doesn't say stop, but instead keeps saying *yes, that too . . . yes, of course, as much as you want, I want it every bit as much as you.*'

There were moments of doubt even at the time, though. He worried that when they'd spent themselves, all of this sweetness would prove to be just a surface that covered something rather pathetic and desperate. Perhaps he'd feel guilty then, or ashamed, or horribly embarrassed? Perhaps he'd realize that he didn't like her? But he told himself no, he *did* like her, and there was no pretence here, no possible misunderstanding on either side that this was the beginning of something, or was anything more than the moment itself.

And actually, he didn't just feel he *liked* her. He experienced something that felt to him like love, and it overwhelmed him. He found himself whispering endearments to her: *sweetheart, darling, beautiful, precious*. 'I knew I shouldn't,' he writes later. 'Even at the time I knew I shouldn't. But I couldn't seem to help myself because she was giving me so much pleasure, so much *happiness*.'

People make rules about love. They say it only counts as *real* love when this or that has happened, or in this or that context, but it seemed to Harry in that moment that love didn't really work that way at all. Love was just a thing that we had inside ourselves, a natural force that allowed us to reach beyond the loneliness of our own heads. And sometimes we held it in, or couldn't quite reach it, or lost sight of it altogether, while at other times it came rushing up in such abundance that we almost had no choice but to let it out.

'Are you okay?' he asked when they'd both come and were lying side by side.

'Of course I'm okay! Don't I look like it?'

'You do, but sometimes, you know, in the cold light afterwards . . . '

'You regret it. I usually do, to be honest. But not this time, Harry. How about you?'

'Me neither,' he said and meant it. 'No regrets at all.'

'That's good.'

Things felt a little more precarious now, it was true. Harry was aware that this was going to feel strange in the morning, but he was still glad that he'd come to her bed and hadn't just crept off to his own (where, as he rather indelicately puts it, just in order to be able to get to sleep, 'I would probably have had to wank myself off imagining what this would have been like'). Life was hard and full of pain, but sometimes it offered a spoonful of pure sweetness that, even if only for a little while, redeemed it completely. Surely only a fool turns that away?

He kissed her, very gently, on that scar on the right-hand side of her upper lip (it was the result, she'd told him, of a bicycle accident when she was nine years old). 'That was lovely, Michelle, so lovely that I can't begin to put it into words. I honestly can't remember when I felt as . . . I don't know . . . as *held* as that. If I ever have at all.'

She kissed him back. 'You posh git! It was only sex.' But he could see she was touched by what he'd said.

'Very sweet,' Cally says. She shakes off a large praying mantis that has alighted on her arm. 'But I must admit, Zoe, that part of me wonders why we should be interested in these people? The Catastrophe was unfolding. The air was getting hotter. The ice was melting. The forest fires were more frequent. All those wonderful creatures were dying out – I mean, have you ever seen those pictures of coral reefs? – and, well, it's nice that these two lonely people found something they had in common, but do we *really* care, when we know what was happening around them and what was coming down the track? I mean, these were people who knew quite well they were fucking up the world but carried on anyway. Why should we give a shit about their love lives?'

We are strolling on the slightly rotten wooden boardwalk that allows you to walk along my street, now that the road itself is underwater. The ground floors of what were prestigious apartment buildings in the early twenty-first century are no longer used except as boat houses, and the boardwalk is fixed at the level of the first floor, where many of the apartments have become shops of various kinds.

'I know that's the important story as far as we're concerned,' I say, 'but I can't help being interested in what life was like for them.'

We've come down from my third-floor flat to get some Shaoxing wine in a store run by a woman called Mrs Thompson, who makes the stuff herself with rice her husband brings back from the paddies in Kent. In the flooded street below us, men and woman pole shallow punts up and down between the dry ground at one end and the Thames at the other. Children and old people sit on the edge of the platform, dangling their legs as they fish for eels in the muddy water.

A six-year-old girl snags one as we're walking past her. The slimy thing writhes in agony on her line, and she slaps it down on to the wooden walkway to saw off its head with an old kitchen knife. 'Three yuan, miss, if you want it?' she says, noticing me looking at her, and she proffers the bloody and still squirming body. I shake my head.

A little further on, a small boy called Joe is fishing by himself. He's about eight years old and has lost both his parents, so he now lives in the flat below mine with an aunt who leaves him by himself all day while she's away at work on the flood barriers. She obviously resents his presence. I've never heard her say anything warm or kind either about him or to him.

'You all right there, Joe?' I ask him, looking into his empty bucket.

'I'll soon catch a load of them,' he says defiantly. 'I'll catch more than anyone because I'm the best.' But his boasting façade is so thin and threadbare that it fools no one. Everyone can see the appalling well of emptiness beneath it, and all the other children avoid him so as not to be contaminated by his loneliness. Whenever he sits here to fish, there's always empty walkway on either side of him.

'Well, good luck with that, Joe,' I tell him, because it makes me feel better if I force myself to be friendly and kind to him, even though I too fear contamination, and even though I doubt my attempts make any more difference to him than a single drop of water would make to someone dying of thirst.

We enter the bare interior of Mrs Thompson's store and she pours us two glasses. Some militiamen pass by outside, their hard boots clomping on the wooden boards, and one of them turns to look towards us in the shady interior of Mrs Thompson's. Darkness isn't a problem for them, of course. Those clever goggles can adjust themselves to any light.

'Your Michelle does seem a bit desperate, I must say,' Cally says when the shadow has passed. 'It's kind of risky, isn't it? Letting out a room and then taking your guests to bed.'

SEVEN

Michelle's diary entries are much shorter than Harry's and, though she does occasionally engage in philosophical speculation, they're usually much more focused on the daily events of her life. Often she just tells stories about things that happened in the shop, which she decorates with her own cartoons. But she's worried about her life. She's aware of her age, and (just like Harry) she has a sense of time slipping away through her fingers.

'I actually liked Harry,' she writes, the day after he returned to London. 'That's the one thing that's different from the other blokes I've been with lately. He seemed a nice man. He listened to me. He treated me like another human being. And okay, I could tell from the off he liked the way I look, but there was no pressure from him, no flirting. Nothing like that at all. I did appreciate that.

'My head was terrible in the morning. So was his. We had a laugh about that, and it hurt so much that we laughed about *that* as well. It all felt a bit weird when we were having breakfast together because he'd said all these lovely things the night before: darling, sweetheart, precious . . . And I knew even at the time it was just because he'd been lonely for a long time, and because he was grateful, and all that, and it didn't really mean anything but still I felt those words were sort of hanging in the air between us.

'But anyway, then it was time for him to go and suddenly, just like that, all his warmth and friendliness shut right down like it had never been there at all, and he was just some stranger who had no interest in me and couldn't wait to get away from me.

'Cheryl could see I was upset about something. I told her it was just a hangover, but when we closed for lunch she got the story out of me. "For fuck's sake, Michelle," she told me, "get yourself on a dating site and find a decent bloke who lives round here and actually wants a relationship. You're throwing away your life.'''

But Michelle had missed the precise moment when Harry's warmth shut down. They'd both stood up and were preparing for what must surely have felt like a particularly complicated farewell hug, when a workman's van drew up outside the house opposite. She went to the window to look out.

'Bloody Poles,' she said. That Estuary accent smeared out the L in 'Poles' and suddenly sounded to him horribly mean and crabbed. 'They've taken so much work from my brother, you wouldn't believe. We'll be glad when this Brexit business is sorted out and they go home.'

To her, I think, this was just a throwaway remark, like a comment on the weather, which she'd made in an effort to make the parting feel less uncomfortably intense. But Harry froze. And in that single moment, his sense of their whole encounter flipped completely and he realized that a combination of sentimentality and lust and booze had blinded him to what she actually was: a woman who hadn't had the curiosity, let alone the ambition, to do anything with her life, or even to rise above the petty small-town prejudices of the people around her.

'You'd think in a dreary little place like Breckham,' he says later, 'anyone with the slightest spark of life would positively welcome the arrival of newcomers. But she didn't even have enough generosity of spirit to feel positive about a few strangers who came to her town for a better life.' The hug had to go ahead anyway – he could hardly get out of it now – but there was no affection left on his side of it. She was doubtless a nice enough woman within her own narrow limitations, but she wasn't really his kind at all, and it had been shallow and embarrassingly desperate of him ever to have imagined otherwise.

'It was really really lovely to meet you, Harry,' she said, still in his arms, and not yet aware of his sudden coldness. But when she drew back from him, she saw it. He knew she did, because he could see the dismay in her face.

'It was lovely to meet you too, Michelle,' he made himself say as they released one another, though he could barely bring himself to meet her eyes.

He walked back to the garage and arranged for his alternator to be replaced, then filled in the waiting time by walking round the streets. Breckham oppressed him: the public library from the 1970s with white paint flaking on its clapboard façade, the United Reformed Church, the tiny dusty museum, the small and shabby park with its swings and slides . . . The word 'provincial' came to mind: a word that means outside of the capital city, but also small-minded, unsophisticated, unambitious, second-rate. You didn't get much more provincial than Breckham.

At one point he became aware that the rather amateurish sign above a small shopfront across the road from him read 'Shear Perfection' and he quickly turned around and walked the other way.

But that was not the end of it by any means! For page after page, day after day, Harry's diary goes over that night and, increasingly, he feels not just shame at the shallowness of his own judgement, but guilt. He feels he's taken advantage of her. She initiated the sex and they'd agreed together that it was just for that night and nothing further would come of it, but she'd been drunker than he was, and more shaken up, and (contrary to Michelle's own impression) Harry feels that he'd been flirting with her all evening. He knows that he has a certain way of behaving in the presence of women to get them to like him, a way of laying on the charm. He doesn't do this deliberately, exactly – in fact, it's almost Pavlovian – and, on a conscious level, he isn't completely sure what it consists of, but he knows when he's doing it, and he knows he was doing it that evening.

But there is one particular aspect that he really struggles with, to the extent that it becomes almost comical to watch him trying simultaneously to name it and to avoid doing so: he fears he abused his social status. This, in our day, seems quite a straightforward idea, but, though his own generation was aware of social disadvantage and talked a great deal about gender, race, disability and half a dozen other social divisions, it was almost as coy and prudish about class and social rank as the Victorians were about sex.

'All my friends are things like doctors and lawyers and academics,' he finally manages to squeeze out. 'So that just seems ordinary to us, and we forget that for a lot of people a doctor or an architect is a *seriously big person*, impressively so, dauntingly so, a bit like a film star would be to me. I am sure Michelle was aware that I was much posher than she is and I'm sure it touched and flattered her that I seemed to find her interesting.'

And then he crosses it all out, so thoroughly that I have some trouble reading it.

Harry struggles on, lambasting himself in a way that seems quite disproportionate to that single drunken encounter. But the reason for that lack of proportion is painfully apparent on every page for, whatever he keeps telling himself, he just can't stop thinking about Michelle. He only has to think about her smile, her voice, the scar on her upper lip, her grey eyes, the way she wriggled into a different position in bed, and he finds himself positively aching with desire. And the loss of that sweetness twists inside him like a blade.

He battles against this. He tells himself that he couldn't possibly build a relationship with a woman whose world was so very much narrower than his own that a handful of hardworking foreigners could feel like some kind of threat. But then he thinks about the sounds she made, or her laugh, or the way her lashes felt when he gently kissed her eyes, or her wry smile, or her hands with their rings and painted nails, and it all feels exactly right, as if there was a Michelle-shaped hole inside him which has ached all his life to—

'That's nonsense,' he tells himself flatly. That was just biology. That was just the pairing instinct at work, driving its hapless human vehicle. He'd felt that way about Janet once. He'd felt that way about his very first girlfriend when he was fifteen. He just needs to get over this and he will feel it again about someone else, someone more suitable, someone who might actually be able to share his life with him.

'Yes, but her smile . . . ' says the other side of him at once.

After a while it all becomes a bit ridiculous, even to Harry himself. 'I'm like one of those cartoon characters with an angel whispering in one ear and a devil in the other,' he says. 'Not good versus evil, perhaps, but reason versus emotion, head versus heart.' (A binary pairing which, as it happens, had been a major part of the collective narrative of Remainers after their defeat. They were the voices of reason, of evidence, of science. The Leavers represented primitive and atavistic emotions: fear of change, hatred of the other, blind adherence to empty symbols.)

'I'm overthinking this,' Harry tells himself, and it's hard to disagree, though in my experience overthinking is usually a cover for *underthinking*, a smokescreen of elaboration to avoid one particular line of thought.

'I need to put this out of my mind,' he says, 'because nothing more can be done with it. The one grown-up conclusion I can draw is that I would very much like to be in a loving sexual relationship again after a very long time without. I should have had a drink with that nice woman Letty I met on the marsh.'

EIGHT

Michelle doesn't write about Harry after that first day, not even a single mention. She talks (as usual) about people in the shop, the amusing things they said, the various troubles in their lives. She mentions an evening watching TV with her mother and her sister Jen, and another time when her niece Jules came over to hers. And she devotes two whole pages to a difficult conversation in a pub with Cheryl. Cheryl's boyfriend was an airman from the nearby American base. It turned out that Cheryl had suggested the drink because she wanted to tell Michelle that she was going to marry him, and they were planning to move to America when his tour of duty ended, along with her two children who Michelle had known all their lives. Michelle had been fairly stunned by this news but Cheryl, perhaps out of guilt at the thought of abandoning her best and oldest friend, had unwisely chosen this moment to have another go at her about getting on a decent dating site, sorting herself out a decent man and starting to build a life of her own. Michelle had suddenly snapped. She told Cheryl to 'get the fuck off my fucking case' and stormed out of the pub. They'd made it up later in a long phone conversation that continued into the early hours.

On the Sunday, Michelle went for a walk with Pongo in the forest that surrounded Breckham. It was a commercial plantation, laid out in a grid, with large blocks of pine and only smaller patches of greener trees, but you could walk for miles there, see foxes and deer and often not meet another human soul at all, once you'd got away from the car parks. (The forest is still there, by the way, but much broken up by squatters attempting to grow things in the poor, sandy soil, which was the reason for it not being farmland in the first place.)

Michelle had a favourite spot, some way from the road and at the edge of a small clearing of pale yellow grass, surrounded by silver birch trees. Hardly anyone but her ever seemed to come here, and she'd seen foxes, and deer, and, a few times, on hot summer days, snakes sunning themselves on patches of earth. (Cheryl had said 'Ugh!' when she told her about them, but Michelle had enjoyed their strange presence.) She had a favourite birch tree. Many years ago she'd even scratched a tiny M into its bark, which was still just visible. She sat down in front with her back against it, took out a packet of cigarette papers and a small bag of dried cannabis leaves and rolled herself what she called a 'spliff'. It wasn't something she did every day, but she did it regularly, buying the stuff from a wizened old friend of hers from her druggy days who she refers to as Splodgy. There was a feeling of autumn in the air, a low grey sky, a smell of mushrooms and bracken, leaves here and there beginning to turn yellow or gold.

She lit up and inhaled. People who live routine lives in small places where nothing much happens have to appreciate the ordinary things that stay the same, and cannabis helped her with that (as I suppose it still helps many people now since, in spite of the militia, you often see those green dama bushes with their spiky leaves growing in the little plots of the poor). The drug stripped away the dull limescale of familiarity to uncover the strangeness and unknowableness of everything, even the streets of Breckham and those houses that to Harry had seemed almost bewilderingly dull. When she was done, she leant back against her tree and, gently stroking Pongo's head and ears, she watched the movements of the dry grass stems in front of her as they made visible the movements of the invisible air.

The forest, as usual, was very quiet, but it wasn't silent. She could hear birds around her – their calls and songs, the whoosh and flutter of their wings – she could hear the rustlings of the leaves, she could hear a branch somewhere behind her creaking whenever the grass in front of her bent in a gust of wind. One of the effects of the drug was to make the sounds seem to be inside her and not just outside, as if her mind and the forest had become a single entity, a single web, with tremors and ripples passing through it.

Three roe deer came into the clearing from the trees on the far side. Pongo tensed and she took hold of his collar so he wouldn't chase after them. The deer spotted her and Pongo immediately but they didn't run, just stood there, side by side, watching the two of them while they watched them back. As she remembered it afterwards one of the deer was brown like most deer, one was white and the other was black. But she'd never seen a deer that wasn't brown before and when she wrote about them she wondered if she'd really seen this detail of their being three different colours, or whether she'd imagined and elaborated it in the dreamlike state that the drug induced, rather like another vivid memory she had of a hawk that had alighted on a branch above her with a little bird in its claws, and how the hawk and its prey swivelled their heads to look at her at the same time and with the exact same beady curiosity, even though one was about to eat the other. She could never make up her mind if that last part had actually happened.

But there were certainly three deer there, and tri-coloured was certainly how she remembered them: one brown, one white, one black, like those threes that kept recurring in the fairy tales that Caitlin liked her to read at bedtime: three sisters, three dogs with enormous eyes, three times that the same event happened, but then something extra happening the third time, after the first two had set up the pattern. She and the deer looked at each other across a space of twenty yards. They knew she was alive, and she knew they were. Apart from that, they were mysteries to one another.

She wouldn't tell anyone about them, but then there were many things she didn't talk about. How much she missed Caitlin, for instance. Or what it was like afterwards, when the lorry had— 'No, no, no!' she muttered. Pongo growled. The three deer started and bolted back among the trees. A fallen twig broke with a snap beneath their hooves, and a crow in their path took flight, its rasping cry echoing among the trees.

She began to roll a second spliff, more as something to occupy herself than because she really needed any more of the drug in her bloodstream. And as she did so she heard a familiar roar from behind the trees to the east where the deer had disappeared, as though there was some great beast in there which they'd awakened. The roar grew louder until, as she'd known would happen, a huge plane with swept-back wings appeared above the tops of the trees, black against the flat grey sky. It was very low, its eight jet engines shrieking as it descended towards the airbase a few miles to the west. Grey wisps of cloud broke over its wings, like waves over a boat in rough sea.

She often saw these planes when she came to the forest. She saw them in Breckham too, flying over her back garden. American bases were part of life at that time along the border between Norfolk and Suffolk and had been for sixty years. Local women formed relationships, as Cheryl had done, with American servicemen who often came from rural, Trump-voting towns that were in many ways quite like Breckham. Michelle had once been out with a taciturn pilot from Illinois called Brett. Cheryl herself was the child of such a relationship. So the bomber wasn't an alien thing to Michelle. These warplanes were a familiar part of her world and they usually only impinged on her consciousness as a noise nuisance. But this time, as it disappeared behind her, she felt as if this enormous black screaming thing had left in its wake a kind of wasteland.

It wasn't that anything had visibly changed. The trees were still trees, the grass was still moving this way and that in the little gusts and eddies of the air. And after the shriek of those huge jets had shrunk into a distant whine, the sounds she could hear were the same as they had been before as well. But somehow the forest's meaning had been stripped away, along with its ability to comfort and reassure. And, as Michelle lit her second spliff, she thought about a conversation she'd had with Jules when they met up earlier in the week. Jules was eighteen, the daughter of her brother Trevor and his second wife, and was seen as the smart one in her generation of the family, just as Michelle had been in the generation before her. She and Michelle had always been close and, when her parents' marriage was breaking up two years ago, Jules had lived with Michelle for several months. But now she'd got herself a place at uni in Leicester to study Marketing, and would be leaving Breckham the following year.

When she came over to Michelle's that week, Jules had talked about a book she'd just finished reading about 'global warming'. And, in the strange meaningless emptiness the screaming plane had left behind, Michelle thought about the melting ice, the fires, the islands sinking beneath the sea . . .

'Cheryl's wrong,' she murmured to her dog. 'I'll be doing everyone a favour if I stay on my own and never have a kid again.'

I've looked at a lot of pictures of Michelle. There are hundreds of them in the extraordinarily comprehensive social media archive we possess today thanks to the mania for data collection of what was then the People's Republic of China. I've even found some short video clips. I can certainly see why Harry found her attractive. And I *like* her too. I like the dry little comments she makes on her friends' posts on Facebook: their pictures of their dogs or cats or their children, the jokes they've recycled from elsewhere in the internet, their blurry pictures of boozy evenings out. Once in a while she posts a picture of something she's made: an arrangement of leaves and twigs, or one of the cartoon drawings she does of regular customers at Shear Perfection, or a second-hand mirror she's bought and done up by painting it gold and gluing little glass beads round it. Her comments are always self-deprecating – 'Bought this mirror for a tenner. Reckon they'll take it back for five?' – and I can see in those comments, and in her face as well, the quality that Harry refers to as wariness, the sense he has of her peeking out from a hiding place. And yet the way she peeks out is friendly and kind.

There's no evidence in the archive that Michelle is particularly interested in politics. She never says anything political herself, but occasionally she will pass on something one of her friends has posted, or respond with a little picture (they were called 'emojis') of a face crying with laughter, or the acronym LOL, which stands for 'laugh out loud'. Her brother Trevor will occasionally make an overtly political statement, always unsophisticated, sometimes poorly spelt, and invariably attached as a comment to some image already circulating on social media. Photos of him show a big, heavy man, ruddy-faced from outdoor work and with a smile that his sisters and mother apparently think of as mischievous and jolly, but which to my eyes contains a great deal of anger not very far below the surface. 'We voted for it! Why don't they get their fucking finger out and make it happen!' he posts at one point, to which Michelle, her sister Jen and their mother Kath all dutifully append a LOL, even though it wasn't really a joke. Another time he posts an American cartoon in which a naive young woman welcomes a dark-skinned man in a turban to her country by holding up a placard that reads 'All immigrants welcome!' only to have him slice her head off with a sword. Michelle puts a cry-with-laughter emoji in response (something that would undoubtedly trouble Harry a great deal), and her sister adds a LOL, but neither of them comment or recycle his post. The same happens when he posts a picture of the president of the European Commission looking drunk: 'And they want *this* clown in charge? Seriously?'

LOL, LOL, LOL, go Michelle, Jen and Kath.

NINE

On the second day of that Suffolk weekend back in August, Richard, Karina, Ellie, Phil and Harry had walked along the shingly beach near the drowned medieval city of Dunwich. As they walked and talked, Harry and Richard found themselves ahead of the others. They discovered they were both keen squash players and, without particularly meaning it, Harry had said, 'We ought to meet up for a game sometime.' Richard had seemed no more enthusiastic than he was and Harry hadn't bothered to follow up: he had enough squash partners and enough friends too. But, to Harry's surprise, a few days after his return from Breckham, Richard contacted him and they arranged to meet in the upmarket gym of which Richard was a member. (The building still stands, although, like many former public buildings, it was converted to basic residential accommodation under the Protectorate, when the rising Thames necessitated the evacuation of some of the lower parts of London.)

Short-legged, potbellied Richard certainly didn't look like much of an athlete, but he made up in sheer determination what he lacked in finesse and inflicted a very thorough defeat on Harry. They retired to the changing rooms where, as Harry records in his diary, he discovered that Richard had 'one of those stubby little dicks and was covered all over with orange hair: chest, back, shoulders, everywhere, like an orang-utan'. Confident, dynamic Richard clearly made him feel insecure.

They had a drink together afterwards. The bar at Richard's gym had soft lights and greenish decor, the barman in shadow against a lavish cornucopia of gleaming glass and golden liquids.

'So, remind me, what kind of work have you got on at the moment?' Richard, who seemed intensely curious about *everything*, kept leaning forward as if not to miss the smallest nuance of what Harry had to say. Leaning back as far as possible, Harry replied that it was basically kitchen extensions and garden studios.

Richard frowned. 'And is that still fulfilling after all these years? It doesn't become a bit samey?'

Harry's hackles rose. 'It does sometimes. But don't all jobs have their boring side?'

Richard shrugged. 'I can't bear boredom. If I get bored of something, I either stop doing it or hire someone else to do it for me. Did you never think of trying something new? I gather from Phil that your ex runs a pretty successful events business. You've not thought of doing anything like that yourself?'

'I'm just not into that kind of thing,' Harry said. He wondered whether to mention his painting but decided against it. It would lead immediately to sharp but unwelcome questions about what he was working on (answer: nothing much), what successes he'd had so far in terms of public recognition (answer: none) and what steps he was taking to take his painting to a marketable level (answer: nothing at all). And while Richard was perfectly entitled to be puzzled why a bright man like Harry hadn't got his sort of drive and ambition, Harry decided he was equally entitled to find Richard somewhat exhausting.

He asked Richard about his own work. Richard told him that, while he'd now built up a huge amount of experience of the financial world, he was already past his intellectual peak. 'What I'm doing now is headhunting bright young mathematicians from half a dozen top universities. I offer them a very good package. I provide them with the structure and the contacts they need to monetize their talents from the off, and if they stay with me I make sure they're very well rewarded. I'm the equivalent of a football player who's moved into management. In the middle part of your life, first-order skills are no longer your strongest suit and you need to adjust.'

Harry felt a need to change the subject. 'So . . . anyway. How about Brexit?'

'What an utter shambles,' Richard growled. 'What a total clusterfuck. History won't forgive the idiots who made this happen.'

('History won't forgive them' is fairly common in the archive. I always smile when I see it. Did they really think we'd be adults who could settle their childish quarrel, and not just more children like themselves?)

Harry knew that the idiots Richard was referring to were the politicians who called the referendum in the first place and the leaders of the successful Leave campaign, but in order to lift the conversation out of this well-worn groove, he pretended to misunderstand. 'What? All seventeen million of them?'

Richard examined him, sucking on his lips. 'Well, since you ask, my faith in British people in general has taken quite a blow. Karina's just come back from a book do in Berlin and she says that, surrounded by all those puzzled, reasonable Europeans, she felt thoroughly ashamed to be British. I mean, for Christ's sake, this wasn't rocket science! Everyone who actually knows anything at all about the economy explained repeatedly during the campaign that leaving would be a disaster. And yet, like a herd of moronic lemmings, our dear compatriots trooped out and voted for it anyway. Crass stupidity. Stupidity and gullibility, seasoned with racism, garnished with narrow provincial insularity, and stirred into a broth of toxic nostalgia for Empire by a motley crew of bigots and opportunists.'

Patient reasonable Europeans . . . ignorant backward-looking Leave voters . . . It was a familiar narrative to Harry and one of which literally millions of iterations can be found in the archive. But as he listened to Richard it struck Harry that it wasn't really a *new* narrative and that it actually predated Brexit. He thought about all those conversations about how European plumbers were so much more reliable than the British ones, European service workers so much more polite and friendly and interesting than rude and uneducated Brits. He even remembered saying such things himself: 'They're such nice people. They work so hard!' And each time he'd experienced a sort of tiny endorphin hit of self-satisfaction, as if being awarded some sort of prize.

'If you're anything like me,' he said, 'you probably don't know many Leave voters.'

'Oh, I know enough of them. There are quite a few in the City: eccentrics who just like to be different, the odd reactionary idiot who wants the whole country to become another Channel Island, and the occasional psycho who wants to make a few million by shorting the entire British economy. I don't talk to any of them if I can possibly help it. For their sake and mine.'

'They don't sound very typical of Leave voters in general.'

Richard snorted. 'They're not. They're intelligent people. Most Leave voters are thick.'

'A bit of a sweeping generalization, don't you think? There are seventeen million of them, after all!'

Once again Richard examined Harry's face for several seconds, chewing on his lower lip and breathing rather noisily through his large hairy nostrils. 'I wish I could agree with you, but I'm afraid it really is rather simple. We live in a nation full of bigoted, mean-minded morons, who are scared of change, incapable of rational thought, and can't accept that the world has moved on since the nineteen fifties.'

'We had the financial crash in 2008. Ordinary folk have seen very rich people, including people who were responsible for the crash, doing very nicely since then, while they—'

'That makes no sense, Harry. If someone is *already* unhappy about the economic situation why on earth would they choose to make things ten times worse? It's been hard for a lot of people, no doubt, not helped by the shitty Tory government, but I promise you that what they've been living through is an absolute *picnic* compared with how it's going to be for them if this shitstorm goes down.'

'I suppose if you're tired of being ignored or taken for granted by the people who run things, you might enjoy voting for something that you know they *really really* don't want.'

Richard sighed. 'That's a lovely, kind gloss to put on things, Harry, and I've heard it many times, but if you look at the data, that really isn't the reason people give for voting Leave. They want fewer foreigners here, they want to "take back control", they want to bring home the three hundred and fifty million pounds they've been mendaciously told the EU takes from them every week, they want to get Brussels off their backs and "have their country back".'

He shook his head. 'Of course if you tell them Brussels *doesn't* take three hundred and fifty million, which they could easily have found out for themselves, or if you explain to them that our economy needs migrants to be able to continue to function at all, they just block their ears. And the worst part is that when you ask them what exactly this wonderful thing is that they can't do now but are going to be able to do when we're outside the EU, they don't fucking *know*, because they don't know the first thing about what the EU does at the moment, and have never even bothered to find out.'

'I guess most people vote with their gut,' Harry said. 'I know I did. I'm more or less a total ignoramus when it comes to economics. I voted Remain because I liked the idea that European countries that have fought each other for centuries have come together in a peaceful union. I found that comforting. When I was on the Continent, I enjoying seeing all the different national emblems on the back of the same Euro coins. But, when it comes to the economic arguments, I have to admit I pretty much accepted on trust that membership of the Union was important for Britain's prosperity.'

Richard had become noticeably cooler. 'It's not just *important* to our prosperity. It's *indispensable*.'

Harry nodded. 'So people keep telling me, and I guess I believe them, though countries have broken away from other countries before, haven't they, and ended up doing all right? I mean, I imagine the American Revolution didn't make *economic* sense at the time, given that Britain was probably America's number-one trading partner?'

Richard didn't respond to this and was now looking towards the bar, rather than at Harry's face. 'Speaking of America,' he said, 'can you *believe* the shit that's going on over there?' And he began talking about the presidential election in which the loutish and wilfully ignorant Trump was doing unexpectedly well.

But Harry was only half-listening. He was thinking about Michelle. He was thinking that, while he didn't like what she'd said about the Polish builders, it wasn't really any more offensive than what Richard had just said about people like her.

'The Right's on the march all over the place,' Richard was saying when Harry started paying attention to him again. 'People on the Left like us need to get our act together and, however well-meaning, we need to stop making excuses for the—'

'We're the *Left*, are we?' Harry interrupted.

Richard frowned. 'Of course. Let's not beat around the bush. Never mind political theology. Never mind Marxist fairy tales. There's no time for that nonsense any more. We Remainers are the Left now, period. We're the good guys. The Brexiteers and the Trumpers are the Right.'

'Okay,' Harry said. 'It's just that you're a millionaire, from what I gather, and you work with banks and insurance companies in the City. And me, well, I'm not a millionaire obviously, but I earn a fairly comfortable living helping well-to-do people with lovely houses make their houses even lovelier.'

Richard studied his face. He could tell that Harry was annoyed and Harry felt each taut muscle in his cheeks and jaw being noted and coolly evaluated. 'What have our jobs got to do with our political views?' the actuarial consultant asked him. 'We both welcome diversity. We're against sexism and racism and homophobia.

We want the brightest and best to be able to get on and succeed, regardless of their background. We believe in decent public services. We believe in *helping* people fleeing from wars and persecution and not treating them like criminals.'

'Of course. Which certainly makes us both liberals, at the very least.'

Richard gave the kind of shrug that means 'so my point is made!' and then glanced at his watch. He was beginning to get bored. 'Karina and I have been talking of putting together a sort of discussion group to try to think about what went wrong and how we can prevent this kind of thing from happening again. We've got some good people who have expressed an interest: politicians, business people, academics. We're both crazily busy at the moment so it may be a while before it happens, but do you fancy coming along? It would be good to have someone there with your take on things.'

By this point, Harry had assumed that Richard had rather written him off so, while he didn't like the idea of the group – he imagined a lot of loud voices and accents ramped up to maximum poshness – he was flattered and reassured to have been asked. 'That sounds *way* too high-powered for me, Richard! I'm basically just a bloke who draws up plans for kitchen extensions.'

Richard shrugged. 'Well, it's up to you.'

'I think I'll pass. It's just not my kind of thing. But thanks.'

'No worries.' Richard showed no sign of being troubled by the rejection, as Harry probably would have been in his position. 'I'm going to head off now. Thanks for the game, mate.'

*

'Michelle didn't actually say anything derogatory about Poles,' Harry writes in his diary. 'She just said she didn't want them taking work from her brother. Now, of course I know she's wrong about that. I know that all the studies have shown that migrants make a—'

He breaks off in mid-sentence. 'Well, I *don't* know that, come to think of it, because actually I've never seen any of those studies. I've just heard people around me assert their existence and have duly asserted their existence myself. Which is interesting because I'm guessing Michelle also relies on what everyone around her says. So it's not really accurate to say that my assumptions are based on evidence while hers are based on prejudice. We're both just repeating things we've been told.'

I don't know where he's writing this. (It makes no difference, of course, but sometimes I just want to know.) Quite likely he's in bed, because he often writes his diary there. But perhaps he's sitting at his dining table or on a sofa.

'When I think about it,' he says, 'I can see how, at first glance, it might seem that immigrants take away jobs, but it does also seem fairly obvious why that's a fallacy. Because immigrants don't just add to the supply of labour, they also add to the demand for it by paying taxes and spending the money they earn.'

I don't *think* he's in bed yet. He's mentioned a few times lately that he finds it hard to make himself go to bed, that his bed seems a dauntingly lonely place, and that he often stays up far too late, fiddling with his phone. I visualize him sitting at a small dining table with the notebook open in front of him and a mug of tea next to him at one end of his flat's combined kitchen and living room, his double-glazed windows shutting out the night sounds of the city to create a strange, dead, hermetic silence that's quite unlike the quietness of the Suffolk countryside or of Michelle's forest. I picture him sucking the end of his pen as he sits there, considering what he's just written and trying to decide what to say next. He's still dressed, as I see him. It's well past midnight and he's very tired, but his mind is too restless to shut down.

'I'm pretty sure that must be true on a national scale,' he writes, 'but I can't see that it necessarily applies locally. I mean, if, say, Polish builders were to increase by 50 per cent the number of builders in Breckham, that won't necessarily increase the *demand* for builders in the area by 50 per cent, will it? It must be *possible* to have a glut of a particular trade, just as it's possible to have the shortages we're always hearing about. And, I don't know, obviously, but perhaps Poles are willing to work for less than British builders? They come from a poorer country, after all. Isn't that one of the reasons we're all so keen on these Eastern European tradesmen? They're willing to do more for less. Maybe in Breckham, Polish builders really *are* making it harder for people like her brother to earn as good a living as they did before.'

He draws a double line across the page here, as he usually does at the end of an entry. But then, perhaps after another pause and more pen sucking, he writes something else:

'I'm very very keen to exonerate her, aren't I? I'm working very hard to make her someone I can like again. And yet whether or not I like her isn't the question, is it? The question is whether I've got anything to offer her? Or her me, for that matter. And the answer on both counts is still no, isn't it, even if she isn't such a terrible racist? We might have got on well in bed, but that's only a part of life, however heavenly, and really and truly it's a small one.

'I've got an unmet need, obviously, but it's not her I need, no matter what my stupid heart tells me. What I need is a new partner.

All this thing has really done is shown me just how *much* I need that.'

He draws another pair of lines, but then discovers he still hasn't finished.

'But I can't stop thinking about her,' he scrawls. I think he must have shut the notebook and pushed it aside, and then grabbed it back later to scribble down this one last thought that had suddenly struck him as urgent. 'I'm forty-six years old, and way too old for this sort of thing, but, however stupid it might be, my heart just aches to see her and hear her and touch her.'

TEN

Charlie was clearing up after a poorly loaded truckload of straw. Jake came over to talk to him.

'All right there, Charlie? I was wondering if you fancied a pint later in the week? I'd like you to meet a mate of mine. He's a very political bloke, and I know he'd like to hear your thoughts on this Brexit business.'

Charlie laughed. He was touched. 'That's nice of you, Jake, but I know fuck-all about politics and that.'

'Me neither, Charlie, me neither, but he won't mind that, I promise you. It's hard to explain, but I promise you Gerald is something quite special. I'm sure as I can be that you'll agree with me.'

They met a few evenings later in the bar of the hotel on the market square. It had a red carpet, upholstered chairs and wood-panelled walls decorated with hunting prints and old cartoons from *Punch*. Charlie had never been there before. And Jake's friend, rising courteously to his feet to shake hands, was unlike anyone he'd ever met in any social context: a man of about sixty with a full head of snow-white hair and a salt-and-pepper three-piece suit. Fussing in the background, Jake was clearly very much in awe of him.

'Wonderful to meet you, Charlie,' the old guy said. His accent was super-posh and, though he wasn't particularly tall, he had considerable presence. His blue eyes fixed Charlie with a confident, open gaze of great intensity, he stood up very straight, and his dress and voice and demeanour all combined to signal authority of an old-fashioned kind which had a powerful magnetic pull. 'I don't know how much Jake has told you about me. My name is Gerald. Gerald Butler. My background is in the British Army, which is why some people call me the Colonel, and I had a second career in the City. But my preoccupation these days is the liberation of the United Kingdom.'

He had stood to attention for these last words but then he laughed and relaxed, and gesturing to a seat, asked what Charlie would have to drink. Charlie was impressed by the fact that he didn't go to the bar, as in a pub and as other people seemed to be doing even here, but signalled to the barmaid to come over.

'What I'm looking for,' Gerald said, 'and what I'm hoping you might want to help me with, is strong, fit, courageous young men, who would be willing, if necessary, obviously, to defend the decision made this year by the British people.' He twinkled at Charlie across the table. 'Are you in?'

'I ... um ... '

The Colonel laughed good-naturedly. 'Don't worry, Charlie. I was pulling your leg a bit there. You've only just met me. Of course you want to know more before you commit yourself.'

Charlie felt himself reddening. 'Yeah. That's the thing. It would be good to hear more and that.'

'Absolutely. Very sensible. But may I first ask you a few things about yourself?'

'No problem.'

'Jacob here tells me you feel very strongly about the Brexit vote?'

'I suppose I do.'

The barmaid came over to take the order. Gerald twinkled at her as well: 'Thank you *so* much, Sarah.' He turned back to Charlie. 'And, if you don't mind me asking, what do you normally vote in elections? Feel free to tell me to mind my own business!'

'I've never voted before. Only the Brexit vote. I couldn't be bothered, to be honest. They're all the same, aren't they?'

'I wonder why you say that.'

'I just don't think it makes any difference who you vote for.'

'Because?'

'Whoever gets in, they'll do what they want, won't they? They'll do what they want regardless and look after their own kind. None of them have got nothing to do with me. They don't know me. They don't know anyone like me.'

Gerald considered this, frowning, his fingertips touching in front of his nose, as if Charlie had said something very profound indeed. 'I understand,' he said slowly. 'At least, I *think* I understand. But the Brexit vote was different, you felt? Why was that, would you say?'

'Well, I knew it would make a difference, didn't I? I *thought* it would, anyway. If I voted Leave, we'd leave. That's what I thought. Something would really happen.'

'Something would happen, and you'd feel you had a part in it? That's fascinating. The way you speak about it, it's almost as if *what* was going to happen was secondary. No doubt you dislike the European Union, like any sensible Brit, but, if I've understood you correctly, you voted this time, more than anything, because you thought that it actually gave you a bit of power. And you liked the idea of that.'

'He *thought* that,' Jake growled, 'but they're trying to wriggle out of it now, aren't they!'

Gerald kept his focus on Charlie.

'You voted for the very first time,' he repeated meditatively, studying Charlie's face all the while, 'because you thought that, this time, your vote would actually *change* something. And being able to change things, being able to influence events, is, when you think about it, the very definition of power.'

'I suppose so, mate.'

'A very famous man once remarked, "Revolutions are the festivals of the oppressed and exploited." A nice phrase, I think, and very true. I think you've just put your finger on why.'

Charlie had no idea what to say. Gerald twinkled at him. 'Do you know who said that?'

Charlie took a wild guess: 'Winston Churchill?'

Gerald laughed good-humouredly. 'It should have been, my dear chap, and I wish it was, but actually it was Lenin. A perfectly dreadful fellow. Quite awful. The first communist dictator. But, credit where it's due, "festivals of the oppressed" really is rather wonderful, don't you agree? May I ask *why* you dislike the European Union?'

Charlie was slightly panicked by the question. 'Well . . . you know . . . because they tell our country what to do. People who aren't British telling Britain what to do.'

Gerald nodded. 'So again it's that feeling of decisions being made a long way away from people like you?'

'Too right,' Jake growled, but Gerald still remained focused on Charlie, his blue eyes fixed on Charlie's face as he courteously waited for his response. Charlie squirmed in his seat a little. Being listened to was an unfamiliar experience and it turned out to be rather unnerving.

'A long way away,' Charlie said. 'Yeah, that's it. People I don't know, a long way away.'

The barmaid came over with their drinks: pints for Jake and Charlie, and for Gerald a little golden glass of sherry. 'You're an absolute star, Sarah!' Gerald told her. He raised his tiny glass in a toast, and Charlie and Jake clunked their pints against it. 'I'd join you in a pint myself,' Gerald explained, 'but unfortunately beer doesn't like me at all these days.' He grimaced comically and pointed to his stomach, then leant forward again to concentrate on Charlie.

'But it's not just foreigners we're talking about here, is it? It's people in London too. Have I got that right?'

'That's very true, mate.'

Gerald nodded, his blue eyes watching Charlie's face with a kind of intense but affectionate curiosity. 'People in London who make fun of your sort of folk. People who you suspect don't even like you, or, which is possibly worse, barely even notice your existence. People who dismiss the things you want, and say you're wrong to even want them. Would any of those descriptions apply?'

'All of them, mate.'

'So London's *quite* far enough away without bringing Brussels and Berlin into it. Am I right?'

'Yeah, you are, mate. That's spot on, as far as I'm concerned.'

'But then, just for once, and for whatever reason, those people in London, who never normally listen to you, said they were going to let you decide something. Call me a bitter and cynical old man, Charlie, but I don't think they *really* wanted you to decide. They only pretended to because they assumed you'd vote the way they told you and then that would settle the matter. But be that as it may, they gave you a choice. And so, for the very first time in your life . . . *Huzzah! Rat-a-tat! Ta-da-da!*' As he spoke, Gerald cheerfully mimed in turn the acts of cupping his hands to his mouth to cheer, beating out a drum roll, and blowing an imaginary trumpet, each one in his characteristic, upright military manner. 'For the very first time in your life, you, Charles Higgins Esquire, went out and voted. Powerful stuff. And I really mean that, by the way. Don't be put off by my frivolity. I hear stories like yours a lot, and I always find them very moving indeed. You took up their offer in good faith and you voted. And, for the first time ever, you really felt involved in a decision about the direction your country should go.'

Charlie was moved too, as if he had never quite grasped until that moment what it was that he'd been part of. There were actually tears in his eyes, which he would have brushed away if it wasn't that by doing so he'd call attention to them. 'Yeah, mate, I was.'

The Colonel reached over the table and patted him on the arm. 'You're moved too, I can see.'

Charlie dabbed his eyes with an embarrassed laugh. 'Sorry, mate. I sort of . . . '

'Don't apologize! Good lord! Why on earth should you apologize? We chaps are allowed to have feelings too!'

Alarmingly, tears still seemed to be forming in Charlie's eyes. 'Yeah, thank you, mate.'

'And yet now, in spite of what they said, in spite of what you were promised, you're beginning to feel that they're going to wriggle out of it one way or another, just as Jake here was suggesting.'

'Exactly.'

'And you really, really don't want that to happen!'

'No, mate, I don't.'

Gerald clapped his hands together in satisfaction. 'Hurrah! Hold the front page! Gerald Butler and Charlie Higgins are in agreement!'

Charlie laughed and Gerald laughed with him. 'But seriously,' Gerald told him, 'I'm very pleased. You seem like a splendid chap and I'd be absolutely *delighted* to have you aboard.'

'Thank you, mate. I'm not sure what I can do, but you know . . . ' Charlie tailed off.

'I'll tell you what, Charlie. Let's not worry too much about details at this point. I'm afraid I need to go in a minute, but what I want to suggest is that you and Jake come out for a little gathering at my house with some of the other chaps I've been talking to, perhaps in a month or so, and we can talk a bit more. You'd not be committing yourself to anything obviously, but I'd be *so* pleased if you came along.'

He stood up. Always polite, Charlie attempted to stand as well, but Gerald gestured that there was no need, and grasped his hand in a strong, dry grip. 'It's been absolutely lovely to meet you, Charlie. Now, let me just catch the eye of the wonderful Sarah there and organize another round for you two chaps. Ah, there she is. Splendid. I will bid you both farewell then, and look forward very much to welcoming you to my home.'

'What do you reckon, Charlie?' Jake wanted to know.

'Nice bloke,' Charlie said. 'Treats you with respect, doesn't he?'

'Doesn't he, though? As posh as you like, but no airs and graces at all. He really *gets* people like us. I think it's from the army. Officers and men side by side. He was a war hero, you know. He won a medal in the Falklands. One of his men was wounded and Gerald fetched him back to safety under Argie machine-gun fire.'

Charlie was impressed. He loved war films. He collected military insignia. He liked to look at pictures of tanks and guns. 'He listens, doesn't he? He doesn't tell you what you ought to think.'

'I know. Wait till you see his house, though, mate. You won't believe it. It's a stately home, Charlie! I'm not kidding you. Tudor, I think he said it was. Or Elizabethan. Anyway, it's a great big brick place out in Breckham St Mary and it's as big the rest of the village put together. You know they used to talk about "the lord of the manor"? Well, that's him! That's only our mate Gerald. He's the lord of the manor of Breckham St fucking Mary!'

ELEVEN

'I wonder if we're *really* the good guys?' Harry writes.

He is sitting by the window in a café that called itself The Truly Delicious Coffee Company. It's about fifteen minutes' walk from his flat in what Harry describes as 'one of the charmingly gentrified toytowns of North London'. He seems to have quietly abandoned the painting idea, but he's taking on very little in the way of new architectural work. Having come in here to reply to emails on his laptop, he's ended up writing in his diary, which he now spends so much time on that it's almost become the focus of his life. He likes sitting in cafés to do it. He likes the hum of other people round him.

'I mean, pretty well everyone *thinks* they're the good guys. And everyone has their own particular shtick to support them in this belief. Millionaires say they're good because they're creating wealth, the landed gentry claimed to be good because they were the backbone of the country. For Christ's sake, even slave-owners had stories to explain why what they did was good and necessary and for the benefit of everyone.

'And let's face it, when it comes to our lot, we're the story-telling tribe. We've got the novelists, we've got the film-makers and the copywriters, we've got the historians and the cultural theorists and the political scientists. All those novels and plays that valorize the experience of people like us: our sensitivity, our refinement, our emotional intelligence . . . All those movies where the protagonists live in nice book-lined Victorian houses . . . When it comes to telling stories about ourselves, we've got more resources than all the other tribes put together. The only trouble is that most of those resources are directed towards—'

'Hello, Harry! I thought it was you!'

He looked up. He knew straight away that he recognized the rather elegant woman standing there, but he had no idea where he might have met her.

'I'm so sorry, I'm afraid I . . . '

She laughed. 'Don't worry! We've only met once and it was nowhere near here. It was out on the marsh near Blakeney.'

'Letty! Of course. Lovely to see you! I'm so sorry. I knew you were familiar but . . . '

The last and only time he'd met her, she'd had on an anorak and a woolly hat. Now she was wearing a very chic blue coat, make-up, a smart short hairdo.

'No need to apologize. Different context. I saw you in here about twenty minutes ago when I was walking past, and it was the same for me. I knew I knew you, but I couldn't think where from. And then you were still here when I came back this way, and it clicked. So I just had to come and say hello. I can see you're busy, though. I won't keep you.'

'No, don't worry about that. Nothing important. Can I get you a coffee?'

She looked at her watch. 'I haven't got very long. But, yes, that would be very nice.'

He bought her a latte and asked her about her son Alex, who it seemed had been having a difficult time in his new school, and about her work, which, at the present time, was mainly to do with disbursing funds to community-based drama groups. 'Not that there's much money to go around with this ghastly government. But what about you?'

'Me . . . ? I'm in a funny in-between kind of place. I've cut back on my work a bit to give myself time to think. I suppose I'm trying to decide what I should do with the remaining years of my working life. My life in general, come to that. Given that I have no children or family to support or provide me with a purpose.'

This last bit turned out to be a somewhat more personal disclosure than he'd intended, and brought him to an unexpectedly thin patch in his protective surface layer. What was he doing at his age, sitting in cafés, and writing page after page that no one but him would ever read? It was the kind of thing that seventeen-year-olds did.

'It may well be,' he added, speaking rather quickly in order to arrive as soon as possible on firmer ground, 'that my role in life is simply to carry on doing what I've been doing for years, which is help people to make their homes a little nicer. And, God knows, there are worse things than that. But still, it feels like a good time to take stock.'

Letty's response was kind; she could tell that he'd come close to some real distress. 'Well, I guess we all worry sometimes about the real value of what we do. I'm always wondering about how much difference it makes in the great scheme of things whether or not this or that little drama group gets some funding to help it put on a show which, let's be honest, not many people will see. But I suppose we just have to hope our little efforts add together into something worthwhile.'

It is interesting that, even as the Catastrophe crept up, and they, by their own behaviour, knowingly drew it closer, people back then still liked to think that they were contributing in some way to making the world a better place.

'Of course it's all very uncertain at the moment with this Brexit craziness,' Letty added. 'Isn't everything *awful* at the moment? Brexit, and now Trump as well, for goodness' sake. I'm just so grateful I've got the place in Blakeney to go to when things just feel too crazy to cope with. My sanity transfusion, I call it. It works every time.'

'I didn't realize you had your own place there.'

'Well, it's not just mine. It was my parents' place – they had a boat up there once as well – but these days my brothers and I look after it between us.'

'We had a place there when we were kids. And a boat too, actually! Up to the mid-eighties, we were up there most weekends during the summer.'

'How funny! We must have run into each other. Did you go crabbing in the harbour?'

'Of course! Ellie and I were always down there with our strings and our old bacon rinds. Mum and Dad had to come and haul us back in when it was getting dark.'

'Me and my brothers, too. So there must have been times when you and I were on the wharf together, just a few yards apart.'

'I suppose there must! No doubt we checked out each other's buckets. Do you remember that? The way that children you didn't know would come just close enough to be able to peer down appraisingly into your personal hoard of crabs? Those carefully opaque expressions as they looked?'

'I do indeed. It was pretty competitive, wasn't it? Do you still have your parents' place?'

'I wish we did. They sold it when we were twelve because they wanted to have more holidays abroad. We lived in Norwich, after all, so we could still go up to Blakeney easily enough. But it was never quite the same.'

'A couple of years ago we talked about selling our place. We nearly went ahead. I could have done with the cash after my divorce, and one of my brothers was thinking about buying a holiday place in Brittany at the time. But I'm *so* glad we kept it. I love our little seaside house. It's a wonderful store of happy memories, going all the way back to when I was five.'

She glanced at her watch again. 'I really ought to go. Thanks so much for the coffee. It's *really* nice to see you. Perhaps we could meet again when we've both got more time?'

Harry had been thinking what a likeable person she was (and very pleasing to look at too), but as soon as she made that offer, he felt himself recoiling from her, just as he'd done on the marsh. This time, though, he was ready for himself. Letty's invitation was a good thing, he told himself firmly. It was exactly what he needed to put behind him his embarrassing adolescent obsession with Michelle. Of course he had reservations, of course he had anxieties and doubts, but they were inevitable. You always knew that behind the face that was presented to you on first meeting someone there must lurk a more complicated and ambiguous entity, just as behind your own slightly boyish good looks were aspects of yourself that were rather less lovable, or perhaps not lovable at all. But these weren't reasons to isolate yourself. You had to push through the ambivalence. It was the price you paid for not being alone.

And after all, it wasn't as if Michelle was an exception to this rule. He'd drawn back from her sharply enough when she made that comment about the Poles. He'd actively disliked her, which had never been the case with Letty. He'd barely been able to look her in the eye.

'That would be great,' he said, looking Letty in the eye without any trouble at all. Then they exchanged phone numbers and emails, and she headed off to her meeting, smiling back at him through the glass as she hurried off. He decided to call her that evening.

TWELVE

'Well, that's good,' Cally says. 'He needs to forget about Michelle. It's getting a bit creepy. He's just using her to project his fantasies onto.'

We are on one of the long walks we often do together across London. It's another of those hot cloudy days where the air is too moist to carry away your sweat.

'That's a bit harsh,' I say. 'It would be creepy if he simply indulged his projections, but he doesn't do that. He knows what's going on. He knows he's putting her into a template that she probably doesn't really fit. He knows she can't *really* be his ideal woman, whatever his foolish heart is telling him. In fact, that's *why* he's leaving her alone! Seems pretty responsible to me.'

'It's not just his fantasies about women he's projecting on her, though, is it? It's his fantasies about lower-class people. His friends are busy demonizing them but he's doing the opposite. It's another whole layer of sentimentality. Setting someone on a pedestal who you'd normally look down on. He's a typical bourgeois, this Harry. He knows he's full of anxieties about his status and importance. He knows he's a bit pompous. And he likes to fantasize about being free of all that.'

The conversation is a little painful to me. Cally fits perfectly into a template of my own and she knows that quite well, although she chooses to pretend she doesn't. Her gracefulness on the one hand, her refusal on the other to take her own gracefulness seriously . . . It's a combination that has completely melted me since she first began to work at the Institute. But she has always made it clear that she wants me only as a friend.

'Did Lenin really say that?' Cally asks. 'I would have thought it was Marx.'

'No, it was Lenin. Of course he was the *ultimate* middle-class expert. He thought that the working classes needed professionals like him to conduct their revolution for them. In that same passage, just a few lines later, he exhorts the leaders of revolutionary parties to show the masses the "shortest and most direct route to complete, absolute and decisive victory". As it turned out, this wonderful route of his led through famine and terror and created a new and brutal ruling class which, seventy years later, would kick away even the pretence of communism, appropriate the hitherto socialized means of production, and become a particularly ruthless capitalist oligarchy of the exact kind that Lenin had claimed to be an expert in overthrowing. So much for expertise!'

My friend smiles. 'And through all those changes, there'll have been people loyally waving the same old flag without even noticing its meaning change.'

We come to the gated area in Hackney, where, behind a high fence topped with razor wire and security cameras, Full Members of the Guiding Body live in large three-storey Edwardian houses not unlike Harry's childhood home in Norwich. They have twenty-four-hour electricity in there, and hot water, and separate bedrooms for each family member. They even have vehicles for their personal use, almost as if they were back in the twenty-first century.

'Apparently they need to live like that because it helps them to give of their best to their work,' Cally says, deadpan, pressing her nose against the wire. 'And of course we *need* them to work at their best so they can figure out a way of helping all of us to live like they do.'

I laugh. 'And that's why they get genetic enhancement for their kids to make them super bright. So they can help us even better!'

But the goggle-eyed security guards are looking at us from the gate just thirty metres away, so we turn away from the fence and follow the road that skirts around it.

'By the way,' Cally says, 'how did you find out about that Gerald guy?'

'I didn't,' I tell her. 'He never existed. I made him up for the story.'

Cally laughs. 'That's a bit random, isn't it, Zoe? Why did you do that?'

'Well, we know a realignment of classes was underway, don't we? Not just in Britain, but right across the Western Hegemony. Old alliances crumbling. New ones forming. I wanted to represent that in the story.'

'Yes, but it didn't work in that way. It was about gradual changes in the stories that members of each group told one another. Not some old gent shaking hands with a power station worker.'

'Yes, I know. But this is a novel, isn't it? I'm giving myself a bit of licence. It has to be about characters and conversations.'

THIRTEEN

On Saturday night, Michelle was quite active on Facebook, commenting on posts made by her friends, adding some new photos, and offering her opinions in real time on the popular televised dance competition known for some reason as *Strictly*, which she was watching at her sister's house. She wrote nothing in her diary that day.

Harry meanwhile was in a French-Indochinese fusion restaurant called Hanoi Jane. It was located inside three eight-metre-high railway arches. The rear half of the middle arch was the kitchen, which was set behind a counter so that the chef and her assistants could be seen at work. The two outer arches were the dining areas. Harry arrived ten minutes early in a new blue jacket that he'd bought for the occasion, and was led to a table at the front of the left-hand arch, beside a tall window made of a single sheet of tinted glass.

The place had been laid out so as to create a mood of comfort, intimacy and modernity while at the same time preserving something of the austere industrial quality of Victorian railway architecture. The walls were the same rough, functional, industrial brick that they'd always been, except that a red star had been stencilled on to them, with a Vietnamese slogan beneath it in giant red letters. Apart from the exclamation mark at the end, the slogan was of course completely opaque to all but Vietnamese speakers, but it carried lingering connotations of a tough, brutal war in which a small communist country had fought off American imperialism half a century ago, and it gave the place a distinct 'alternative' edge.

It is an interesting feature of the period that, while middle-class gentrification tended to result in the pricing out of lower-class residents in formerly working-class areas (and, incidentally, the pricing out of non-white residents, given that ethnic minorities were under-represented in the middle classes), the new settlers, if we can call them that, felt a need to preserve a certain 'authenticity' or 'grittiness' that they associated with the area's past. (The adjective 'urban', with its additional connotations of 'radical', 'alternative' and 'edgy', was often used in branding as a way of capturing this much-sought-after 'gritty' and 'authentic' quality.) So industrial structures such as dye works, warehouses, power stations and so on were often refitted in such a way as to retain, and make a feature of, their former unadorned functionality.

Harry himself had designed several conversions on exactly these lines – he didn't really *just* work on kitchen extensions – and he admired the clever way it had been done by the designer of Hanoi Jane. But, as he sat there waiting for Letty, he found himself thinking about this practice of deliberately retaining 'industrial' features and comparing it to the habit prevalent among his friends and acquaintances of *proletarianizing* their language. (The affectation of glottal stops, for instance, or the adoption of the once exclusively working-class term 'mate' as a means of addressing people.) It seemed to him that his tribe lived in fear that, in the process of refining itself, it had become in some way inauthentic and no longer organically part of its surroundings in the way that it imagined less sophisticated people to be. So it felt this need to wrap itself in the mantle of those it had displaced, hoping that some of their earthy magic would rub off.

'Ellie and I grew up in Norfolk,' he writes later. 'I don't think either of us has even a trace of a Norfolk accent, yet very occasionally, if they know where we come from, someone or other will claim to notice a slight Norfolk inflection in the way she or I pronounce some word, and we feel ridiculously pleased and proud.'

But what he was particularly noticing about this kind of place was that Michelle wouldn't feel at home here. Although it seemed to celebrate the workplaces of industrial labourers, this bare-brick style didn't really signify 'working class' at all, and he was quite certain that she would read it, just as he did, as 'posh' and 'trendy' and 'middle class'. So the way his tribe liked to proletarianize itself was not about reaching out to actual living working-class people but about acquiring for itself the imagined magical tributes of those it had replaced. 'Like tribal warriors,' Harry thought, 'devouring the still-beating hearts of their valiant but vanquished enemies.'

But at this point he was brought back into the world by the arrival of Letty. As he'd done himself, she'd gone to some trouble to look her best for the occasion and was beautifully wrapped in an interestingly asymmetrical dress in deep red, with large gold earrings. They gave each other a peck on the check. She'd never been to the restaurant before and complimented Harry on his choice as they settled down at the table. He told her that his sister's friend Karina was a food writer and he'd asked her for a recommendation.

'Not Karina Stoke? Gosh!' Karina was well-known – she had a regular feature in the *Guardian*'s weekend magazine – and, as he supposed he'd intended, Letty was impressed by Harry's connection with her.

The waiter came with the menus and they ordered wine. Harry learnt that Letty had grown up in London and had lived in various parts of the city all her life, apart from three years in Brighton where she studied for her English degree and a one-year stint in Kenya in the nineties with her then husband.

The food, when it arrived, was artfully presented, arranged in the middle of clean white plates in a cross-hatched pattern, almost like abstract paintings, with little streaks of various brightly coloured sauces. (Harry couldn't help wondering about the complicated relationship between this artfulness and those bare-brick 'urban' walls.) I don't know *what* they ate, but there was probably meat or fish in both the starter and the main course, because one of the most striking things about life in Britain in the early part of the twenty-first century is just how much *flesh* everyone gobbled down. Even people on relatively low incomes typically ate meat or fish every day, and not infrequently several times a day, absurd as that seems now. But this was of course a Ponzi-scheme society that was only possible because it was able to defer its inevitable collapse to a point some way off in the future. Harry knew this perfectly well – he sometimes refers to it in his diary – and we know Michelle did, and so no doubt did Letty, but people in those days were somehow able to know and not know this fact simultaneously, just as the two of them doubtless also knew and didn't know that, even though they weren't conspicuously wealthy, they were significantly richer than most of their compatriots and so *hugely* rich in comparison to the majority of people on the planet that there was no way that the material resources of the Earth could support a lifestyle like theirs for anything but a small minority of its more than seven billion human inhabitants.

Harry asked Letty about her time in Kenya. She told him it was both fascinating and exasperating. 'Lovely people. Beautiful country. Awful corruption. Lousy politics.' And she went on to say that, of course, the problem with countries like Kenya is that they were artificial creations. Their boundaries were drawn up for the convenience of colonial powers, and made no sense at all in terms of the pre-existing language groups, cultures and allegiances, so that people had been lumped together who were historically part of completely separate nations, and separated off from their own ethnic kin. The Maasai people, for instance, with whom she and her husband had worked, had their own unique language and culture but were more or less equally divided between two separate states.

Harry was immediately interested in this. 'Arbitrary boundaries,' he writes later. 'People who had nothing in common being shoved together, people with the same language being split up, as European Empires carved up the African cake without a thought for the preferences of the people who actually lived there. It's one of those universally accepted truths that members of my particular tribe repeat to one another when the topic of Africa comes up: a dinner party truism that we pass back and forth, like ants passing back and forth the pheromones that bind them together into a single entity.'

He took a sip of wine. 'It's a funny thing,' he said, leaning forward slightly. 'What you've just said is something I've heard and read many, many times. African countries are artificial constructs. They were imposed, not chosen, and this causes conflict and makes nation-building difficult. I know I've said it myself more than once and I've no reason to think it isn't true. Yet when our own compatriots express concern about Britain being incorporated in a huge multinational construct of that kind, or when they question whether making our society even more multicultural is necessarily a good thing, we don't even allow it as a point of view. We say it's prejudiced nonsense and we call them racists and bigots.'

Letty's face changed. She was bewildered and at the same time worried. This was pretty unorthodox stuff. What else was he going to come up with? Had she completely misread what kind of person he was? Was *he* a racist? Was he going to turn out not to be her sort of person at all?

'I don't think I follow you,' she said. 'What are you saying exactly?'

'I'm rather interested at the moment in where our ideas come from. Us liberal Remainers, us *Guardian*-reading types, like to imagine ourselves to be the reasonable ones, don't we? And we like to point out the dishonesty and lack of logic of the other side. And yet we ourselves . . . Well, I'll give you another example. That bus—'

She knew immediately what he meant, as anyone at that time with the slightest knowledge of British politics would have done, for the bus was constantly being referred to by the Remainer side as an example of the Leavers' perfidy. It was a large red bus, and the 'Leave' side had painted it with the demonstrably false claim that Britain sent £350 million to the European Union every week, which could otherwise have been spent on the National Health Service.

'You're not going to defend that, surely?' Letty exclaimed. She was *really* troubled now. Everyone she knew, including even her stubbornly Leave-voting father, agreed that the bus was incontrovertible evidence of the deep dishonesty of the politicians who had campaigned for 'Leave', and it had become a cornerstone of the Remainer narrative about the unfairness of their defeat. 'It was deliberately misleading,' Letty said. 'We get half that money back as a rebate and most of the rest of it as—'

'Oh, I know it was misleading. Absolutely. But it occurred to me recently that it was equally misleading for people on the Remain side to talk up all the projects that the EU finances in this country.'

'But they *do* fund projects in this country, Harry. Good God, I should know! I've helped all kinds of community projects apply for funding!'

'Of course they do. But if it's dishonest to say we pay all that money to the EU when in fact most of it returns to us, then surely it's equally dishonest to say that we benefit from EU funding, when in fact that funding is really our own money coming home?'

'I suppose,' she said without much conviction. It was obvious she couldn't see what point he was making. It just seemed to her trivial and nit picking. She looked exasperated, flustered even.

He smiled, apologized for being contrary and asked her about her son.

I suppose he was tired by the time he got home. He writes a few pages in his diary, but he doesn't tell us how he and Letty parted or whether they agreed to meet again, and he doesn't offer any general thoughts on Letty herself, or what he now feels about her. After describing that conversation about the bus he simply draws a line.

'The thing you feel you've lost,' he writes. 'The thing you can't reach. The thing you're not allowed to reach. It's always so much more powerful, more intense, more vivid, than things that are actually present.'

FOURTEEN

Christmas was a very big thing in England in the early twenty-first century. A former pagan festival overlaid with Christian meanings, it still flourished in those largely irreligious times, complete with a new tongue-in-cheek mythology to take the place of the Christian story. This new narrative, which no adult believed but which was told to small children as if it was true, centred on the cheerful and rotund figure of Santa Claus, who was the owner of a toy factory, and travelled the planet with bulging sacks of consumer goods. It was a kind of cargo cult, a festival of consumption so prodigious that, in countries like Britain, it formed a significant component of the entire national economy, an event whose impact was discussed on the financial pages of newspapers.

Decorations began to appear as much as two months before the day itself and special Christmas music was played in the shops, referring to a rich, if shallow, iconography of reindeers, snow, warm fires, sleighs, family reunions, seasonal food, Santa and presents, presents, presents. Millions of trees, grown specially for the occasion, were chopped down and installed in people's homes, to be covered in electric lights and shiny balls and then discarded in the New

Year. Millions of turkeys, raised specially for Christmas dinners, were slaughtered. Thousands of tonnes of gifts were imported on container ships from Old China, many of which would never find a place in the life of their recipients, and an appreciable portion of which very soon would be going all the way back to China for disposal, for Britain had already filled up so many landfill sites with discarded goods and packaging, it struggled to find space for more.

'Michelle and Cheryl wish a very Merry Christmas to all our lovely customers!' says the greeting on the Facebook page of Shear Perfection. 'We're closed now but we'll be open again as usual 27ᵗʰ–31ˢᵗ, so come and have a makeover for that New Year's Eve party, or perhaps that new look to set you up for 2017.'

Michelle seems to have enjoyed the preparations for Christmas. She writes about trips to supermarkets with her mother and her sister. She speaks of a present-buying outing to Norwich with her niece Jules, and a 'Shear Perfection girls' night out' to a club in Cambridge. When the day itself arrived, Michelle, Kath, Jen and Jules worked all morning at Kath's house to prepare the feast and set out the room it would be eaten in. In her family, at least, this seems to have been strictly a woman's task.

Trevor was the first to arrive along with his new girlfriend, Sandra. Then Jen's husband came with two out of their three grown-up sons. Jen's oldest son was accompanied by his wife and two small children, the children clutching toys that they'd unwrapped at home earlier that morning: a large blue plastic truck that could be remotely controlled and a doll that could say more than twenty different things.

Everyone made themselves at home in the Christmas setting which Michelle and the other three women had arranged for them. Pongo slept in the hallway. Jules fetched drinks. Michelle played with the children. Jen and Kath put the vegetables in serving dishes and mixed up gravy and white sauce from packets. Later, after the meal, Cheryl would call by with her partner and her two children, and, as everyone became drunker, family members who weren't present would make video calls to the whole group. Many photographs were taken on phones, and some of them can still be found on the Facebook archive. There's a picture of Michelle pulling a comical face under a sprig of mistletoe while her brother-in-law Ken kisses her on the cheek. There's a family group taken by Michelle herself, Jules at one end looking like a younger version of Michelle, arm-in-arm with her cousin, Jen's youngest son. Michelle's mother Kath is in the middle, for nominally she's the matriarch, but she's very small and fragile and slightly dazed-looking, so the figure that draws the eye is big, red-faced fifty-year-old Trevor, who stands grinning beside her with an arm round her shoulders, wearing a pair of fairy wings and waving a wand. 'Couldn't fit our Christmas fairy on the tree' is Michelle's caption.

At one point Michelle took Pongo out for a walk in the nearby streets, which were always quiet but were now almost completely deserted. Many of the houses had twinkling lights outside them, or signs that read 'Merry Christmas', or electric snowmen and reindeers that blinked on and off. (There was no real snow. Even back then, snow fell only rarely in that part of England.) She looked through windows at other families in the yellowish glow of electric lights, eating, drinking and watching TV. In some of them the curtains were already drawn, and the TV light flickered round their edges.

When she came back in again, the children were playing in the hallway with their new toys, and all of the adults apart from Kath were slumped in the overheated living room in front of an old war movie they'd all seen many times before, which had just got past the opening credits. Kath was bringing in a tray of tea and chocolate biscuits, with a crumpled paper hat still on her head.

Michelle couldn't bring herself to surrender to that stupor. She knew it wouldn't feel like contentment and that it would at best be numbness, a profound boredom that was endurable only because there was no will left to do anything else, a kind of warmed-up death.

'Oh, for fuck's sake,' she said, 'we're not watching this *again!*' And, in spite of protests from Trevor and her brother-in-law Ken, she flipped off the TV and organized a game of charades. (Facebook photos: Michelle pretending to be a cat of some kind, holding up her claws; Jen looking very embarrassed and uncomfortable and not obviously looking like anything at all; Trevor standing on one leg in a parody of a ballet dancer; Michelle draining back a very large glass of red wine ...) After that it was time for Michelle, Kath, Jen and Jules to start laying out the next meal.

She drank far too much that evening, and staggered back to her own house arm in arm with Jules, who made her a cup of tea, fed the dog, helped her up the stairs, and then went to bed herself in the spare room.

FIFTEEN

Both of Harry's parents were dead – his mother had died a long time ago, in fact, when he and Ellie were in their early twenties – so his only real family now consisted of Ellie, Phil and their two teenage sons, Josh and Nathan. As it happened, Richard and Karina had decided to spend Christmas in Australia ('We needed a break from the Brexit madness') and had invited Ellie and Phil to make use of their house in Suffolk over the holiday period. Harry went to join them there.

By Harry's account, this wasn't an entirely successful plan. Nathan and Josh, who were sixteen and fourteen, were resentful about being separated from their friends in London and were soon ostentatiously bored, withdrawing into their phones in front of the TV. Phil had always found teenage behaviour very difficult and had a savage row with Nathan in the afternoon of Christmas Day, creating a dark cloud of resentment that was still hanging over the family on what was called Boxing Day.

'I feel like throttling Phil when he's like this,' Ellie confided to Harry. 'Would you mind taking him to the pub or something?'

It was a mild, sunny afternoon. Harry and Phil walked three miles through fields and what Harry calls 'a mysterious, mushroomy-smelling, marshy wood, full of shadow and light', to the nearest village. It was very much a middle-class pub, Harry records, its decor of bare stripped wood a variant of the stripped-down 'industrial' look he'd observed in London.

On the way over Phil had talked about how hard he found it to cope with his sons' behaviour, and how he sometimes found himself hating 'the self-centred little bastards and their sense of entitlement to bloody everything'. But the walk had calmed him and by the time they reached the pub he was ready to move on to other things. They ordered beef sandwiches and beer, and talked about football, Phil plunging into this reassuringly safe topic with obvious relish and relief.

'Burnley are whining that Sissoko didn't get sent off after that high tackle because he went on to set up that second goal for us. But just look at the video, for Christ's sake! There was no *way* that was a red-card offence. A yellow card was *exactly* right.'

They spent a good fifteen minutes on football but in the end they couldn't avoid coming back to Brexit, and to what was happening in America.

'A lot of people just can't cope with change,' Phil said. 'That's what Trump was playing on. He peddled the illusion that the world could somehow be wound back to how it once was in the good old days. And of course that's exactly what the Leave voters want as well: to stop the world, to stop history.'

'But isn't it us who are getting upset about change right now?' Harry said. 'We are the *Remainers,* after all. We're the ones who are complaining about things not being "normal". We're the ones saying, "This doesn't feel like my country any more."'

This doesn't feel like my country any more. Harry remembered a tedious old man on a coach journey many years ago who'd said those words, after a very long and bitter story in a dreary Midlands voice about how the street he'd lived in all his life had once been full of people like himself but now, except for him and his wife, was entirely populated by Bangladeshis. But Phil was so mellowed by beer and by the arrival of their beef sandwiches that he just grunted and let Harry's point rest. In fact, the sandwiches were so delicious that even Harry, who never talks about food, pauses to comment on them in his diary. For several minutes they munched in contented silence.

'There are all kinds of funny inversions and contradictions these days,' Harry finally said when the sandwiches were gone and had been washed down. 'Like, for instance, we liberal types still don't forgive Mrs Thatcher for destroying coal-mining communities in the eighties but when Trump says he wants to help the coal industry in Kentucky we all groan.'

'Oh, come on, Harry. Coal is a relic of the past. *Everyone* knows that. In fact, that's a perfect example of what I was talking about. Trump was cynically getting votes by pretending that an obsolete industry could be protected indefinitely.'

'Okay, but "You can't protect an obsolete industry against the modern world" is pretty much exactly what Thatcher said, wasn't it? No doubt Kentucky once had tight-knit coal-mining communities too. I read somewhere that the state already has one of the worst opiate problems in America. Yet we're not really interested. Our sympathies have moved elsewhere. Who we care about and who we don't seems to largely depend on who we currently need to feel morally superior to. And, let's face it, working-class people are *so* last century. If anything they've become the bad guys.'

'Well, some of them really *are* the bad guys. The Leave vote was highest among white working-class voters. Based in large part, one suspects, on a racist preoccupation with immigration.'

'But that's another thing, Phil. We're so *dishonest* with ourselves. Immigration is a case in point. We tell ourselves a fairy story in which a virtuous *us* wholeheartedly welcomes it, and a wicked *them* is wholly opposed, but—'

'They're abusing foreigners in the streets right now, Harry.'

'Who is "they"?'

'Okay, it's a small minority, obviously, but—'

'*Most* people think it's necessary to control immigration, Phil. And that includes members of immigrant communities, and it includes me, and it almost certainly includes you as well. I can't believe there are really many folk who would honestly want a completely open border.'

'Why not? That's exactly how it should be, isn't it?'

'How it should be, perhaps, in a sort of aspirational sense, but come on, Phil, you don't really want us to abandon border controls right here and now in the world we actually live in, do you? It would be chaos. Our systems would be completely overwhelmed. Communities would fall apart.'

Phil shrugged. 'Well, okay, but this is silly, Harry. No one is *proposing* that we abandon border controls completely!'

'*Exactly*! No one is. But by telling the story the way we do, by presenting ourselves as *for* immigration – and therefore good, generous, welcoming, tolerant – and presenting our political opponents as *against* it – and therefore bad, narrow, racist, bigoted – we magically exonerate ourselves from responsibility for the ugliness of border controls and project all the blame for them on to the other lot, *even though we ourselves accept such things as necessary evils*. Do you not see how dishonest that is?'

He watched Phil consider this: clever, donnish, with his long thin limbs and his shaven head. 'Particularly,' Harry added, 'when you take into account that people like you and me tend to live in largely white British areas, where very few recent immigrants could afford to live.'

He decided not to mention the fact that Phil and Ellie had actually moved to their present home south of the river in order to be in the catchment area of a good (and largely white) school.

'Your politics seem to have moved to the right lately, Harry,' Phil observed as they trudged back from the pub, the sky already darkening. 'I used to think of you as more of a lefty than me.'

Harry didn't answer this straight away. He knew, of course, what Phil was referring to, and he knew it had to do with Michelle. Meeting her had made him want to defend people like her against the caricatures that his friends seemed to want to reduce them to. But it wasn't *just* that, because the shift had begun before he met her. He was already feeling disillusioned with his own tribe when he met her and the fact that she came from outside of it had been a big part of her appeal.

He swallowed. 'I don't think I've changed my views exactly,' he said. 'But what's been striking me a lot lately is how we stage-manage things to make us look like the good guys. It's almost as if we have to claim the moral high ground in order to be able to dismiss people we don't want to have to listen to or care about.'

They walked for a while in silence. The mushroomy wood was dark and cold now.

Phil turned on the torch that was built into his phone and a barn owl was caught in its light as it glided over a nearby field with ghostly white wings. (The creatures went extinct about a century ago.) 'There are really nasty people leading the Leave side,' he said, speaking quite firmly. 'Liars, haters, naked opportunists, racists. That's a fact, Harry. It's not just our projection. It's a bit sentimental to pretend that everyone is equally good at heart. Sentimental and dangerous.'

'All I'm saying is that the other side have done a better job of making people feel that they've been noticed and heard.'

'Well, perhaps,' Phil said, 'but you could have said that about Hitler.'

Ah, Hitler! Here he comes! All students of the period notice how the Second World War still loomed in the imaginations of people in 2016, rather as the Warring Factions period looms in ours. There must be literally millions of references to the Nazis in social media posts about Brexit. The Remain side equate their opponents with Nazis, and even coin the word 'Quitlers' to describe them. The Leave side liken the European Union to the Nazi Reich, and themselves to the plucky little Brits who, in British mythology, had faced the might of the German war machine alone. I suppose this helps to explain why the study of history is important and why it still continues, to a limited degree, even now when so many other aspects of intellectual life have become unaffordable luxuries. We need to cover up our nakedness, and the past is one of the places we go to find clothes.

Harry sighs. 'You *could* have said it about Hitler. But my point still stands. If our tribe can't persuade people we've got their back, there are others they can turn to. It's like borrowing money. When reputable banks aren't interested in helping you out, you end up going to loan sharks.'

They fell silent again, trudging along the path, and Harry wondered gloomily what Michelle was doing now, and whether she ever thought about him.

'As to whether I'm still on the Left,' he finally said, 'I used to think I was well to the left of Blair, but now we've got Corbyn, and I think he's too left wing and not pragmatic enough. I wonder sometimes where exactly *is* the sweet spot that would fit exactly with my own degree of leftiness? Does it even exist? Or is my problem that I want to *believe* that I'm one of the good guys but I actually quite like things how they are. I can't help feeling that the kind of vaguely left-wing politics that people like us subscribe to is a bit like going to church a few generations ago: conventional piety, an outward show. It doesn't really change the way you lead your life, but it reassures you that you're on the right side.'

They'd reached the road that ran in front of the cottage. There was a pavement for pedestrians on this stretch, so Phil had turned off his torch and was searching his phone for the day's sports news. 'Well, Marx would be with you, I suppose,' he observed as he did so. 'Liberal values just a fig-leaf over the— Ha! Bad luck, Harry! You were beaten three–one by Reading.'

Back in the cottage, Ellie and the boys had found their way to a much more cheerful place in Phil's absence. With the stove in the living room blazing, coloured lights glittering on the Christmas tree, the curtains drawn tightly against the cold and dark outside, and Nathan's music playing, the three of them were assembling an evening meal under the old black timber beams of Karina and Richard's large and beautiful kitchen.

After they'd eaten and cleared the table – the same table where Harry had once sat listening to Richard and Phil roaring and thundering about Brexit – all five of them settled down to a lengthy board game called Risk and were very soon completely immersed in a loud, cheerful and protracted battle for global domination. Ellie and Harry grew tired of this after about an hour and, having allowed their forces to be overrun, they took their glasses of wine through to the living room, to sit on those beautiful sofas in front of the log-burning stove, while the other three continued their ruthless war with undiminished enthusiasm.

'Remember last time we were down here together sitting round that table and everyone was banging on about the referendum?' Harry said. 'I was thinking about it just now – how angry and upset everyone was, how outraged – and do you know who it suddenly reminded me of? Uncle Jack! Uncle Jack and that awful friend of his he used to insist on bringing with him when he came to visit. What was his name? That chap with the little moustache and bad breath who used to tousle our hair and slip us each a fifty-pence piece? Do you remember how the two of them would sit there in the living room going on about the *blecks* and the *wahts* in their whiny, pinched Rhodesian accents?'

Ellie pulled a bewildered face. Uncle Jack was their maternal grandfather's older brother, who had returned to the UK from the British colony of Rhodesia when it finally became independent as Zimbabwe. 'Oh, come on, Harry! Uncle Jack would *definitely* have been a Leaver!'

'Of course he would. But, all the same, our Remainer script sounds exactly like those interminable conversations he used to have with old racist whatshisname with the moustache. *Credulous*

people stirred up by leaders who are only out for themselves . . . '
Harry counted off the points on his fingers. '*Russian interference . . .*
Rabble-rousers promising them the earth . . . The country's going to go
to the dogs . . . The ones who voted for it are going to be hit the worst,
but they weren't capable of understanding what they were voting
for . . . Think about it, Ellie, it's all there! We were like a bunch of
disgruntled Zimbabwean whites at the beginning of majority rule!'

Ellie shrugged. 'I really don't see it.'

'No really, Ellie, it's perfect, because it's exactly the same thing. A
formerly dominant group suddenly finding that the levers they used
to pull are no longer connected to anything.'

Ellie was unconvinced. 'It's not really comparable, though, is it,
Harry? I mean, Brexit really *will* be bad for the country, especially
for the people who are worst off.'

'So was Zimbabwean independence, for Christ's sake! It was
economically disastrous! The agricultural sector collapsed. The
currency became worthless. Et cetera, et cetera. Uncle Jack shook
his head and said he and his chums had told us so all along, but
he completely missed the point. Because it *had* to happen, didn't
it? Even if it did make things worse for a generation – or two
generations, for that matter, or three – it was just one of those things
that had to happen. And just like us – *just* like us – the one question
that never once occurred to him and whatshisname was how white
Rhodesians like themselves might have brought this on themselves.'

Ellie smiled non-committally and shrugged. 'I've been meaning
to ask you, Harry. How are you getting on with Letty? You seemed
so keen to choose the right restaurant, I got the impression it was
really important to you. And afterwards you told me the evening
went okay, but you didn't seem to want to talk about it, and you've

gone completely silent ever since.'

Harry turned his wine glass back and forth between his fingers. 'It was fine. I think I may have worried her at one point when I got a bit contrary. You know how I sometimes do?'

'*Sometimes?* You're always doing it these days. Phil says he can't tell any more whether you're kidding or being serious.'

'I'm not sure myself sometimes, to be honest. It bothered Letty a bit. But we moved on to other things, and we had a perfectly pleasant time. It certainly wasn't a disaster. And at the end we exchanged hugs and pecks on the cheek, and agreed to meet again. As far as I can tell we both meant it. But she was going to spend Christmas in Provence with an old friend of hers who lives down there, so we said we'd be in touch in the New Year. I'll give her a call then.'

'I'm not hearing a lot of enthusiasm.'

'Oh, she's really nice. She likes a laugh. She's bright. She's interested in things. She's lovely to look at. Of course it's early days, but . . . '

'*Still* not getting much enthusiasm, Harry.'

'No. I suppose not.'

She shrugged. 'Well, never mind. You can't expect to click with everyone, even if they *are* nice. Maybe you just need to keep looking? You're a good-looking man, you know, and a very lovable one too. There'll be plenty of others interested.'

Harry shrugged. From the dining room came the sound of a handful of dice flung down on the wooden tabletop.

'It must be very hard for you, Harry,' his sister said. 'Having to start again at the beginning. But it's not all bad. There are times I envy you, you know. I'm sure Phil does too. He and I are fine, don't misunderstand me, but it would be fun in a way to start again. I mean, I know Phil loves me, but I wouldn't mind being with someone who felt able to actually tell me so more than once in a blue moon!'

'He's a good bloke and he loves you very much.'

'I know, and I'm grateful to have him. But my point is I know you feel sad and left out, and I know you could do without that at this time of your life, but it's exciting too, isn't it? There's a good side to it as well as a bad one.'

'You're right, but . . . ' He hesitated, unsure how much he wanted to tell her. 'Okay, the truth is that I don't believe this is to do with Letty specifically, I think it's to do with the state of my heart. I don't think I'm ready.'

Ellie sighed. 'Oh come on, Harry, you really do need to let go! You and Janet were *so* unhappy for *such* a long time. It's been over a year now since you split up. You're forty-six years old. Don't waste any more time over it.'

Again he hesitated. In the next room, Phil crowed with triumph as his forces overran some strategically important territory and Nathan howled in protest.

'I'm not talking about Janet,' Harry said quietly. 'It's someone else.'

This took Ellie completely by surprise. '*Really*? Who? Since when?'

He sighed. 'Okay, I'll tell you, but you're going to think I'm being pretty stupid. I stayed over in Breckham when my car broke down on the way back from the coast, and—'

'You met someone in *Breckham*?' She was even more surprised now.

'I stayed with this woman Michelle who lets out a room. We got talking. We drank a lot of wine. We ended up in bed together, and . . . Well, I know it's silly but I can't stop thinking about her.'

'Is she married?'

'No, she's single. Single and childless like me. She had a child who died, in fact, so actually *very* like me in that respect.'

'So, what's the problem? Doesn't she want to see you?'

'I don't know. I haven't been in touch.'

'Why not? If you really liked her, why on earth not?'

'She's not like us, Ellie. She's a hairdresser. She left school at sixteen. I'm pretty sure she voted Leave.'

Ellie laughed. 'Well, whatever Phil might think, you *can* vote Leave and not be the devil incarnate.'

'You certainly can. But—'

'But you're thinking it would be difficult to sustain a relationship with someone who didn't share your values? It would, actually, wouldn't it? Still, if she really meant that much to you . . . '

Just talking about this, just having Ellie discuss it as something that needed to be taken seriously, had made him almost light-headed. That this odd little story could actually be spoken out loud and still remain real seemed miraculous. And he noticed to his amazement that the glass in his hand was trembling. He put it down on the coffee table, wordlessly acknowledging the strangeness of this with a half-bewildered, half-embarrassed glance at his sister.

'I don't know what's going on in my head, Ellie. I had a lovely evening with Michelle. I honestly haven't been that happy in another person's company for . . . oh, I don't know, it actually feels like for ever. But in the morning . . . well, there was this moment when she made a comment about bloody Poles coming over and stealing people's jobs, and I thought, "What the fuck am I doing here?" I disliked her so much I could barely even look her in the eye. And I felt ashamed of myself for being so desperate as to be able to overlook the obvious gulf between us.'

'And yet . . . ?'

'And yet that passed. The dislike didn't last. I realized that most people I know say equally hateful things almost routinely without even noticing it. And I actually think that part of her appeal is that she *isn't* like me. Isn't like *us*, I mean. Isn't one of our kind. I know it's a funny thing to say, but this Brexit business . . . Well, you've noticed me becoming rather contrary on that subject . . . I haven't changed sides exactly, I certainly haven't changed my personal views, but it has made me less tolerant of our own sort of people. I look at Twitter a lot – I'd be far too embarrassed to tell you just *how* much – and you should see the ugly sneering contempt that our tribe directs towards hers. We're such a *smug* lot. It never occurs to us that, just possibly, other people might see things that we don't see.'

Ignoring the content of what he was saying as if it was nothing more than background noise, Ellie watched him with narrowed eyes. 'Is she very pretty?'

He shrugged. 'I guess so,' he said and then surrendered to her stern interrogative gaze and laughed. 'Who am I kidding? Yes, she is. *Very*. I found her incredibly attractive physically. I was aware of it as soon as she came to the door. I even liked her voice on the phone.'

'And you had a lot to drink?'

'Yes, a bottle of wine each.'

'And lovely sex?'

'Yes. Initiated by her. Absolutely unbelievably lovely.'

His sister nodded. 'And the grown-up part of you is thinking that the lovely time you had with her was a lot to do with being drunk and good old-fashioned lust, and probably couldn't be replicated in the cold light of day?'

'Well, exactly.'

'And yet you can't seem to shake off the thought that just possibly it *could*?'

'I suppose that's it.'

'Well then, you need to see her again, don't you? See her when you're not drunk and you're not in bed together.'

At this point, Harry says, he became so agitated that he could no longer even bear to stay in one place. He leapt up and began pacing about. From the dining room came another shout of triumph, this time from Josh: 'I am now officially the king of South America!' He could see them through the open door, the father and his two sons, all three leaning intently over the board. Phil glanced quizzically in his direction for a moment, but Nathan had just thrown the dice, so he returned his attention to the battle.

'But that wouldn't be fair to her,' he said. 'She needs to get on with her life. She's thirty-eight, she could still have a kid if she got a move on. She really doesn't need some guy who may well not be able to offer her anything barging into her life and wasting her precious time.'

'Well, she's a grown-up, isn't she? She can make those calculations for herself.'

Harry was elated by that thought, but Ellie was severe. 'Of course, she might not want to see *you*. That's possible, isn't it? She might have exactly the same kind of doubts. And you've left it for so long! If I were her, I'd be a bit suspicious if you got back in touch with me after all this time. I'd wonder if you just fancied another shag. But if she said no, that would at least be an end to it, wouldn't it? And if she says yes . . . well . . . who knows? Maybe you'll find you actually do get on. The worst that could happen is an uncomfortable few hours.' Ellie laughed, gesturing to him to sit with her again. 'You're in a real state about it, aren't you? I don't think I've ever seen you like this!'

He sat down and rubbed his hands over his face. 'I can't remember feeling this way since I was fifteen.'

His sister laughed. 'Poor Harry. You've gone short of love for a very long time, haven't you? You're like a starving man who's unexpectedly been given a meal. And the cruel thing is you don't need to be hungry at all.'

To Harry's own surprise he burst into tears. Ellie went to shut the door through to the dining room and then sat beside him and put her arm round his shoulders.

'There's food all around you, bro,' she said. 'You just need to learn how to eat again.'

He went up to bed soon afterwards, not wanting to have to deal with Phil and the boys when their game was over. But he was far too agitated to sleep and his entry for 26th December is one of the longest in the entire collection of notebooks. He is haunted throughout it by the awareness that he has two distinct images of Michelle in his mind that don't connect up with one another, like two halves of a stereoscopic photograph that can be seen separately but refuse to align into a single 3D picture. On the one hand there is the perfect Michelle who fits his own longing like a key in a lock: the one he couldn't help himself from calling sweetheart and darling because of the torrent of long-buried love she'd drawn out of him. On the other hand there is the Michelle he'd barely been able to look in the eye. 'I feel like King Midas,' he writes, 'except the other way round. I see gold but I'm afraid to touch it, in case by doing so I turn it into dust.'

He remembers that there were two Janets as well, but then corrects himself. Actually, there were three: one that he'd loved, one that he'd hated, and one that he'd simply coexisted with, as you coexist with a workmate or a next-door neighbour.

'We don't really know anyone,' he thinks. 'Even the people we know very well, we don't know well enough to see as a single whole. And as to the rest of the world, well, we're just guessing, we're just projecting our own fears or desires on to whatever little fragments we think we've glimpsed. Dear God, I don't even know *myself*! Essentially what I was doing this evening was laying out the mess inside my head and asking Ellie to tell me what it meant and what I really wanted.'

He draws two lines across the page.

SIXTEEN

Charlie was invited out to Gerald's house in the week between Christmas and New Year. Jake passed the invitation on and picked him up in his car. The village of Breckham St Mary was about four miles away from the town of Breckham and, if it had been a little bigger, it would have been the kind of place that Harry refers to as 'Tory toytowns'. The pretty old houses were built in a mixture of mellow brick and flint. The pub had a thatched roof. There was a large and handsome church, also faced with flint, with a tower and high, graceful leaded windows of clear glass which, as Jake and Charlie arrived in the village, were pouring out a soft golden light to warm the night around them as if the church were the village's glowing hearth. The overall effect was like being inside a Christmas card. All that was missing was snow.

Gerald's house and grounds stood opposite the church and behind a high brick wall. They reached it through an ornate gateway topped by a big carved animal with bat-like wings that looked down at them from a perch above the capstone. A number of cars were parked on the gravel in front of the house and a row of tall pointed windows, not unlike those in the church, gave out a glow that dimly illuminated them in a way that felt slightly dreamlike because it created a kind of island in the darkness. The upper reaches of the house were black against the stars. The Christmas-card world was surprisingly close to the world of Gothic horror.

A servant, or what Charlie took to be a servant, met them at the door and led them through to the dining hall, which was two storeys high with a gallery at one end that once had been used by musicians to entertain the owners of the house and their guests. Grotesque heads and coats of arms decorated the roofbeams and the gallery's wooden balustrade, and tall leaded windows alternated with big, dark portrait paintings. There was a young man with a moustache in a polished breast plate, a severe old patriarch in an Edwardian suit, a tall, haughty woman dressed in lace . . . But where one might have expected a long table, there were rows of plastic chairs, most of them already occupied. About forty men were there, some of them Charlie's age, some nearer in age to Jake. He recognized a number of them from school or from the pubs in Breckham, or both. There were no women among them – though this didn't strike Charlie as odd because, in his world, men and women tended to do things separately – and everyone there was white apart from one young man with freckles and curly hair who looked as if one of his parents was black. Some of the men were talking to one another, but in subdued, self-conscious voices. They were all a long way away from where they felt at home.

A small platform had been set up below, and just in front of, the gallery. Gerald stepped up on to it. 'Gentlemen! Could I have your attention, please!' He was wearing a blazer with brass buttons and a regimental tie. 'I'd like to welcome you all to my home. And thank you so much, once again, for taking an interest in my little project. As you know, what we're trying to do here is to build up an organized body of men willing, if necessary, to defend our country against a possible enemy within. We're still at an early stage, sorting out our ideas, feeling our way, thinking over the options, but I think tonight's speaker will be very helpful to you. His name is Steve Finch. I only met him quite recently but I like to think of him as a friend; and he's been doing a lot of thinking about where we are and where we need to get to. I feel sure you'll find his ideas very interesting. I know I do.'

The big man who took Gerald's place on the stage wasn't at all how Charlie would have imagined a friend of Gerald's to look. He was about fifty, his face large, round and suntanned, his head shaved bald, and he had tattoos on his arms and neck. He was well built but somewhat overweight, with a pronounced beer belly that thoroughly filled the dark blue T-shirt that he wore tucked into his jeans. When he spoke it was with a strong Birmingham accent.

'I'm not who you expected to meet in a place like this, am I right?'

The whole gathering laughed, grateful for the release and pleased to be looking at a man who seemed to come from a world like their own. No one had felt comfortable inside this enormous, strange and slightly sinister-looking house.

'Truth is,' Finch went on, 'I wouldn't have expected to meet *myself* in a place like this. And I certainly wouldn't expect a bloke like Gerald here to be calling me his friend.' Gerald, who was standing just to the side of the stage, made a humorous gesture to indicate that the surprise was mutual but entirely pleasing. 'Gerald and his kind were the enemy, that's how I would have seen it in the old days. Because, let's face it, the man's a toff and, if there was one thing in the world I hated, it was toffs.'

Finch contemplated their host. 'Colonel Sir Gerald Butler . . . Seriously! Who would have believed it? We still disagree about a lot of things, mind you – a whole lot of things, in fact. I'd go so far as to say that he still is my class enemy in a way, but in this world you have to form alliances, and when you form an alliance you have to learn to respect your ally. And I have to say that's not been hard in this case because there's a lot to respect about the Colonel. He's a man who cares deeply about this country and its traditions, for one thing, and he also happens to be a war hero who risked his own life to save one of his men.'

Finch winked at his audience. 'But that's enough of that, eh? Sir Gerald's head is *quite* big enough already without me puffing him up even more. I'll move on, and tell you something about myself and how I ended up being up here on this stage in front of you, in what looks, let's face it, like the set for a sixties horror movie. As you can probably tell, I'm a working-class boy from the Midlands. My parents were factory workers, so were my grandparents, and so was I when I started out. I worked for a company that made wheels for bikes and motorbikes. The company still exists, as a matter of fact, but it's shifted all of its production to a factory in Vietnam where people work long hours for only a few quid a month. How about you guys? From what I gather most of the factories near here have closed down too. The Thermos glass factory in Thetford, the Kwalpak suitcase factory in Breckham . . . How do you earn a living these days?'

He pointed to various members of the audience. There was a delivery driver from Brandon with earrings and a red beard, a shelf stacker in the Breckham Tesco, a young man with acne who cleaned the stands at the race course at Newmarket, a guy from Mildenhall who was out of work . . .

'I've been there, mate,' Finch told him. 'I've been there. My sympathies.'

He turned his attention to the room at large. 'Right! Now then, everyone, show of hands: how many of you are in a union?' Less than half put up their hands. Finch nodded. 'Not what they were, unions, are they? I was a keen union man myself, just like my dad, and I became a full-time union organizer and an activist in the Labour Party, standing up for the workers against rich bastards like Sir Gerald here. Up the revolution!'

He laughed grimly. 'Fun fact about the Labour Party: it was set up by the trade union movement, specifically to get working-class people into parliament. How's that working out? Let's look at the last four Labour leaders. Corbyn and Blair both went to private schools. Milliband was the son of a university professor. Brown's dad was a Church of Scotland minister. Oh dear! Not very working class at all. In fact, none of them could really claim to be any more working class than Gerald here, and at least he doesn't pretend to be anything other than what he is. Nope, the Labour Party isn't the party of working people any more, as you probably knew already. It's sloughed off the unions that set it up. It gets half its support from posh university towns. But then manufacturing is yesterday's news, or so we're told. That's Asia's job now. Britain isn't a country that makes things these days, it's a *knowledge economy*. It's all about financial services, and advertising, and IT, and biotech – the kind of stuff that happens in London or in wealthy, techy towns like Cambridge, just down the road from here.'

He shaded his eyes to look out into the room. 'So how come you lot are still out here in the sticks in Norfolk and Suffolk? You, mate, are scrubbing beer and tomato sauce off of the stands at Newmarket, but how come you haven't grown a hipster beard and set up your own PR company in Shoreditch? And you, sir – you over there – why are you stacking shelves in Tesco's when you should be splicing genes in some swanky lab in Cambridge, or maybe writing software for the driverless vehicles that are going to put our delivery-driver friend here out of work? This is a globalized world, don't you know? We're competing in a global marketplace. No room for dinosaurs. You either adapt or die! Didn't you get the memo?'

The audience was silent, stunned, resentful. Charlie, who'd always had difficulty detecting sarcasm, was also very confused. Wasn't this man supposed to be on *their* side?

Finch laughed. 'Ha! Good luck with all of that, guys. Good luck with even *living* in one of those places! I was in Cambridge yesterday, as a matter of fact. Dropped by for a pint with an old Labour Party mate of mine, and I happened to look in an estate agent's window. I saw an old three-bedroom council house for sale that was just like the one I grew up in back in Brum – no extensions, nothing, just a bog-standard nineteen-fifties brick semi with three smallish bedrooms – and, I kid you not, it was on the market for . . . wait for it . . . five hundred thousand pounds. You'll have to excuse my French, your colonelship, but seriously, *five hundred thousand* fucking pounds! No one cares any more about you dinosaurs out here in the sticks, but sure as hell no one's going to let you move anywhere else.'

He studied the faces of his listeners. 'When I finally started to get all this, my first thought was to go full lefty. The Labour Party had sold us out, I said to myself, but there was still communism. But you know what? That's a con too. You show me *one* communist country where working people are really in the saddle and aren't being screwed over by some tyrant or other, or some bunch of oligarchs with their fingers in the till. So these days I take a different view. There are always going to be bosses. There are always going to be blokes like Sir Gerald in his Elizabethan mansion here, whatever you choose to call your political system. But that doesn't mean we've got no power. I was reading this book the other day—'

Here Finch broke off, pretending to look hurt, as if someone in the audience had expressed incredulity. 'I know. Hard to believe. But I did. Get me! I read a book.' There were a few chuckles, but Finch wasn't satisfied with that and hammed about to coax a more generous response from his listeners. He pretended to open an imaginary book, very gingerly, as if it might explode at any moment, and then recoiled in amazement at its contents. It was well done and he got his laugh. He had a knack for building up tension and then releasing it.

'It was a book about China, as a matter of fact,' he went on. 'Amazing country. Amazing people. I won't hear a word against them. Those guys were living in cities when us lot were still swinging from the trees. And they've had this wonderful idea for more than two thousand years that they call *Tianming*, the Mandate of Heaven. What it means is that, yes, the Emperor gets to rule the country, and yes, Heaven will help him do it, but *only* if he looks after the people. If he stops looking after them, if he disrespects their traditions, if he starts to imagine that him being Emperor is just the way things are and, to hell with the plebs, he's going to do whatever he damn well likes . . . well, then Heaven withdraws its support, the Emperor stumbles, and the people sweep him aside.'

Finch gestured the act of sweeping as he spoke.

'And, you know what?' he said. 'I think that's pretty close to the situation we're in right now. For a long time this country's been run by people who don't really care about us, who barely even bother to conceal how much they despise us, and yet think they can do whatever they want and we'll just put up with it. But they've got that wrong, haven't they? We're not having it any more.'

Someone cheered, and Finch gave him a thumbs-up. 'We aren't, though, are we, mate? Seriously! You're not having it. None of you are. That's why you're here. Give yourselves a round of applause!'

They all clapped, and a few men cheered raucously.

'But we're British people,' Finch said, 'so we're going to be reasonable about it. We've given them fair warning. We know that if we don't have this lot in charge, we'll have another lot instead, and we could do without the hassle if we can possibly avoid it. So we're giving them a chance to change their ways. If they show they're willing to listen to the British people, fair enough. If not, we chuck them out. And I'm not just talking about voting the Tories out and getting Labour in, or anything like that. We've seen through that game. I'm talking about getting shot of the whole bloody lot of them: Labour, Tory, Liberal, the whole shooting match. If they don't get their act together, we sweep it all away.'

'Brilliant,' Jake shouted excitedly. 'Spot on!' And he began to clap loudly. Charlie clapped too then, and the rest of the audience quickly joined in.

'That was indeed spot on!' said Gerald, climbing back up on to the little stage and grasping Steve Finch by the hand. 'Splendid stuff, Steve! Absolutely splendid stuff! I told you he was worth listening to, didn't I? Let's give him another round of applause, eh? Let's give him a cheer! Come on, chaps, stamp your feet! Let's really show our appreciation!'

And the Colonel watched, beaming benignly, as the audience duly delivered a great deal of noise, which echoed from the ceiling of that strange woody place, releasing tension all the while, so that they all began to feel comfortable, in spite of everything, in Sir Gerald's Elizabethan hall.

'But now it's time to talk about what happens next,' Gerald said. 'What Steve and I have got you here for is to ask you to join a kind of army. I see some of you flinching at that, but don't worry. I'm not asking you to break the law. No illegal firearms. No dodgy explosives. No paramilitary uniforms. None of that at this stage. But there will be a *lot* of hard work. I want to make you as fit as any soldier in the British Army, and as tough, and as disciplined, and as skilled. I want to teach you about self-defence and hand-to-hand combat. I want to take you to firing ranges and show you how to handle a gun. All perfectly legal, as I say. We're not rebels, remember. We're loyalists. We're preparing ourselves to defend our beautiful country and its way of life against enemies who would do it harm.'

Gerald beamed at the little crowd. 'So, chaps! Who's with me?'

'I am!' yelled Charlie. 'I'm with you, mate!' And to his absolute delight, the whole room cheered him.

SEVENTEEN

Cally doesn't like those bits at all. She thinks I should stick to the diaries and not make stuff up. And she says that in any case, this whole Charlie story is ahistorical. It's like writing about the Wars of the Roses and giving them tanks. 'Admit it, Zoe,' she says. 'That's the Patriotic League you're describing there, the Patriotic League in all but name. You're conflating completely different periods of history. You know perfectly well that the earliest mention of the Patriots as an organized force won't be until many years later.'

We're drinking the stewed green tea they serve up in glasses in the Institute's rather dingy tearoom.

'If we confine the historical account to actual records we might achieve greater accuracy,' I tell her, 'but we do so at the expense of realism, and our histories will be skewed towards the small minority that records its own life, and the even smaller one that has its life recorded by others. I don't want to write that sort of history.'

A huge praying mantis alights on the edge of our tin table and stands there trembling. Cally smiles, but says nothing. Little motes of dust glitter and gleam in the beams of yellow light that are streaming into the room from its three rather grubby south-facing windows, making visible the invisible air.

'You are right about the Patriotic League,' I concede. 'The Patriots don't emerge as an entity for some years. But I'd argue that, even back in 2016, we can see the battle lines of the Warring Factions era beginning to emerge. A realignment of classes is taking place, and the new stories that are beginning to be told are already prototypes of the positions that will later serve as flags on the battlefield. For instance, the meanings of words like 'liberalism' or 'the Left' are mutating rapidly. And something resembling the Liberal faction of the future is beginning to part company with what will become the Democrats.'

Cally makes that side-to-side movement of her head that signifies that one acknowledges a point only with very major reservations.

'And, most obviously of all,' I tell her, 'we see the resurgence of a narrative of national and cultural solidarity that will provide the ideological raison d'être of the Patriots. You can hardly deny that, Cally! It's right there in the record. And that being so, is it really *so* fanciful of me to imagine that early prototypes of the Patriot militias were already beginning to form?'

'Well, okay, but the ideas you've put into their mouths are completely unrealistic,' she says. 'We're familiar with *Tianming* these days because we've only recently emerged from Chinese rule, but I very much doubt that someone like Finch would have come across it back then, let alone refer to it in a gathering of that kind.'

'Probably not. But he would have made that same point in another way.'

'I wonder. And in any case, the language would have been *much* more inflammatory. *Foreigners are a menace . . . Anyone who disagrees with us is a traitor* . . . That kind of thing, not all this reasoned argument.'

'True. All the various groups were working themselves up into an absolute lather back then. But I wanted to strip away the lurid iconography of villains and heroes they indulged in and try to understand what was going on beneath it.'

Cally sighed. 'It's a strange project, Zoe, and I can tell you for certain that the Guiding Body won't like it. They won't mind you telling the story again, but they'll want it told their way. You know that. They'll want you to identify their precursors and then make them unambiguously into the heroes of the story.'

'Of course. Everyone always wants that. Many people think that's what history's for.'

EIGHTEEN

Hello Michelle,

*Did you have a good Christmas? I hope you don't mind me
writing. I've been thinking a lot about the time I stayed at yours
in October when my car broke down, and I was wondering if
you'd like to meet up again? We seemed to get on so well and I
thought perhaps it would be nice to meet up for lunch somewhere
and see if we get on in different circumstances? I quite understand
if you'd rather not, and please don't feel obliged in any way. But
this is just to say, that if you felt like it, I would like to see you
very much indeed.*

Happy New Year,
Harry

I don't know if this was the final version, but it is the last of several
drafts in his notebooks. He sent it off, or something like it anyway,
on the 28th December, via the accommodation website he'd used to
find Michelle in the first place.

He was half-expecting a reply the same day, because in one of the stories he'd constructed in his mind, Michelle felt pretty much the same as he did. But there was no reply that day, or the next day, or the day after. Every night he records the absence of a reply, and analyses what it means to him. 'In many ways, I'm relieved. This has been such a strange episode, such a powerful obsession. Part of me will be very glad to have finally laid it to rest.' But at the very same time he hopes she *will* reply, and keeps imagining the heart-stopping moment of seeing her name appear in a list of new emails.

He went to a New Year's Eve party at the home of some friends of his called Jerry and Dave. They were friends of Janet's too, and there was a distinct possibility that he'd see her there, though he hoped he wouldn't. He had a great deal to drink and talked to a lot of people, quite often about Brexit.

'It's just crazy, isn't it?' said a very small bald man whose name he didn't catch. 'And so unnecessary, that's the maddening thing! It was all about settling a quarrel in the Tory Party. *Nobody* really wants it.'

Harry's contrariness had by now become an almost involuntary tic. 'Apart from slightly over half of the electorate, obviously,' he observed.

He waited for the standard responses to this, and ticked them off one by one as they duly arrived . . . *Dishonest campaign* (tick), *A lot of people didn't vote* (tick), *It was really just a protest vote* (tick), *A lot of them are changing their minds already* (tick), *Younger voters voted remain and they're the ones who are actually going to have to live with it* (tick). Did the little bald man really think he wasn't already familiar with these well-rehearsed positions?

'I guess they could rejoin the EU later then, couldn't they,' Harry observed, 'in five or ten years' time, when enough of the older voters have died to be sure of a majority?'

The small man was mildly disconcerted by this response. 'I suppose so. But we'd never get our opt-outs back.'

'But why would we need opt-outs if we think the EU is a good thing? Why wouldn't we want to be a member on the same terms as everyone else?'

Jerry had come to join them by this point, a slim, dark-haired man who edited an arts magazine. He and his partner Dave had both been part of Harry's friendship group at Cambridge. 'You're both very bad men!' Jerry told them. 'You know perfectly well that Brexit is officially banned from this party.'

Harry pretended to look remorseful.

'Oh, all right, go on then,' Jerry said, rubbing his hands, 'let's indulge ourselves. I won't tell Dave if you won't. Let's have a *really good moan.*'

The small man was up for that and, as he and Jerry talked, Harry counted off various other standard observations. *This is a representative democracy and parliament doesn't have to abide by the referendum* (tick), for instance, followed surprisingly quickly by: *We need another referendum* (tick). After these two there appeared, in quick succession: *Embarrassed to be British* (tick), *But of course Scotland is wonderful* (tick), *EU being so patient with us* (tick), *Shambles* (tick), *Utter shitshow* (tick), *It's the EU people living here I feel sorriest for* (tick) and *the NHS would crumble without them* (tick). Harry had become very conscious lately of how much of conversation, any conversation, was not about exchanging ideas or information but about collectively rehearsing a position and obtaining little strokes of mutual validation.

'When I was a kid,' he writes later, 'I used to wonder how grown-ups could bear just to talk for hours on end, without playing, without *doing* anything at all. But of course they *were* doing something, and the thing they were doing was very much like the grooming behaviour of chimpanzees. We humans reinforce the bonds that link us together, not by eating each other's ticks and fleas, but by harmonizing our views and providing each other with agreeable little endorphin hits of fellow feeling.'

Harry imagined other parties across the country where other tribes were doing the same thing. *Why can't they just get on with it and leave?* (tick), *Remoaner civil servants are dragging their feet* (tick), *It's an establishment conspiracy* (tick), *EU are playing us for fools* (tick), *If only the Remoaners would get behind the country* (tick), *Apparently democracy is only a good thing if it comes out the way they want* (tick).

Quite probably Michelle was at a party right now where they were talking just like that. Perhaps she was being chatted up at this very moment by the handsome and sun-tanned proprietor of the local Toyota franchise, and wasn't even thinking about the peculiar email she'd received a few days ago from that architect from London she'd spent that embarrassing night with. Of *course* she wasn't going to reply to him! She was an attractive woman with options. Why would she take a risk with a man like Harry, when she must get plenty of offers from attractive men in the world she knew?

Harry swallowed. 'Funny that a wealthy nation of sixty-five million people can't recruit enough doctors and nurses from its own population, though, isn't it?'

The small man and Jerry looked at him, puzzled. 'My guess is that most British people don't fancy the appalling conditions that junior doctors have to work in,' Jerry offered.

The small man agreed. 'The working hours these days are just awful, from what I gather.'

'I suppose there'll never be an incentive to improve those conditions,' Harry said, 'if we can just hoover up doctors who've been ready-trained for us elsewhere. I sometimes wonder about the countries they come from, though. Can they afford to train up doctors for us? Don't they need doctors themselves?'

'I don't know the answer to that, I'm afraid,' the small man said. Jerry made a humorous face to express his own equal ignorance.

'We have an agreed conversational path,' Harry writes the next day, 'and we all walk along it together. It's rather like the narrative strand of a story. It feels real, it creates the illusion that there's a hinterland behind and around the events you're being told about, but really all you're being given is a single line of words, and nothing at all on either side.'

People used to go from one New Year's Eve party to another back then, so new folk arrived at the party from time to time, and Harry eyed each set of arrivals to see if Janet was among them. Not that it would be a calamity to see her, of course – the two of them were on perfectly friendly terms – but it would be painful, and it was something he felt the need to brace himself for.

At about eleven fifteen a small group arrived. The first to come into the room was a designer called Rodney, a very tall black man in his mid-fifties with a rugged face and a booming actorly voice. He was a friend of Harry's, but perhaps even more a friend of Janet's and she often commissioned work from him. Harry wondered if she was going to be with him. But no, as his companions followed

Rodney into the room, Harry's wife wasn't among them. One of the group was Rodney's charming and gentle Italian partner, Franco, the other two were a man and woman Harry didn't know. As he'd done at previous gatherings, Harry noticed that Rodney was the only guest in the whole room who wasn't white, and thought about how strange that was in a city where more than a third of the population was black or brown.

Another group arrived at half past eleven (all white also, he notes), but he didn't know any of them and Janet wasn't among them. And then, at about quarter to midnight, three more slightly drunk white women came in.

No, Janet wasn't among them either. He saw that straight away, but as one of them turned and looked down the room in his general direction, he realized it was Letty. She obviously knew Rodney quite well, because, after being greeted by Jerry, she went straight over to him to hug him, and it was only a few minutes to midnight when she finally turned away from Rodney, and noticed Harry for the first time.

'Oh, Harry!' She threw her arms round him and kissed him wetly on the cheek. She smelled of warm scent pleasingly mingled with fresh sweat and booze. She must have been dancing at her previous party. 'How nice to see you!'

He thought this was going to be a standard cheek-peck greeting from which he'd be released straight away, but she held on to him. 'It really is lovely to see you!' she told him, leaning back so she could look into his face.

'You too!' He beamed at her. 'How was Provence?'

'Not that great. Alex was very bored. But we got by. You?'

'We got by too. My nephews were also bored. But we had some fun, all the same.'

'So are we going to meet up again? I wasn't sure, after last time, whether you . . . you know . . . '

'I wasn't sure whether you "you know" either!'

'Really? I must admit I thought at one point you were going to come out as a UKIP supporter, but apart from that I enjoyed our evening very much.'

'Me too. And don't worry, I'm a fully paid-up North London wishy-washy liberal. You really don't get much wishy-washier than me.'

Michelle wasn't going to get back to him, he told himself. It had been three days. She would have replied by now if she was at all interested. And that was all for the best, really. The whole thing had been a bit silly. He'd almost certainly spared himself a lot of embarrassment.

'I'm much too drunk to make arrangements now,' he said, 'but yes, let's sort something out very soon.'

Someone had turned on the TV, letting in the sounds of various festivities from across the country so as to create, as Harry puts it later, 'however vague and superficial, however stage-managed, a sense of a single nation moving together through time.'

Letty was still holding his arm and as Big Ben struck the twelve strokes of midnight, she pulled him to her and kissed him on the mouth. Then they both turned round to be welcomed by their companions into the year 2017.

NINETEEN

Harry spent most of the next morning in bed, with coffee and a jug of water beside him, readjusting his fluid balance and cossetting his sore head. He played with his phone. He wrote many pages in his diary.

'It felt good being kissed by Letty,' he writes. 'Whatever Ellie says about my lack of enthusiasm, I like her very much and I appreciate the fact that she likes me. That's enough for the moment, isn't it? Surely that's all you can realistically ask for when you hardly know each other.' Realistic was a good word, he thought. The opposite of obsessing like a teenager about someone you really didn't know at all. He'd email Letty later today or in the morning at the latest.

But there's a shift in tone on the very next line. 'What's changed? What's made me feel suddenly so much warmer towards Letty? Does one kiss really make a difference? Am I that trivial? If so, no wonder a good fuck blew my mind!'

He looked briefly at Twitter. 'I'm just going to come right out and say it,' someone called Damon had just tweeted, 'Nazis. Are. Evil.' Damon had duly received 322 'likes' and sixty-three replies thanking him for his brave and unflinching stance.

'Jesus wept,' Harry muttered, tossing his phone aside (as I imagine it) to pick up his notebook.

After a while he began to brood about Michelle's New Year's Eve.

'His name is Lee. He owns a Toyota dealership, or maybe an up-and-coming garden centre. He's divorced from the woman he met at eighteen before he made his money and is now looking for a beautiful woman who will adequately reflect his status. He has dark wavy hair, a square jaw, expensive shoes. He works out at the gym four times a week, wears Brut and is a member of the Rotary Club. He votes Tory, owns a brand-new convertible sports car and has a timeshare in Lanzarote with its own private pool where he'll soon invite Michelle to come and spend a week with him. He likes to spend his money but he knows he hasn't got much taste, and he'd love for her to help him turn his big hollow new-build pseudo-Georgian house into something more like a—'

Harry draws a line across the page to make himself stop.

'I wonder how it feels to be Rodney,' he writes, 'going to these North London parties where he's the only black man. I must ask him sometime. He plays on it, of course, setting aside that upper-class accent of his to make acidic comments in his grandmother's Caribbean dialect. And we all love that. We lap it up, us North London whiteys gathered round him, pink and clueless as babies. It's like he's blessing us in some way. It's like he's absolving us.'

He flipped through Twitter again. There was a lot of New Year stuff going on in there, but plenty of the usual things too: Brexit, Trump, people expressing outrage about other people's utterances, or triumphantly accusing one another of not caring, of being hypocrites, of being inconsistent. 'So many people desperate to prove that they are GOOD and someone else is very, very BAD,' he thinks. 'Like a gigantic suburban street in which people wait eagerly behind their lace curtains for something to happen that they can all condemn—'

He was interrupted by his phone pinging to indicate an incoming message. It was a text from Letty.

> Lovely to see you last night, Harry. How's your head? Mine's terrible. Mad week at work coming up, but how about meeting at the weekend?

He stared at the speech bubble on the little screen, examining his feelings. You couldn't call this elation, he had to admit. You couldn't deny a certain ambivalence. But he'd been through all that already, hadn't he? It was just the way things were. You needed to face it and push on through it or you would always be alone.

So he replied:

> Let's do that. Saturday night? My head's terrible too. Shall we think about a more detailed plan when we're feeling more human again?

He laid down his phone. 'This is life,' he writes, rather defensively, as if his sister was present and had remarked on his obvious lack of enthusiasm. 'Not miraculous. Not revelatory. Not an orchestra swelling up in a crescendo of ever-increasing bliss. Just people getting to know each other and seeing if they get on. You can't ask for any more than that.'

He felt tired and closed his eyes. It was eleven in the morning by now but he thought perhaps he'd try to snatch another half-hour of sleep before finally getting up. He had just settled into the uneasy half-dreams of a hungover brain, when the phone pinged again. It was probably Letty, he thought, acknowledging his reply, or suggesting a place to meet. Or maybe Ellie sending him a New Year message. Let it be, and he'd read it later.

But he couldn't settle back into sleep and so, in the end, he surrendered, sat up and looked at his phone.

Hello Harry, It's Michelle. I'm sorry I have not replied before, but I haven't been checking the b'n'b emails over Christmas and I've only just seen your message.

It's nice to hear from you. I was quite surprised to be honest because I really didn't think you'd be getting back in touch.

I would like to have lunch with you, yes. I don't know when you were thinking of but we don't open the salon on Wednesdays, so that's always a good day for me.

Anyway, I will wait to hear what you've got in mind. Happy New Year to you too,

Michelle

His hand was trembling. His heart was pounding. In a way his feelings were just as ambivalent as his feelings about the text from Letty, but they were far more powerful in both directions. There was dread in there, real dread, a sense that he'd blundered into something he should have left alone, but at the same time there was a dazed, childlike amazement that this woman who had been an idea in his mind for the last two months had suddenly, magically, become a real person again.

'Enough dithering,' he told himself. 'Enough see-sawing. I need to see this through.' And he replied at once, suggesting that he pick her up from her house at eleven thirty on Wednesday, in three days' time, and take her to a pub he knew of in the village of Breckham St Mary. He'd once eaten there with some friends from Cambridge after a walk in the nearby forest.

Her reply came back almost at once. A strange feeling, to know that right at this moment she too was focused on this same conversation so that, although she was ninety miles away on the map, in another less literal kind of space she was right there with him.

That sounds lovely, Harry. See you then.

And then, once more, she was simply ninety miles away, invisible to him and moving on to something else.

He sat for a while, trying to make sense of what was happening inside him. Then he sent an awkward email to Letty explaining that, lovely as it had been to see her again, he was 'in a funny confused place at the moment and I think perhaps we'd better not go ahead with another get-together. I'm so sorry for being in a muddle about this.'

TWENTY

I've heard rumours of an insurrection in Greenland: some of the Inuit people there are said to have risen up against the settlers who outnumber them these days ten or even twenty to one. I've seen grainy pictures, taken from planes or satellites, of streets in tropical cities strewn with skeletons, killed not by war or famine or disease but by pulses of heat so intense that the human body can't endure it for more than an hour or two. I've heard that the fine grey dust that falls on London from time to time comes from vast forest fires in the tropical zone. Large areas of the Earth these days are barely habitable, and very little news comes out of them. There are whole nations that are completely silent. But then again, news is carefully filtered for us by the Guiding Body in the interests of social cohesion and psychological health, so we can never be sure that we have the whole picture. This may very well be wise. It reduces the risk of widespread panic. But it also means that the present time is rather a mystery. One of the attractions of the past is that it's easier to see. Cally wanted to know why we should care about the lives of people two and a half centuries ago, and I think that's one of the reasons. And its remoteness makes it comforting.

*

Harry arrived back in Breckham, that nondescript little town with its Victorian clock tower, its war memorial, its slightly shabby old-fashioned hotel. An app in his phone directed him. 'At the roundabout, take the third exit onto Thetford Road.' 'In one hundred yards, turn left on to Forest Drive.' He entered the former council estate where Michelle lived.

The drive from North London had taken him about two hours, back up the M11 and then on to the A11 and the A14, switching back and forth between the parallel streams of metal and plastic and rubber. It wasn't very far at all back in those days, but it struck him that Breckham was more remote from the world he knew than cities on other continents like New York or Sydney or Toronto.

'Turn right on to Woodland Road . . . You have reached your destination.'

He parked his car and climbed out. He remembered standing here in almost this same spot, before he'd even met Michelle, and for a few seconds he stood there again, under a flat grey sky. He was wearing that smart blue jacket of his, and, after much deliberation, a white and blue striped shirt without a tie. His feelings were extraordinarily intense, but so confused that he couldn't name them, or even tell whether they were positive or negative overall.

He pressed the bell. A few seconds passed and then there was movement behind the frosted glass. The door opened and there she was.

Just for a moment she was simply a human being standing there, a human being like any other, no more and no less, so that it seemed strange that he had expended so very much time and emotion on thinking about her. But in the space of about a second, all the connotations that she'd acquired in his mind came flooding back, wrapping themselves around her again, clothing her in meaning, turning her into a kind of miracle in human form, an idea that had become flesh.

'Michelle!' he croaked, wondering what kind of hug or kiss was appropriate when you greeted someone you'd only met once but had slept with. She solved the problem for him by kissing him lightly on the lips.

'Hello, Harry. Nice to see you. I'll just go upstairs and get my bag.' She was wearing a brown leather skirt and matching boots, and a cream polo-neck top. 'Come inside for a minute.'

He hadn't expected it but there was someone else already there in the living room. 'This is Cheryl, Harry. My best friend. You remember I told you about her?'

Cheryl stood up from the sofa. She was a tall black woman with light brown skin and curly fairish wavy hair that was very meticulously layered and highlighted. She wore a good deal of make-up and bright red lipstick. She had sharp, green, interrogative eyes.

She let him shake her hand, but did not grasp his as he did so. Michelle left the room.

'It's good to meet you, Cheryl. Michelle talked about you when I came here before. You're her business partner, right?'

'That's it. We run the salon between us. You're an architect in London, apparently?'

He wondered whether Michelle had asked her friend to be here to give her a second opinion, or whether Cheryl herself had taken the initiative.

'I am,' he told her. 'I'm afraid it's not quite as glamorous a job as it sounds. It's mainly a matter of—'

'Michelle's been through a lot of shit, you know. She's a lovely person. I couldn't wish for a better friend. But she's had a tough life. She doesn't need anyone else to mess her around.'

'I know she's been through a lot. She's lost a child. I don't know if she told you, but that happened to me as well, so I do know what it does to you.'

Most people received the news of his loss of Danny with at least a nominal expression of sympathy, but Cheryl ignored it completely. 'I won't lie to you, Harry, I don't have a good feeling about this. If you haven't got anything real to offer her, please, please for her sake, let her be.'

'I appreciate your concern for your friend, Cheryl, but I can assure you—'

But then Michelle came back in. She'd put on a short white coat and was holding a small cream-coloured bag with a gold chain. All three left the house together, Cheryl to climb into her own immaculate white car, Michelle and Harry to get into his battered red one. As he drove off, he glanced round at the woman beside him. He couldn't quite believe she was really present.

'Did Cheryl come over just to check me out?' he asked, when they were on the road through the forestry plantation that led to Breckham St Mary.

Michelle laughed. 'Well, we do normally meet up on a Wednesday so we can catch up on paperwork. But yeah, she definitely wanted to have a look at you. She thinks I'm too trusting.'

He glanced across at her again. Those grey, naked eyes. Then she laughed. 'Hey! Look at the fucking road, Harry!'

'Sorry. Truth is I can't quite get my head round the fact that you're actually here.'

'Well, I am here and I don't want to end up wrapped round a tree!'

'Cheryl seemed very worried that I might let you down in some way, or betray your trust.'

'She's very protective of me. She knows I've made some bad choices before.'

'I'm not sure what to say. We don't know each other very well. We can't know in advance what will happen, can we, or how well we'll get on? So neither of us can guarantee anything. But I do want to be absolutely straight with you.'

She laughed again, a little uncomfortably. He realized he'd come over as intense. 'Okay,' she said. 'I believe you.'

'Cheryl's your closest friend, yes?'

'Yeah, we've been friends since we were kids. We both started school in Breckham when we were fifteen, so we were like the two outsiders that none of the other girls wanted to be with because we weren't from round here.'

Harry laughed. 'No! Really? But you came from Romford. It's not exactly the other side of the world!'

'Well, it might not seem far away to you, but believe me that's a long way in Breckham. Cheryl got teased for coming from *Brandon*, and that's only ten miles away.'

'You're joking?'

'I'm not. They gave her just as hard a time as me.'

'Because she came from Brandon? Not because she's black?'

'Well, that too, I suppose, but there were a few coloured kids in our school. We've got these big American bases round here, and women get together with black Air Force guys. It was more that no one wanted to hang out with people they hadn't grown up with.

And believe me, it wasn't just the kids who were like that. It was the grown-ups too.'

'But you're not like that. How can you bear to be in a town where people are so – I don't know – intolerant?'

'What? You're saying it's not like that in London?'

His first impulse was to say that it wasn't like that at all. Cosmopolitan, dynamic, Remain-voting London was one of the heroes of the story his friends were telling, along with wonderful progressive, Remain-voting Scotland. But he made himself reflect on what London was actually like, and not on the projections that were currently being laid over it. 'I suppose it's more like that than we Londoners like to think. We stick with our own kind and keep our distance from the rest. You can get apps these days that tell you what kinds of newspapers people buy in the street you're thinking of moving to, so *Guardian*-readers can avoid finding themselves among readers of the *Mail* or the *Telegraph* or the *Sun*. But we don't really need the apps, if I'm honest. We can tell at a glance whether it's our kind of street, our kind of people, and if it's not we avoid it. I guess it's the same everywhere, one way or another. People feel threatened by folk who are different.'

'I reckon. So yeah, anyway, me and Cheryl became best friends. We're good for each other. She's a bit harder than me. More of a fighter. So she stands up for me sometimes, or helps me stand up for myself.'

'And what do you do for her?'

'Hmmm. Good question. I suppose I help her take her armour off a bit, if you know what I mean. Or I like to think so, anyway. We've had a few rough patches. It was difficult between us after I lost Caitlin. Lots of the other mums didn't want to be around me at all, and she found it very hard. But we seem to have got through it.'

'It was like that with us, too. Our friends didn't feel comfortable around us. But listen, Michelle. We have that loss in common, and that feels special, but if there was an app that worked on people instead of streets, it would tell us that we weren't the same kind of people at all, wouldn't it? We probably don't read the same papers. We probably don't have the same ideas.'

'I've never met an architect before, that's for sure.'

'I've never met a hairdresser. Except when they cut my hair, obviously. I won't lie, I worry about that difference between us, but at the same time it's one of the things that fascinate me about you. I don't know why, but it does. It's as if I've grown bored of my own kind.'

Michelle didn't answer at first. Harry's exhaust pipe spewed sulphur dioxide into the wintry forest. 'I don't know what you want me to say,' she finally said. 'I'm just . . . *me*, you know?'

He realized he'd said a stupid thing. It was as if he'd told a black woman, 'You fascinate me because you're black.' Who wanted to be an object of fascination because of their demographic category?

'I put that badly. I'm sorry. You fascinate me full stop, Michelle. I've only spent one evening with you, after all, but I couldn't put it out of my mind. And I don't want to lie to you or tell you sweet nothings, or . . . ' He tailed off. 'I'm sorry. This is what comes of thinking about you for two months without getting in touch. I've had so many conversations with you in my mind. *So* many. I forget that you couldn't really hear any of them.'

'Don't worry about it,' she said.

They reached the pub. It was called the White Horse and had a thatched roof.

'Did you really think about me a lot?' she asked, as they climbed out of the car.

'Yes. A *lot*. You could ask my sister. She'd tell you what a state I got myself into.'

'I thought about you, too. Actually, I know what you mean about being different. I liked it that we were different but we seemed to get along anyway. It was . . . well, okay, I'll use your word . . . ' She put on a ridiculous, ultra-posh voice like the Queen's, 'It was *absolutely fascinating.*'

'Oi!' Harry exclaimed in mock protest, and then he attempted an imitation of her Essex speech, smudging the Ls in her name into a kind of W: 'You taking the piss, Michelle?'

'And that's supposed to sound like me, is it? Jesus! I'd stick to drawing houses if I were you.'

She took his arm as they entered the pub. A waiter took them to the table that Harry had booked, and helped Michelle out of her coat. The place was panelled in wood, and instead of the 'edgy' industrial chic beloved of liberal middle-class Londoners, it evoked, as Harry puts it, 'the more traditional fantasy, beloved of another section of the English middle class, of a mythical Merrie England of roaring fires, silver tankards and rosy-cheeked landlords'.

'This is a nice place,' she said. How precious she seemed to him, sitting just across from him in her silver teardrop earrings. She had a completely different way of being a woman from Letty, or Ellie, or Karina, or almost any woman he could think of, animated by a different kind of spark, and he was terribly drawn to it.

'Now this was my idea,' said Harry, 'so it's my treat.'

She looked momentarily puzzled – she'd obviously made that assumption already – then smiled, said thank you, and turned to the menu.

'I was really surprised to get your email,' she said.

'You mean after leaving it so long?'

'I was surprised you got back in touch at all, to be honest. You seemed keen to get away as quickly as possible that morning. I thought we were getting on all right and then suddenly you were desperate to be off. I talked about it with Cheryl and she said she knew exactly what had happened. She said it was the moment you remembered you had a wife.'

'I do have a wife, Michelle. I told you that when we met before, didn't I? But we've not been together for over a year now and we're in the process of getting a divorce. She left *me*, actually. I'm sure she'd feel a bit weird about it if she knew I was here with you, but she wouldn't see it as something I wasn't entitled to do.'

She examined his face, those raw grey eyes slightly narrowed. 'I believe you, Harry. And, for what it's worth, I told Cheryl I believed you.'

'I've got a lot of faults, Michelle, as I'm afraid you'll find out. I'm a bit lazy. I'm prone to let other people sort things out for me. I'm a wimp when it comes to arguments. But one thing I don't do is lie to people. Not on purpose, anyway.'

'Not on purpose? Can people lie by mistake?'

'I have to watch out that I don't get carried away by my own enthusiasm.'

She was still watching his face intently, her small narrow fingers, with their glossy cream-coloured nails, absently twiddling her glass. 'So I imagined that, did I?' she said. 'That moment when all your warmth turned off like someone had flipped a switch.'

He took a breath. There was no point in any of this unless he was truthful, but he hadn't anticipated the sharpness of her interrogation. 'No, you didn't imagine it. You said something I didn't like that morning, and it made me feel that you and I were much further apart that I'd thought. And just in that moment the whole thing seemed like a bad mistake. I don't know if you remember, but some Polish builders drew up outside and you—'

'And I said I'd be glad when they went back home because they're taking work from my brother Trevor.'

'That's right. And I won't lie – I didn't like that at all.'

A stony hardness came into her eyes that he hadn't seen before. (But of course this was only one of the Michelles he hadn't seen. There must be so many of them.)

'Well, it's true,' she said with a shrug. 'It's just a fact. Trevor's boss isn't much of a businessman, but they were doing all right until that lot set up in Breckham and it's much harder for them now. I don't see why I should be pleased about that. It'd be the same if someone came in and set up another salon next to Cheryl's and mine and charged half of what we do.'

'But those Polish builders are just trying to make their way, the same as your brother, same as anyone. I don't suppose they'd have come all this way at all if it wasn't difficult to make a decent living back home.'

'I've no idea what it's like in Poland, but yeah, maybe if I lived there, I might do the same as them. But . . . '

'But that doesn't mean you have to be glad about them being here?'

'No. Exactly.' She frowned. 'What did you think, Harry? Did you think I was being racist or something? My best friend's a black woman, as you noticed. My own mum's half-Italian.'

'You're quarter Italian? You didn't tell me that! But if that's the case, I would have thought that—'

He broke off, dismissing what he'd been about to say with a wave of his hand. 'You're descended from migrants, so why aren't you in favour of immigration?' was, when he thought about it, a very silly and superficial question not just in one but in several different ways, including one whose silliness he himself had explained to his brother-in-law only a week previously. 'I suppose what I didn't like is that you seemed to be blaming those builders personally, given that they're every bit as entitled to be here as they would be if they'd come here from – I don't know – Sheffield. You hear of Eastern European people being abused in the streets these days, or attacked, when all they've done is move here to do a job.'

Michelle shrugged. 'Well, I don't abuse those guys in the street. I say hello, I smile, I laugh if they make a joke. Trevor takes it more personally. He *is* a bit racist, if I'm honest – me and his daughter are always telling him off for it – but I'm pretty sure even he isn't rude to those blokes when he meets them. He's an awkward sod at times and, as he admits himself, he's really thick, but he's got a kind heart deep down.'

'I'd be interested to meet him.'

She laughed, a little bitterly, refusing to be deflected. 'So, anyway, you didn't like what I said and you wished you hadn't slept with me, but then you changed your mind again and emailed me. How come?'

She was poised, defensive, almost hostile.

'I didn't like what you said. It seemed mean and small-minded, like the kids in your school being unfriendly just because you came from Essex. But it struck me that it was no worse in its own way than things I hear my friends say. In fact, no worse than things I've said myself. And I kept thinking about you, and how close we'd felt that night, and how—' He broke off. He was determined to speak the truth, but that was proving surprisingly difficult. Absolute truth was against all the normal rules of social interaction, and perhaps even beyond the reach of language.

Michelle waited, still turning her wine glass absently back and forth between her fingers. She wore rings of various kinds on all of them, even her thumbs.

He looked straight at her, into her grey, flayed eyes, their rawness somehow at odds with her neat, groomed presentation. 'And, like I said before, I couldn't stop thinking about you. In the end, I talked about it with my sister Ellie, and she told me I was being stupid, and I should get in touch with you. She said you were a grown-up and you could decide for yourself if that was what you wanted.'

Michelle seemed to soften slightly. 'I remember you telling me about your sister. She's a doctor, yeah?'

'She is.'

'Do you think she'd like me?'

It was a surprising question and it momentarily threw him. 'Er . . . yes, I think she would. The same as I do.'

'She's your twin, isn't she? What does she look like?'

He took out his phone, found a picture of Ellie taken at Christmas.

'She looks nice,' Michelle said. 'Really pretty, too.'

'Well, everyone says she looks a lot like me, so I'm good with that.'

She kicked his foot under the table. 'Talk about fishing for fucking compliments, Harry!'

The waiter came for their order. Harry asked Michelle about her family. 'It sounded as if you were very close. I remember you saying both your brother and sister moved to Breckham when you and your parents did, even though they were both married by then and had kids. That must have meant giving up jobs, and all sorts.'

'Well, my mum and Jen are practically joined at the hip,' Michelle said. 'Jen always says Mum's her best friend. They see each other every day. They do all their shopping together. No way was Jen going to settle for being seventy miles away. It would have done her head in. And that left Trevor on his own. His first marriage was breaking up by then, and he's a bit of a mummy's boy himself deep down, so he sort of followed on.'

'That is a *very* close family!'

'Do you think? I don't think we're closer than most people's. Cheryl sees her mum most days. And they go shopping to Cambridge or Bury nearly every weekend.'

'I suppose I'm just comparing your family with people I know. I mean, I see my sister every six weeks or so, and when my dad was still around, I went up to Norwich to see him maybe six times a year. More when he was very ill, obviously, but until then once every couple of months at most.'

'Well, not all families get on. Jen's husband Ken fell out with his brother when he moved to Breckham and now he never sees him at all.'

'Oh, I don't mean that. I get on very well with my sister. I got on perfectly well with my dad. It's just a different kind of family life, I suppose. Most of my friends' families are spread out over a wide area and only see each other once in a while. My wife Janet's parents are in Scotland, for instance, her brother's in Madrid, her sister's in Los Angeles.'

'Wow!'

'And I honestly can't think of any woman I know who would say their mum was their best friend, or see her mum every day unless she was ill or something.'

She frowned. 'Are you saying there's something *wrong* with being that close to your mum?'

'No! Not at all,' he said, though actually the idea of family members being that involved with each other felt to him quite stifling, in much the same way that he found the idea of living in Breckham stifling, and to his ears there was something a bit pathetic about a daughter saying her mother was her best friend, like a woman who'd never quite grown up. 'I'm just noticing a difference. It's as if we came from different countries, and I was noticing your country has different customs.'

Michelle nodded. 'Well, family's important in my country. Although I wish Jen would make a few friends her own age. What's she going to do when Mum's gone?'

Their food arrived at this point. Platefuls of meat, I expect. Or, if not, something made with cheese. They couldn't get enough of their animal products back then: a third of the dry land on Earth was given over to feeding the animals they used for food. Michelle picked up her knife and fork. 'I'll tell you one thing. You talk about completely different things from any bloke I've ever been out with.'

'Really? What did they talk about, then?'

'Oh, their jobs, how much money they earned, their cars. Maybe their motorbikes, if they had them, or boats or stuff like that.'

Harry smiled. 'Like bowerbirds.'

She stared at him in bewilderment. 'What's that?'

'You've not seen them on the nature programmes?'

'I don't really watch nature programmes, to be honest.'

'Well, they're a kind of bird that makes a little structure called a bower to attract a mate, and fills it up with pretty things to impress her.'

'Yeah? I guess it is a bit like that. Trying to impress me. It gets a bit boring, to be honest. Like I give a damn what kind of bike they've got, or how much it cost. But you . . . I really can't tell if you're trying to impress me or not. You haven't even mentioned your job. You haven't mentioned your money or the things you own. And I mean, you're an architect. You must be doing all right, but you've got that little Renault which must be at least ten years old, with dents and scratches all over it.'

'That seems strange to you, does it?'

'Well, it's up to you what car you drive, isn't it? But most people I know like to have a decent car.'

'I did like him,' Michelle writes later. 'He's lovely to look at, he's way more interesting than most blokes, and he's a better listener too. But he is *weird*. He was really stressed about those Polish builders. It's like he doesn't know there's a world out there where everyone says stuff like that. And then, after we'd finished the main course, we got on to Brexit and I told him I'd voted Leave, and he got all tense again and made me explain exactly why. I felt I was being tested, to be honest. I felt he liked me a lot, but he was worried I might turn out to be someone he *wasn't allowed to be with*. Like that funny kid we had at school back in Romford – Cathy, I think her name was – who had to wear a headscarf all the time and wasn't allowed to be friends with anyone that didn't have the same religion.'

Michelle told Harry she didn't like the idea of having to take laws that came from Brussels.

'Well, we help to make those laws too.'

She laughed. '*You* might, Harry, but no one ever asks me.'

'Well, I don't mean you and me personally, obviously, but we can vote for the European Parliament and we can choose our own government, which sends ministers to the European Council.'

'With loads of other countries, though.'

'Twenty-seven. But we have the same say as all of them.'

'Well, why can't we just make our own laws and leave them to make theirs, like it used to be? Plus I don't care what you said about me and those Polish guys, I don't like us not being in charge of who comes to this country and who doesn't. That should be for us to decide.'

'Well, we are still a separate country. We've got our own government, our own foreign policy, our own army, but one of the great things about being in the EU is that you and I are entitled to live and work in any one of those other twenty-seven countries whenever we want!'

That just made Michelle laugh. 'Well, whoop-de-do! Why would I want to live in another country? I haven't lived anywhere but Breckham since I was fifteen! I mean, don't get me wrong, I love going to Spain or Greece for a holiday, but why would I want to live there? They speak a different language, they do things differently. I like having people round me I can relate to.'

'Your Italian grandpa adjusted, I suppose?'

'Well, sort of, but he had to, didn't he? He came over here because he needed the money, but all his mates were Italian. In fact, never mind Italian, most of them were Sicilian like him. He didn't have much time for north Italians. I don't know if it was really true, but he always claimed he couldn't understand their language. Yeah, and anyway, Harry, he came over here before the war. There was no EU then, was there? But people were still allowed to come over here if there was work for them. What's wrong with that? Plus, I don't see the point of sending all that money to Brussels, when we could—'

'That three hundred and fifty million quid a week? We were lied to about that, Michelle! We get a rebate from the EU. The real figure's under two hundred million.'

Harry was looking so serious that she had to fight an urge to burst out laughing. He seemed to think that what he'd just said would be shocking news to her. 'Oh, I know that. Of course I do. They were always arguing about it on TV. But it's still a big number, isn't it? And I don't know about you, Harry, but once numbers get into hundreds of millions, *big* is all they really mean to me.'

She poked at the food left on her plate. 'And anyway, politicians *always* exaggerate. They always promise things that won't happen. That's not news, is it? You have to decide with your gut in the end, don't you, and hope for the best? They're all out for themselves, anyway, or out for their sort of people anyway. But at least our politicians are in England. At least they speak the same language as us and live in the same country.'

She watched his face, puzzled and amused. What she was saying seemed to torture him, yet to her it didn't seem controversial at all.

What struck Harry was that Michelle was barely even aware of all the arguments that his fellow-Remainers had been rehearsing obsessively since the vote in June. All this time, the people of his tribe had been getting themselves more and more angry and distressed about a menacing and unknowable Other, far beyond the edge of the pool of light in which they lived: a brutish, loutish, hate-filled Other, which, for its own primitive reasons, had committed an act of pointless and even spiteful vandalism against something that to his people was integral to how they saw themselves. But Michelle and her friends hadn't been listening. They'd been part of a completely different conversation about the way that the centre of power was moving ever further away from them, both literally and metaphorically, and no longer cared about what mattered to them or how they wanted to live.

'And you're not bothered at all by the consequences of leaving?' Harry asked. 'Because you know, whatever the Leave side said, the fact is that our whole economy's tied up with Europe. It'll take years, maybe decades, to readjust.'

Michelle laughed, not so much at what he said, as at the earnestness with which he said it. 'Do you really think that's an argument for staying, Harry? Sounds to me like a reason for leaving.'

'A reason for *leaving*? How come?'

'Well, if we're already so tangled up in it that it'll take years to disentangle ourselves, doesn't that mean we should get a move on and get out before we get tangled up even more?' She smiled. 'Reminds me of my garden shed, actually. It's got ivy growing all over it. You know what ivy's like, it pokes itself in between the planks and slowly breaks them apart. It'd take me ages to clear it all off, but if I don't do it, it'll be an even bigger job next year, and in the end I won't have a shed at all.'

'But I don't think of Europe as creeping ivy,' Harry protested. 'I think of it as extra connections, like extra helping hands. I mean, this is one world, isn't it? There's only one planet. Only one human race.'

'We've got to look after ourselves first, though, haven't we? I mean, you and all your friends, you've got nice houses, I'm guessing, you have nice holidays abroad, you have nice— Oh wait . . . scratch that . . . I was going to say you have nice cars.'

'Bloody hell, Michelle. Leave my poor car alone!'

She smiled. 'What I mean is that you look after yourselves first, yourselves and the people near you, don't you, the same as everyone else does? So, okay, you *talk* about one planet and one human race and all of that, and it's true in a way, but at the same time . . . '

The waiter came and cleared their plates.

'But at the same time we're hypocrites,' Harry said.

'I used to go out with a bloke called Brett from one of the American bases we've got round here. We met this other American guy in the pub once. I think he was a professor of some sort, and he started going on about how America was stolen from the Indians, and it was terrible, and they should have it back. In the end Brett said, "Okay, so find out which Indian tribe used to live where you live now and give them the deeds of your house." The poor bloke didn't know what to say!'

Michelle glanced at the dessert menu which the waiter had given her.

'Mind you, I'm just the same. I worry a lot that we're fucking up the world. You know, with this climate thing, and plastic and everything. It really bothers me at the moment, I don't know why, the idea of everything coming to an end. None of my friends seem worried and Cheryl says I'm nuts, but sometimes it keeps me awake at night, like this huge black bird hanging over me. I say to Cheryl, "You've got kids and one day they'll have kids too. What kind of world are they going to have to live in?" But she tells me I'm just obsessed. "You don't do anything about it any more than I do," she says, "so how are you helping anyone just by worrying?"'

*

That sort of statement is quite powerful when you know that people like Harry and Michelle were indeed fucking up the world, and that theirs was the first generation in history knowingly to fuck up the world, and yet *still carry on doing it*. That's why some people these days refer to their era as the Age of Selfishness. But I do sort of get it as well.

It's lonely and stuffy inside my damp little flat and I lean out of my window and watch the life below me: the mantises hunting for moths on the wall, the boats nudging round each other, the people passing back and forth on the wooden walkway. It's a kind of company, and it cheers me up.

As ever there are children and old people fishing and from time to time there's a little flurry of activity and laughter as another eel is lifted from the water, either to have its head lopped off on the walkway there and then or to be tossed into a bucket and killed later. Little Joe's down there as usual hunched beside his bucket, pretending to be the genius fisherman utterly absorbed in watching his line, so as to explain why there's no one sitting near him. But I'm looking to cheer myself up, not to make myself unhappy, so I turn my attention to a couple of little girls a few metres along from him who are shouting triumphantly after catching a particularly large eel.

Normally I'd enjoy the spectacle of their delight but, I suppose because of my unease about Joe, I find myself wondering for a moment what it's like for the eel to be suddenly yanked out of its world by a sharp, barbed, stinging thing that clings to its mouth and can't be shaken off. But I brush away that thought as you brush away a fly. I don't doubt eels are capable of suffering – I can't really see why their capacity for pain should be any less than mine – but I haven't enough peace and contentment to spare just now to worry about little boys who no one loves, let alone to worry about eels.

I sometimes think this lies at the heart of our human dilemma. Without empathy we're nothing, but unless we set limits to empathy, none of us would ever be happy at all.

Harry drove Michelle back to her house. When he pulled up outside she gave him a soft kiss and invited him in.

'I don't know,' he said. 'Perhaps we should just leave it like this today?'

She pulled back from him, frowning. 'Oh, for fuck's sake, Harry. Don't tell me I've said something wrong *again*?'

He laughed and grabbed her hands. 'No, Michelle, not at all. Nothing like that, I promise you! Right now the only thing that's holding me back from having my hands all over you is that we're sitting here in full view of all your neighbours.'

'Same for me,' she said. 'So if we go inside, we both get what we want, don't we?'

'But this is all too quick, isn't it? We need time to think. Time to work out where we might be going. Sex is like a drug. It makes you want more and more of it, and—'

'And stops you thinking straight?'

'Yes, exactly.'

He was still holding one of her hands in his lap. She moved it slightly so the back of it brushed against his growing erection through the fabric of his trousers, and gave a little snort of laughter. 'And you're going to think straight in that state, are you?' She opened the door of the car. 'Come into my house, Harry. If we're making a mistake, well, we're making a mistake and we'll just have to deal with it. But you can't spend all your life telling yourself you can't have what you want.'

She didn't offer him tea or coffee, but led him straight up to the bedroom. She pulled off her polo-neck top while he threw off his jacket, and they stood there and kissed, him in shirtsleeves, her in her bra. When he began to fumble at the zipper on her leather skirt, she dragged him down on to the bed.

'Do you want another child?' Harry asked her suddenly, pulling back to breathe.

'*What?* Jesus Christ, Harry, I thought you were the one who didn't want to move too quickly!'

'I didn't mean *now*! I meant, in general. Is that your plan in life?'

'Yeah, I would like to try again.' She laughed. 'You know . . . if the right guy was to come along one day.'

'I love the idea of making a baby with you.'

'Well, it's not going to happen now, mate,' she told him. But when they joined together, there was a new intensity to it and she pulled him into her as deep as she possibly could, as if to ensure that every drop of him would find its way into her womb.

'But all this will fade soon enough,' he thought, as she cuddled up against him afterwards, purring and kissing his neck. 'This bliss. This lovely, simple, sensual heaven. This is just the honey that nature dishes out to make us do what it wants. Then it makes us hungry again and sets us back to work.'

Michelle frowned. 'Are you okay?'

'Do you actually want *me*?' he asked her.

'Of course I want you, Harry! I'd have thought that was obvious!'

'Me as me, I mean. My body, my mind. Not me being an architect and going to Cambridge and all that shit, but just me.'

She sat up abruptly. 'What the *fuck* are you saying, Harry? Are you suggesting I'm just after your money?'

'No, of course not. You're not like that at all. I was just wondering what it really is that draws us to each other, and whether it's real and something that will last once we've seen through each other. Because we will see through each other, you know. That's how it works. We'll discover we're just two human beings.'

But Michelle was still working through her initial reaction. 'Just after your money? Because, let's face it, one thing a car like yours really says is that this is a guy who knows how to flash the cash!'

His car genuinely bothered her, Harry realized, in one of those fleeting insights that are swept away immediately by more pressing matters. This wasn't just a joke. It seemed perverse to her that a man in a prestigious and well-paid job would own such an unimpressive vehicle.

He reached for her hand but she pulled it away.

'I could ask you that exact same question, Harry. Do you really want *me*? *My* mind, *my* body. Well, actually forget the body part. I *know* you want my body. But do you want me as a person? Or is it just a bit of a thrill for you to leave that posh world of yours up in London and go with a woman who's common and talks like I do?'

'It *is* a thrill. I don't deny it. I'm tired of my own kind of people. Our self-importance, our self-righteousness. It's much more than a thrill, though. I love the way you aren't like that. But I'm wondering what you and I would be like when we were too tired for sex, and we knew all there was to know about each other. What would we talk about, do you think?'

'Well, what do you talk about with anyone?'

'I don't know. Politics. Art. Books. Movies. Football. People we know. Crap mostly, I suppose.'

She started pulling on clothes. 'I'll make us some tea.'

When he followed her downstairs she had placed two mugs on the breakfast bar.

'You *worry* too much,' she told him. 'If we enjoy seeing each other, then we can see each other. If we stop enjoying it, we can stop. That how it usually works, isn't it? Where's the problem? Why do you have to try and figure it all out in advance?' She put on her super-posh voice, '"Oh, but you and I are so different, Michelle!" I mean, for fuck's sake, Harry, if that really bothers you, then we can end this now. And if it doesn't bother you, why do you have to keep on and on and on about it *all the fucking time*?'

'I do, don't I? It must be really annoying.'

'It is. So do you want us to meet again?'

'Oh God, yes, Michelle! *Very* much! I couldn't bear the idea of not seeing you again.'

She shook her head. 'You are weird, Harry.'

'It's true. I am weird. You're making me see that about myself. But that being so, do you want to see *me* again?'

'Of course I do, you twat.'

'I'll go home when I've drunk this tea,' he told her. 'But why don't you come down to London next time? I don't know if there's anything in particular you'd like to do, but I was thinking maybe we could go to an art gallery or something? I can see from the way you've done up your house that you've got an eye for colour and design.'

'Yes, that would be nice,' she said, but there was suspicion in her voice, and she frowned.

'What's the problem?'

'I've seen those movies,' she said. That sudden coldness had come back. She would be quite frightening, he realized, when she was really angry.

'What movies?'

'Those ones where some ignorant peasant from the sticks gets taken up by a kind posh person, and suddenly her eyes are opened and she sees what she's been missing, and she goes to uni or something, against all the odds, and ends up becoming a famous writer or something, all thanks to him.'

He was about to break in. 'No, let me finish,' she told him. 'You need to hear this. I'm just me, all right? There are a lot of things in my life I'm sad about, but I'm fine with being this kind of person. I like doing my customers' hair and nails and chatting to them about their cats and their grandchildren and the latest *Strictly*. I'm happy living where my mum and my sister and my brother live. I've not been sitting here waiting for some fucking knight in armour to come up from London and turn me into someone like you.'

'I don't want to change you into anything. I like you just as you are.'

She nodded. 'That's good. Because you'd be disappointed otherwise.'

'But I thought you might like looking at pictures. It's a way of spending time together. Something to talk about, you know? Like going to the movies, except you don't have to keep quiet for two hours and sit in the dark. Of course, if you prefer, I could just do the bowerbird thing and boast about my car.'

She laughed. '*That* car? You've got to be kidding.'

L ucy greeted the concierge by name – she had known her for several years – and passed on through the hallway to the glass lift. It rose through a shaft that was also glass, so she could see the dark boats passing over the glowing water below her, and the city's towers and bridges glittering with light. She never tired of that sight.

Lucy was twenty-eight and a lecturer in political science at the London School of Economics and she was visiting her father who lived, with his second wife and their son, in an apartment on the eighth floor of this building. It had its own balcony garden, and even a small tree, thirty metres above the river bank. Lucy was very bright, and knew it. She was one of the rising stars in her field, but she was aware of the importance of building a reputation beyond her institution and beyond her own academic peer group, and was a frequent, funny, acerbic contributor to several social media platforms. 'Scholar. Feminist. Politics nerd. Ski fanatic,' read the self-description on her Twitter home page. 'I block bores, bigots, bots, bastards, Brexiteers, etc. Preferred pronouns: She/Her'. She had nearly 15,000 followers.

Her father greeted her at the door and they embraced warmly. She had his red hair and his green eyes though not his short legs, which meant that she was nearly a head taller than he was. The two of them were very close. They shared the same restless energy, the same intolerance of fools, the same bewildered impatience with the kind of people who fretted and dithered and refused to grab hold of their lives. She knew he was immensely proud of her.

In the creamy living room, with its long curved sofas, Lucy's stepmother, Karina, was laying out bowls of interesting and unusual nibbles: dried meats, peas coated in something blue, deep-fried plantain chips . . .

'Lucy, you're here!' Karina exclaimed. She and Lucy had never had a very close relationship, but they got along, and they kissed each other amiably enough. Her brother Greg came in – her half-brother strictly speaking, and eleven years younger than her – greeted her a little absently, grabbed a handful of the nibbles and retired to his room. Like Lucy, and like his father and mother, he had a tremendous capacity for focused work, and he was obviously in the middle of something. By himself in his room, with his headphones, his laptop and his electronic keyboard, he would work away at ideas for songs for hours at a stretch.

On three of its four sides, the living room had triple-glazed glass in place of solid walls. At the far end, the glass could be slid back to join the apartment to the small Babylonian garden where that little Japanese tree stood in its blue porcelain urn. To the right the glowing river and the brightly lit towers on the northern bank were framed and made brilliant by the night. To the left, in the neighbouring apartment block, small figures moved, as if in an open doll's house, among the miniature lamps and furnishings of their own softly illuminated glass-walled rooms.

The guests began to arrive. First was a Labour MP, from the centrist pro-EU wing of the party (she was a friend of Karina's from her previous career in the law), and her partner who was an analyst for a merchant bank. Next was an American-born economist who played squash with Richard, along with his textile designer Spanish wife. Then another friend of Karina's turned up, the director of what was normally described as a 'left-leaning think tank' and his husband who was an IT entrepreneur. After that came the couple who lived in the flat below – a fund manager and her lawyer husband – followed by a sociology professor who taught at the School of Oriental and African Studies. Richard had met him at a party.

'Karina and I would like very much for this to become a regular thing,' Richard said, as he moved round the seated guests with opened bottles of white and red wine clasped in his large hairy hands. 'Our idea was that this should be a discussion group, a kind of book group if you like, but not necessarily focused on books. We might look at a book sometimes, of course, but we might simply discuss a topic chosen by one of us. Or we could ask people to come and speak with us, in this case my brilliant daughter Lucy. Whatever the format, the focus would be on our current political crisis, but with a view to exploring longer-term solutions, rather than indulging in yet another "Isn't Brexit awful?" sort of gathering, which we've probably all had enough of already.'

'But *isn't* it awful!' the textile designer said in her charming Spanish accent. 'Isn't it *worse* than awful? Let's at least say that before we begin!'

Lucy watched them with her bright, interested eyes, checking them out in turn and noticing, for instance, that the sociology professor, a rather good-looking if humourless Asian man, had not been amused by the textile designer's intervention.

'I'm interested in constitutions,' she told them when they'd all been given drinks. She spoke without notes, trusting to her knowledge of her subject, her knack of engaging people, and her ability to think on the spot. 'Constitutions aren't just words and pieces of paper. They're machinery. They're machines whose specific purpose is to keep various currents and forces in a kind of equilibrium, so that a state retains some sort of stability and doesn't just fly apart. Some constitutions don't work and crumble very quickly – there are countries which go through constitutions like boxes of tissues – but others are very durable. The Anglo-Saxon countries have a bit of a genius for this particular kind of machinery, and both the British and American constitutions have demonstrated their ability to evolve and adapt over a very long period of time, while continuing to maintain just enough rigidity to hold together. But even the best of constitutions contain flaws, chinks if you like, which, if they're allowed to widen, will eventually break them. And we're starting to see that happen now on both sides of the Atlantic. In each case, the flaw that's becoming apparent is that, while both constitutions contain many subtle and ingenious safeguards, neither is well defended against decisions that are simply wrong, not necessarily in a moral sense – that's a subjective judgement, after all – but in the sense that they're based on assumptions that are demonstrably and objectively false.'

Lucy looked at the people gathered there on her father's long cream-coloured sofas. They were all between their late thirties and their fifties. She was younger than any of them by at least ten years. You couldn't say they were old or past it, but there were almost certainly intellectual barriers by which they felt constrained – relics of the old order of the late twentieth century – but which did not constrain her at all.

She talked about constitutions in different countries, the various systems of checks and balances that had been devised. She discussed the tension that existed between making a constitution too inflexible to be able to respond to changing times and making it so easy to amend that it was barely any different from any other kind of law. She compared the kinds of constitution that endured and the kinds that failed. Then she returned to the flaw in the British system.

'Representative democracy requires anyone seeking political office to put together a broad coalition that can obtain the support of a sizeable proportion of the population, and that's generally a good thing. The majority isn't necessarily right, of course, but widespread consent is key to stable government and that underlying principle is so valuable that we can and should live with bad electoral calls if their only result is a government that can be thrown out again in a few years' time. What we're discovering now, though, is that it's entirely possible within our constitutional arrangements for a majority to vote for something that *isn't* easily reversible and which is likely to do long-term, and even permanent harm not only to society as a whole but to the liberal settlement that made the vote possible in the first place. And that's something we surely *shouldn't* try to live with. The difficulty is that, when most of the electorate lack the knowledge, the interest and, in some cases – let's admit this for once – even the intellectual ability to make informed judgements about complex matters that require specialist knowledge, we're always going to be vulnerable to this kind of threat. And that's a serious weakness. Being representative is highly desirable, but sometimes being right is even more important.'

She paused for a moment to take stock of her father's guests. They all seemed to be on board so far. She noticed a woman on the same floor in the neighbouring building looking out of her window, a silhouette against the warm glow of her room.

'So how do we protect our system against stupidity?' Lucy asked. 'How do we protect it, for that matter, against judgements that even intelligent and thoughtful people might make in the absence of appropriate expertise? The problem is that, while each of the three branches of government acts as a check on the others, we lack a sufficiently robust check on the not often mentioned fourth branch, which is the electorate itself. We're squeamish about that because we assume that letting the people decide things is a cornerstone of the liberal state, and we forget that rationality and respect for evidence are at least as important to the preservation of the liberal order as is what we now call democracy. For, make no mistake, without rationality and science the whole edifice comes tumbling down.'

'Ban referendums,' said the fund manager. 'That's the solution. Go back to being a *representative* democracy.'

'A step in the right direction,' Lucy said, 'but the voters can still elect a parliament that makes stupid decisions.'

'Require party manifestos to be approved by an independent, non-party panel of experts, whose job is to check for accuracy and viability,' suggested the IT entrepreneur.

'Mandatory training for MPs?' the lawyer wondered. 'Or minimum qualifications to *become* an MP?'

'Or better still,' said the woman who *was* an MP, 'proper, thorough political education in schools. It's crazy we don't think that's necessary for a healthy democracy!'

'I read about a sort of jury-type system that someone's suggested,' said the textile designer. 'Instead of public votes being taken by the whole electorate, a cross-section of the electorate is picked out by some random process, and then these people are provided with intensive training in economics and so forth before they take the vote.'

Lucy nodded. 'All good ideas, but how about an entirely new kind of upper house? Scrap the Lords as it stands and start again. No more hereditary peers, no more peerages handed out as thank-yous to supporters, or as a way booting nuisances upstairs, but instead a chamber that brings together outstanding thinkers in all of the relevant fields, chosen on a non-party basis by their fellow professionals. Economists chosen by economists, lawyers chosen by lawyers, and so on. A House of Knowledge, a kind of benign, non-partisan guiding body. And then give it teeth. Give it an absolute veto on legislation, not just delaying powers like the House of Lords has now, meaning that the lower house *has* to negotiate with it, and has no choice but to fix or change things that the relevant experts can see won't work.'

'Gosh!' said the MP, sounding simultaneously shocked and excited. 'We really *are* thinking outside the box, aren't we?'

'Times like these call for that, though, don't they?' Lucy said. 'It's clear to all of us, surely, that something fundamental needs to change? And the hard fact is that there are much rockier times ahead. Climate change, population growth . . . In the coming decades this is going to be a world that's much harder for a lot of people than it is now. A lot of difficult and unpalatable choices will need to be made, and we know that it's *precisely* at such times that old-fashioned representative democracy is at its weakest. Because, as we're beginning to find out, people who don't want to hear bad news are very vulnerable indeed to snake oil salesmen.'

'It seems to me,' said the sociologist, 'that your guiding body idea would be taking us right back to what the House of Lords originally was: a chamber which exclusively represents the interests of a particular class.'

'That's not true at all,' Lucy said flatly. 'The old aristocracy was there by right of birth, but experts can come from any class and any background. No one would be there as of right. It would be something you had to earn.'

'Well, okay,' began the sociologist. He was annoyingly attractive with his large dark eyes and his lean limbs. 'But the fact is that—'

'The upper house is only part of it, though, isn't it?' Richard broke in. He'd been sitting quietly up to now, watching Lucy's confident performance with fatherly pride. 'Do we not have to think about the franchise itself?'

'Interesting,' said the American economist. 'In the first French republic, there were active citizens and passive citizens. They all had the same legal rights, but only the active citizens participated in politics.'

'Gosh!' exclaimed the MP, as if she'd been shown a shockingly erotic image.

'So we're talking now about a qualified franchise, are we?' asked Karina.

Lucy shrugged. 'It's worth considering. Or maybe a weighted one, with votes for all, but multiple votes for the best qualified. It might help, though I'm not entirely sure it would be necessary if we gave sufficient teeth to the new upper house. But we do need to do something because this is a crisis. The liberal order is in danger and we really have got to be willing to think the unthinkable if we're going to save it. And the truth is this isn't just about the referendum. Every election involves making judgements about how best to manage a highly complex and highly dynamic global system, which few people really understand at all. That's okay in comfortable times when people are willing to listen to the advice of people who *do* have some expertise, but not when they're angry and fed up and the experts are telling them stuff they don't want to hear.'

'But a qualified franchise would be going right back to the nineteenth century,' objected the sociologist. 'It's precisely what the Chartists were fighting against!'

He was a bit of a prig, Lucy decided. The kind of person who let other people make the difficult choices on his behalf, but reserved the right to criticize afterwards.

'Not at all,' she said. 'In the nineteenth century, the qualification was based on property. You could be as stupid and ignorant as you liked and still get a vote if you owned a big enough house. What we're talking about here is a qualification based on the ability to understand the issues being decided. That's an entirely different thing.'

'Not *entirely* different,' the sociologist pointed out. 'There's a pretty strong correlation between—'

'But let's not get bogged down in that,' Richard suggested. He'd risen to his feet a few minutes before to fetch more wine, but had paused to watch this exchange. 'I'd suggest that the best use of our time right now is simply to generate ideas, allow ourselves to think thoughts which we'd normally dismiss out of hand, and not worry too much at this point about details and snags. Let's come back to those later.'

'This is all so fascinating,' Karina said, 'but I wonder, would everyone like a quick break before we carry on?'

'Good idea,' Lucy said. Richard went for the wine, the lawyer left the room to use the toilet, the economist began a private conversation with the director of the left-leaning think tank, and the textile designer crossed the room to speak to the fund manager, who happened to serve on the board of the same charity as herself.

Lucy walked to the north-facing window to look out at the ravishing spectacle of those enormous, empty office buildings blazing with electric light across the water. She loved this golden city, this pinnacle of human achievement. It was like a magnet drawing in wealth and talent and ambition from across the globe. And the more it drew in, the more brilliant it became and the more powerful its magnetic pull.

'Noocracy,' the sociologist said, coming up behind her. 'The rule of the wise. Plato's philosopher kings. That's what you're talking about, isn't it?'

'I think I prefer the word epistocracy. The rule of the knowledgeable.'

'I can see two snags. One: being clever or knowledgeable doesn't make you selfless. Two: there's one important thing that the cleverest people in the world know far less about than ordinary folk.'

'Oh, yes? And what's that?'

'What it feels like to be an ordinary person.'

She laughed politely. What an insufferable prig he was!

TWENTY-TWO

Harry and Michelle met at King's Cross station. She was wearing her white coat, grey ankle boots, and a neat grey dress, and carrying a small overnight bag. It was a Saturday and she'd arranged for Jules to help out Cheryl at Shear Perfection. Harry had a taxi take them to Tate Modern. These days the gallery has become the brick ruin we just know as 'the Modern' and it's often flooded. It was very briefly a Liberal stronghold during the later stages of the Warring Factions, and was heavily shelled by the Patriot forces. But back in Harry's day it was another instance of an industrial structure (in this case an enormous coal- and oil-fired power station) that had been refitted to serve a completely different and more refined purpose, while deliberately retaining some of the proletarian glamour of its original function.

When Harry and Michelle visited it, there was an exhibition going on of a twentieth-century Cuban artist who no one now remembers, but whose work bore some similarity (at least to my eyes) to the art of Picasso, who *is* still known, if only to historians like myself. Michelle seemed to enjoy being there. She held Harry's arm and leant in closely against him to look at the often cartoon-like pictures, pointing out details and happily discussing with him what they represented and why they had been done in this way or that way. She'd never been to a proper art gallery before, she said, unless you counted the museum in Cambridge which she'd visited a couple of times on school trips, but, as she recalled, most of the stuff there was mummies and old statues. 'If you asked me to name some famous artists,' she told him, 'I'd have a job to give you five of them. That's how much I know.'

'Well, it's nice to know about the history behind a painting,' Harry said, 'because that's sort of the language that the artist is using. But it's also good to leave all that behind and just see where the image itself takes you, and that's probably easier for you than it is for me.'

'You were right,' she told him a bit later, 'this is way more fun than going to a movie. Once the film starts you might as well not be with anyone at all. But I'm not being funny or anything, but don't you think a kid could have done some of these?'

He laughed at that. He found it rather endearing that she should come up with this thought as if it had never occurred to anyone before. 'Dear God, Michelle, you sound like my *grandmother*!'

'Well, maybe your gran was right. I mean, this one here ... Don't get me wrong, it's nice to look at, and I'm really loving being here, but if you saw it in a junkshop or something, wouldn't you think some kid had done it?'

The cartoon-like image in front of them included an eye that seemed to be part of a mask, a sideways mouth, two breasts drawn in rough outline and some stylized leaves. To the extent that it was flat and heavily outlined, with no concessions either to three-dimensional space or to naturalism, it did bear some resemblance to children's pictures. 'I can see what you mean,' Harry said, 'but I really don't think so. I've done enough painting myself to know there's an awful lot of skill in those brushstrokes.'

'Okay,' she conceded, 'but the *idea* of it.'

'I think even the idea of it is *way* more sophisticated than anything a kid would come up with. I really am quite certain that if I saw it in a junkshop I wouldn't think a kid had done it. But I get your point. If I saw it out of context, would I immediately think it was a work of art that deserved to be hung in a famous gallery like this? If I'm honest, I'm not sure. I do wonder sometimes, when I look at art, whether the emperor is really wearing clothes, or whether it's us who clothe him in our minds? But then that's true of a lot of things.'

In fact, it might be true of the two of them, he thought for a brief moment: two strangers, each one clothing the other in meaning. But he didn't say that. He turned away from the bleakness of that idea, and they moved on to the next picture.

Two women came into the room as they were about to leave it. With a sudden cold shock, Harry realized that one of the women was Letty. He tried to steer Michelle away from the door again, muttering something about a picture they'd missed, but Letty had already spotted him. 'Oh hi, Letty!' he croaked, and he would have hastily released his arm from Michelle's if she hadn't in the same moment tightened her hold on him, having realized that they as a couple were about to greet someone she didn't know.

'Hello, Harry.' Letty looked enquiringly at Michelle.

'This is my friend Michelle,' Harry said, and Letty inclined her head. She didn't introduce her companion. It was an older woman, perhaps her mother or an aunt.

'Hello, Letty,' Michelle said in her perky little Essex voice. 'I was just saying to Harry that a kid could have done some of these pictures.'

Letty visibly flinched, and so did Harry. In fact, he cringed. Michelle seemed so *small* all of a sudden. Not just small physically, though she was shorter and more petite than Letty, but small in her naivety, her lack of culture, her provinciality. Even her way of speaking, which normally delighted him, made her seem to him now like some sort of silly chirpy little Essex sparrow. People like himself and Letty were cultured and educated, connected to a body of shared ideas and knowledge that gave them substance and depth and gravity, and the lack of all that in Michelle made her seem so tiny by comparison that Harry felt the kind of shame that he would have felt if Letty had caught him going out with a sixteen-year-old or one of those young Filipino women that certain middle-aged men found on the internet. An old-fashioned phrase of his father's came into his mind: *Dolly bird*. Cultured, grown-up, capable Letty had caught him with his little dolly bird and he was so ashamed that he could feel his face burning and the roots of his hairs prickling and crawling. Yet all the while Michelle clung to his arm.

'It would have to be a pretty talented kid, don't you think?' Letty said. She smiled thinly at Harry, her eyes narrowed, and she continued into the room with her companion.

'Who was she and what the fuck was happening there?' Michelle demanded, as Harry hurried her into the next gallery. She released his arm so she could stand and face him, turning her back to the rest of the room. 'That's not your *wife*, is it?'

'No. She's someone I met quite recently. In fact, it was just a couple of days before I met you. Out on the marsh at Blakeney.'

Michelle looked blank. 'It's in Norfolk,' Harry said, unable to conceal his irritation at her ignorance even of the county she lived in. 'On the coast near Sheringham. Later I ran into her in London, and I went out for a meal with her.'

'During the time you said were thinking about me every day?'

'Yes. During the time I was thinking about you every day and *trying very hard not to*. I thought perhaps she'd help me put you behind me.'

'Did you sleep with her too?'

'No. She went abroad and I didn't see her again after that meal until we ran into each other again at a New Year's Eve party. We talked about meeting again, but then I heard from you so I put her off.'

Michelle studied his face, hard eyed. They were only a few yards into the room, and people were moving round them on either side, like a river parting round some obstruction, glancing at the two of them as they passed. 'You know what, Harry. I can see it now. You weren't just embarrassed to be seen with another woman, were you? You were embarrassed to be seen with *me*.' People were looking quizzically across at them and giving each other amused little smiles, but she seemed oblivious to all of this. 'You told me you wanted to be honest with me, so fucking *be* honest. Tell me if I'm right. Or prove to me I'm wrong.'

The honest truth was that he was *still* embarrassed to be with her. It was that Polish builder moment all over again. She was one of the small people and he felt as if everyone in the room must be wondering what he was doing with someone like her and what it said about his maturity and his self-esteem and his attitude to women. 'Okay,' he said. 'Fair enough. Let's go outside, shall we, and we'll talk?'

Without answering him or waiting for him, she began to walk very quickly through the remaining rooms of the exhibition and out on to the landing, where there was a row of lifts to carry visitors up and down to the several floors of the cavernous industrial building. He hurried after her. They didn't speak to each other or look at each other's faces as they descended side by side, or as they strode through the people milling around on the ground floor and out into the space in front of the gallery where a wide footpath, these days usually submerged, ran above the bank of the river.

'Is this outside enough for you?' she demanded.

'Yes, of course. Listen, Michelle, I'd have been embarrassed to be seen with anyone. Only a few days ago, I agreed with her that we'd arrange another date, and there I was with you. It must have looked as if—'

Michelle shook her head firmly. 'But it wasn't just that, was it?'

He looked down into her face. He could still see that 'smallness' which he now saw was the essence of that entirely different way she had of being a woman from someone like Letty, or Janet or his sister Ellie. (There was something light and birdlike about it, as if her bones were filled with air: perhaps that was why loutish Essex types referred to women as 'birds'?) He wondered if, all along, he'd really just been turned on by the fact that he could look down on her, and if so what kind of man he really was?

'No, you're right,' he admitted. 'It wasn't just that. You embarrassed me. It's not your fault at all, but you did. And okay, if you want the truth, I felt ashamed.'

'*Ashamed?*' Her white-hot fury had once again drawn the attention of people all around them, but he was no longer worried about that. He felt himself reeling as if from a physical blow. 'What the *fuck* did I do, Harry, to make you feel ashamed? You introduced me to that woman, she was looking daggers at me and I had no idea why but I did my best to be friendly. What more did you expect of me? What the fuck else could I have done? Okay, I'm not one of your sort and she is. But you knew that already, didn't you? You fucking mention it often enough, for Christ's sake! But hey, if you want to be with someone like her, well there she is. I'm sure she's got loads more to offer you than I have. Go after her, why don't you? Be my fucking guest!'

'No . . . it's not—'

'Is this why you keep going on about us not having enough in common, and not wanting to waste my time? Because you know that whenever you meet anyone you know, you'll be so fucking ashamed of me that you'll go bright red and stammer like you did up there? Because you did, you know, Harry. You went bright fucking red, just because you were with me, and you were so embarrassed you could hardly speak. Well, I'll tell you something. If that's what you've been worrying about all this time, you were right to worry. You *should* have left me alone. You *are* wasting my time. And if you really cared about my feelings at all, you would have thought about that before you asked me out. Why would any woman want to be with a man who was embarrassed to be even seen with her?'

He tried to touch her hand but she shook him off. 'Listen, Michelle,' he said, 'please listen. You find my car embarrassing, don't you?'

'Not like that, though!' Her grey eyes were bright and fierce, like the eyes of a wild animal that's been backed into a corner and has no option but to fight to the death. 'Not so as I'd feel so ashamed if someone saw it that I'd go red in the face and wish I wasn't with you at all!'

'No, I understand that, but hear me out. You'd prefer it if I had a decent car, yes? Me driving that car makes you uncomfortable?'

She shrugged. 'Well, I can't see why you don't get a decent one.'

'Exactly. Because among the folk you know, having a nice car's a bit like wearing decent clothes, am I right? It's a simple matter of self-respect.'

She shrugged. 'Something like that.'

'Well, believe it or not, I don't know anyone else who gives a shit what kind of car I drive. Okay, a lot of my friends have nice cars, but I literally don't know anyone apart from you who'd even think it was worth mentioning that my car was battered and old. Because that kind of thing doesn't happen to matter to my kind of people. But my tribe has its own equivalents, and one of them is *knowing stuff*. That, for us, is as important as wearing decent clothes. And I know it was stupid, Michelle, I know it was petty of me, I know you didn't deserve it, but I was embarrassed that you knew so little about art that you spouted that tired old cliché about how a kid could do better than that. None of my friends would say a thing like that. Not one. And never mind my grandmother – whatever I said in there, she was a cultured woman and she'd never have said it either – you'd have to go back generations in my family to find anyone who would. So yes, I was embarrassed. I was embarrassed by what you said, even though I know that, just like cars, that sort of thing doesn't really matter at all.'

People passed this way and that. Seagulls alighted on the path and on the railing by the river, looking around for opportunities with their cold yellow eyes. He wondered if what he'd just said was really close enough to the truth. For it wasn't just what she'd said that had embarrassed him, was it? It was who she was. Even if she'd just said hello, he'd still be feeling like this.

'You were embarrassed when I said it in front of her,' Michelle said, 'but when I said the same thing to you a few minutes before . . . well, okay you laughed at me, you said it was like talking to your nan – even though you're telling me now that even your nan wasn't that fucking stupid – but you didn't seem to *mind*. In fact, you actually admitted there was some truth in it. You said you wondered sometimes if artists were like that emperor in the story where no one dares tell him he's got no clothes on.'

'It's true, I did.'

'So how come you were embarrassed when I said something you think is true?'

It was a good question and he had to think before he could answer it. 'Because "A kid could do it" really is a very old cliché,' he said. 'It's quite possibly *the* most clichéd thing that people say when they don't know anything at all about art. And I was particularly embarrassed by you saying it because I was already embarrassed by the situation.'

'I know *exactly* what embarrassed you,' she told him. 'You thought, "What sort of sad fuck do I look like to Letty, turning down a beautiful sophisticated woman like her for a thick little chav from Norfolk who might be pretty but knows fuck all about anything?"'

Harry had promised to be honest but, if he was to keep that promise, he'd have had to admit that what Michelle had just put to him was an almost exact description of how he'd felt. 'You're not thick,' he finally said, and at first he was addressing himself as much as her. 'You're no more thick than I am. You've just spent less time being educated, and don't live among highly educated people, so of course you're not so familiar with the things they talk about. And you're not a chav either, whatever that means.' (I've looked into the word 'chav', incidentally. It's definitely pejorative and, though its precise meaning is rather hard to pin down, it always refers to people who are of a lower class than the speaker.) 'You and I have different backgrounds. We grew up with different expectations and among different kinds of people. If we carry on together, we're going to find that difficult. I don't think I'll find your people easy to be with, either. But . . . '

Somehow, while he'd been speaking, his feelings had completely changed again. Standing there in front of him shivering in her neat grey dress, Michelle seemed inexpressibly precious to him.

'But what?'

'Oh Michelle, I'm trying hard not to get carried away, I'm trying not to say silly over-the-top things, but . . . '

She peered up into his face. Behind her stood that huge industrial shell that had once stunk of soot and engine oil and hummed with brutal energy, but now contained gluten-free salads, and miniature bottles of cabernet sauvignon, and those strange, arch creations that constituted art in the latter part of the Western Hegemony. 'But *what*, you stupid man?'

'Well . . . okay, if you really want the truth, I look at you now and I just . . . I just *love* you.'

He admits to himself later that 'some dumb, vain, adolescent part of me actually believed that when I said that she'd melt', but of course that wasn't what happened. Instead, Michelle exploded, her anger blasting through him like white-hot shrapnel, devastating the contents of his mind, and reducing what had been furnished rooms inside his head into splintered wood and crumbled masonry.

'Oh, for fuck's sake, Harry! This is *mad*! This is totally fucking mad! Ten minutes ago you were so ashamed of me you wished you could just make me disappear into the ground. *Ten minutes ago!* And now *this*! You do *know* that loving someone doesn't just mean wanting to have sex with them, don't you?'

'Yes, of course I—' began Harry.

But she was in mid flow and wouldn't be stopped. 'It means wanting to be *with* them,' she said. 'Wanting to be with them when they've got their clothes on! Wanting to be with them when other people are there! And being fucking *proud* of them.'

Harry had never been good with rage. Overwhelmed by the fierceness of her anger, he shook his head repeatedly while holding up his hands as if to ward off the blast she was directing at him. He tried to turn away from her towards the river where (so he later remembers) a tug was shoving six barges, lashed together into a single block, against the force of the turbulent water. But she wasn't having that.

'Look at me, Harry! Look at my face so I can see you've heard me! I don't want to be *anyone's* guilty secret!'

'I *do* want to be with you,' he told her, wondering what he really meant by his words even as he was speaking them, given that she was quite right, and that ten minutes ago he had indeed felt exactly the opposite. 'It's not just about sex. It really isn't. I'm sorry about what happened. I'm ashamed of having been ashamed. I'm completely crap when it comes to things like that. But I . . . I think I want you to help me be someone else.'

She shook her head. 'Oh no. No, no, no. No chance, mate. I'm not having that either. That's what Fudge used to say. He'd hit me and call me names and then he'd cry and say he didn't want to be that way but he needed my help to change.'

Again Harry turned away from her, not in anger, but because he needed respite, and this time she didn't stop him so he walked over to the railing that separated the path from the river. The tide was going out, and that tug and its barges were still beating their way slowly upriver against its flow. He had a tendency, he knew, to get carried away and speak his feelings in the moment rather than restraining himself until he'd made a realistic, grown-up appraisal of his state of mind. He could see this was a weakness. It was selfish of him, and childish. And now, in a flash of insight, he realized that it was also extremely manipulative. When it was convenient to feel love, he felt and expressed it, but when it wasn't convenient, he shut love down at once and felt something else entirely.

For a moment, presented with this ugly reflection of himself, a surly child stirred inside him. 'But it's not only me who's been impulsive,' he muttered to himself. 'It's her too.' Not just once, after all, but on two different occasions she'd wanted to go right ahead and have sex with him when he'd tried to be grown-up about it and suggested they needed to be careful!

But his moment of insight had been just powerful enough not to be extinguished in that way, and he recognized the game that his inner child was trying to play. He'd played it often enough, after all, with Janet, deflecting self-examination by telling himself that she was just as bad or worse.

He turned back to Michelle. 'I've honestly never hit anyone since I was nine years old,' he told her. 'And as for calling people names, well Janet and I said some pretty brutal things to each other, but I'm fairly sure that if she were here, she'd confirm that being a bully is not one of my many faults.' He reached his hands towards her. She didn't reach back. 'I do get why you're angry with me, though, Michelle. If you wanted to call it a day now, I'd understand. All I can say is I don't want to.'

She studied his face, her raw grey angry eyes searching his troubled brown ones. Her coat was still inside the gallery and she was hugging herself against the cold. Finally she nodded. 'Okay. So what do you want to do now?'

'We'll forget the gallery, yes?'

'I'm sorry, Harry, I know you paid a lot of money for that show, but I don't want to be in that place any more.'

'I understand. Me neither. Let's go and get your coat and bag and go somewhere else.' He put his arm round her shoulders and pulled her against him to rub her back. 'You're absolutely freezing, aren't you?'

As they queued at the cloakroom, he asked what she usually liked to do when she came to London. She said the only reason she ever came to London was for shopping trips with her mum, or Jen, or Jules. 'I remember we had a school trip here once,' she said, 'to a big museum with dinosaurs and whales and stuff like that.'

'The Natural History Museum? I used to love that place. I haven't been there since I was a kid either. Do you fancy going there now?'

Michelle took pictures in the Natural History Museum and at one point had a passer-by take a picture of the two of them together, standing in front of a dinosaur skeleton, which she went on to post on Facebook. (Harry was uneasy about that, and confides to his diary that he didn't like the idea of people in Breckham he didn't know studying him, evaluating him, teasing Michelle about him . . . But he knew better than to speak this thought out loud.) I've spent a long time looking at that picture, the two of them side by side, arm in arm, their heads leaning together, each putting on their photo smile. They seem quite happy together in that moment and there really is something alike about the two of them. However different their backgrounds and their outlooks, there's a similarity in their stances on the world. For one thing, I notice their size. Harry had become suddenly aware of Michelle's physical smallness during the encounter with Letty, but, though he is much more stockily built than her and half a head taller, he's not a big man himself. For another thing, they're both good-looking people, but neither has that particular kind of self-confidence that often goes with good looks.

They both separately report in their diaries that they had a happy time in the museum among the dinosaur bones and the stuffed animals that they'd both enjoyed as children, almost as if they were children again now. A few times, Harry admits, he was shocked by her lack of knowledge – she seemed to think that cavemen lived alongside dinosaurs, for instance – but he was strict with himself about this. After all, what did he really know himself? It wasn't as if he truly understood the world around him. He had no idea how his phone worked. He didn't really know what electricity was (okay, he knew it was 'electrons', but where did that really take you?). He had no idea what he was looking at if he lifted the bonnet of his car. And, in spite of hundreds of hours of Brexit conversations, he had to admit, if only to himself, that he was still a little unclear about the precise difference between the 'Customs Union' and the 'Single Market'.

There existed in Harry's tribe a certain level of shared general knowledge that allowed him and his friends to feel that they were reasonably well-informed: you knew humans appeared long after the end of the age of dinosaurs, you knew that cubism's rejection of the literal representation of the world might seem childlike but was in fact a carefully thought-out strategy . . . But these bits of shared knowledge worked in rather the same way that a few leaves painted in detail at carefully chosen points on a canvas deceive the eye of a viewer into thinking they are looking at an entire forest-full of leaves when in fact, apart from those few, all that's really there is a mass of paint in various shades of green.

'*I* feel embarrassed now,' Michelle said, when he had to remind her that a whale was a mammal. 'You must think I'm such an ignorant woman.'

He kissed her and said everyone was ignorant about most things, and the world was still pretty much a mystery in spite of science and TV and computers and all the rest. 'I reckon we just don't notice that most of the time, because we all know just enough to get through our day, and deal with the people around us.'

'My flat's like my car,' Harry warned her, as they climbed the stairs. 'It does the job, but it's nothing special.' He was worried that she'd expect something stylish – he was an architect, after all – but he'd done nothing to his rather anonymous rented apartment beyond hanging a few pictures and moving in some of the furniture from his old house.

Michelle seemed to find no fault with it, though. He poured her a glass of white wine and while, at the kitchen end of the flat's open-plan living space, he finished preparing a fish dish whose ingredients he'd got ready in the morning, she wandered around the main part of the room looking at his things.

'Who's this old guy?' she asked, picking up the miniature enamel portrait that was still lying unhung on his mantelpiece.

'Gideon Providence Roberts,' he said. 'The man who supposedly turned my family into posh middle-class types like me.'

'He looks a miserable old sod.'

'He does, doesn't he? He was all about self-discipline and self-improvement, by all accounts. Not much fun at all, I imagine. I think that was done in about eighteen hundred.'

'You actually know your ancestors back that far? I don't know mine any further than my grandparents.'

She looked at the books and magazines strewn on the glass coffee table in front of the TV. There was a sketch pad and some pencils there, and she asked if she could see what he'd been drawing.

'Be my guest.' He slid the fish into the oven. 'But there's not much in there, to be honest. My big plan to become an artist hasn't really got very far.'

She leafed through the pages. He'd done various deliberately stylized drawings of trees, and the view from his window, and ordinary household objects, trying to find his way to a visual language that wasn't just a rehash of someone else's. 'They're good, Harry. I reckon if you turned these into paintings and hung them in that gallery, no one would know you weren't a famous artist like the bloke we saw today.'

'That's nice of you but no. I have got reasonably good basic drawing skills, but I'm beginning to think that's as far as it goes.'

'Can I draw something?' she asked him.

'Yeah, of course, go ahead.' He assembled the ingredients for a salad and chopped them up. When he looked up again she was completely engrossed in what she was doing and didn't even notice him watching her. There was something rather touching about her rapt face.

'You're really getting into that!' he said at length. 'At one point you were actually sticking out your tongue!'

'Oops. I did that when I was a kid. Trevor always used to tease me about it.' She snapped the pad shut. 'That fish is smelling nice.'

'It'll be ready in half an hour or so. Aren't you going to show me what you've done?'

'Oh, don't look at it now. I was only having fun.'

'Let me see it.' He sat beside her and picked up the pad. Her drawing was in a completely different league from what he'd anticipated. She'd done a recognizable and very competently executed pastiche of the cartoon-like pictures they'd seen in the Tate.

'Bloody hell, Michelle, that's *good*!'

'Oh, come on, Harry, it's just a scribble.'

'No really, Michelle, I know about drawing, it's part of my job, and, trust me, that is *good*.'

'Well, thanks.' She seemed oddly indifferent to his praise, almost as if she hadn't heard what he was saying.

'Seriously,' he persisted. 'That's a real talent you've got there.'

'Well, I was okay at drawing at school. I quite enjoyed it.'

Harry was puzzled. Why wasn't she pleased that he was impressed? 'No, I mean it, Michelle,' he said again. 'I'm not being nice, that really is *good*!'

She shrugged. 'Okay, great. But why are you making such a big thing about it? I'm still just me, whether I can draw or not.'

Harry was puzzled. 'Well, of course, but . . . '

'But now you've got something to tell your friends about when they think I'm just a thick chav?' She put on her posh voice. '"I know she doesn't seem like much, but you should see her art. It's *absolutely extraordinary*."'

'Oh come on, Michelle! I'm just saying your drawing is good.'

He went to check the fish. It wasn't actually necessary to do this but he felt hurt, and he needed a moment to get over his disappointment that she'd gone right back to their row outside the Tate. As he opened the oven, though, it struck him that she was completely right. His feeling on seeing her drawing hadn't just been pleasure. It had also been *relief*. She had shown potential. She had demonstrated that, given the opportunity, she was capable of being something other than what she was.

The fish was, of course, fine. He pushed it back. 'Okay,' he told her, still standing behind the kitchen counter. 'I understand what you're saying, but the fact is I was very happy to have you here in my flat before you started that drawing – surely you could see that? – and I would have been equally happy to have you here if you hadn't drawn anything at all, or if your drawing had been completely crap.'

'You're happy to have me in your flat, Harry, I know that. But what about outside? What about meeting your mates?' She didn't leave him time to answer. 'You know what I hate? I hate it when there's been a plane crash or a bomb's gone off or something, and when they talk on the news about the people who've died, it's always the one who's just got a scholarship they go on about, or the one who was about to climb some mountain in Africa or something. Like their deaths mean more than the others. Like achieving stuff is the only point of being alive, and the only people who matter are the clever people who do clever things.'

She picked up the drawing she'd done, glanced at it, and put it down again. 'I don't want to be your project, Harry. I don't want to be improved by you. And if you ever again make me feel like you're so ashamed of me that you wish I was someone else, that's it, all right? That's the end of us.'

Harry was annoyed. 'Fair enough, but let's make a deal, shall we? If I promise not to do that again, I want you to promise not to be *so fucking defensive* that I can't praise your talents or tell you about something I think might interest you, without you accusing me of trying to improve you. It's not a crime to be good at things and to want to get better at them, for God's sake! It's not a crime to learn! You like *Strictly*, don't you? Isn't that what *Strictly*'s all about? People learning to do difficult things, and working at it, and getting good at them?'

The edge in his voice made her flinch. She was no better than he was at facing anger.

'No, of course it's not a crime to be good at things,' she said, with a rather forced shrug, looking away for a moment to avoid his suddenly fierce gaze. But then she returned to the attack. 'But why do you have to be so fucking *serious* about it? That's what gets me. I don't mind you saying my drawing's good. I know I'm quite good at drawing. I do pictures of our customers to make them laugh. But it's just for fun, isn't it? That's all. It's just for the fun of it. But for you it's got to be *art*. It's got to be something *serious*. It's got to be this big *important* thing that you're going to develop, so you can make pictures that everyone will look at in a gallery and whisper about, and frown, and say how *extraordinary* it is, like they're in a church or something.' She'd put on her 'posh' voice again to say the word 'extraordinary'. 'What's wrong with you people that everything you do has got to be important and serious and extraordinary?'

Harry said nothing for a while and then, to Michelle's surprise, he crossed the room for that old picture of his ancestor and laid it down on the coffee table in front of her. 'I blame this guy. He was a farm labourer on a big estate in Gloucestershire, but he was very able and hardworking, and he impressed his boss so much that he lent him the money to go to university and study the law. Eventually he became a successful solicitor and ended up marrying his boss's youngest daughter.'

Michelle had picked up the picture and was looking down at it as he spoke.

'As a matter of fact,' Harry said, 'Gideon's boss had made his fortune from a slave plantation in St Lucia, but we don't talk about that. The important part of the story is that Gideon made himself respectable by having a good brain and through sheer hard work. And he brought up his eleven children to work hard too, and improve themselves, and make good marriages and get the best possible education, so as to be sure of keeping the position in society that he'd established for them. And they brought their kids up that way in turn, and so on, and so on, except that after a generation or two we couldn't really congratulate ourselves any more on having clawed ourselves up from the gutter, so we had to find other ways of making ourselves feel like we were something special: our connoisseurship, perhaps, our sensitivity, our advanced liberal values.'

She was smiling now, he saw to his relief. 'And that's called being middle class,' he said, with a bow. 'That's how we're brought up. I was even brought up to remember that my ancestor Gideon, this miserable, driven-looking old bastard, was the one who made it all possible!'

She handed him the picture and he returned it to the mantelpiece. 'So there's your answer, Michelle. That's why we're like this. That's why we're so fucking earnest and self-important and obsessed with bettering ourselves, and that's why, I suppose, we secretly envy people who aren't middle class for being free of all this pressure and all this stuff we're supposed to live up to.' He sat down on the sofa beside her. 'Bettering ourselves! I wonder if the world would be in the mess it is today if people in the past had just relaxed a bit more and not kept trying to make things better all the time.'

Michelle looked at him with widened eyes and gave him her lopsided smile. 'Bloody hell, Harry! Have you finished? I wasn't expecting a fucking lecture!'

'I wasn't expecting to give one, to be honest,' he said.

They clinked their glasses together and drank, and began to kiss with warm wine-tasting lips until the timer on his oven pinged to say the fish was ready.

'I felt like everyone in that room was seeing me as a silly ignorant common little woman, who didn't know enough to understand about being quiet and respecting the art,' Michelle writes later. 'And it made me think how Mum must have felt when Dad got angry with her because she didn't know something, or she didn't get something, or she forgot something. I remembered me and Dad sitting at the tea table, and her out in the kitchen fetching the ketchup or the mustard or something she'd not remembered to put on the table. "How in God's name did I end up with someone like you, Kath?" he went when she came back in. He usually pretended it was just a joke but sometimes he'd get really angry. "You haven't got two brain cells to rub together, have you?" he said once and then he stood up right in the middle of a meal and left the room, leaving Mum to clear the table. I didn't offer to help her either. I went and watched TV with Dad so I didn't have to see those pathetic little tears in her eyes, and I didn't even try to tell him off for what he'd done. "You've got a halfway decent brain," he said. "For God's sake use it, girl! Don't end up in a place like this. Don't end up with someone you can't respect." And I just looked at the telly and didn't say anything at all.'

She draws a line, like Harry does, to end that thought. 'I'm not going to change,' she writes. 'Not for Harry, not for anyone. I don't want a better job, I don't want to live in a better place. There's nothing wrong with just being ordinary.'

I don't doubt that she meant it, but I still don't quite believe it myself. I can't help thinking that part of the attraction of Harry was that he offered an honourable way out. To leave Breckham behind her for the sake of a career, as her father had wanted, perhaps seemed too cold and disloyal for her to contemplate. But to leave for love . . . ?

They had a happy day on Sunday. They both agree on that. They stayed late in bed. Michelle did one of her cartoon drawings of Harry. They had lunch in a café and walked in a park. They talked about their childhoods.

But after he'd dropped Michelle off at the station on the Sunday evening, Harry felt strangely numb and didn't know what to do with himself, ending up sitting at his dining table, flicking through Twitter on his phone.

'I will never forgive the people who've done this! Never!' someone or other had tweeted apropos of Brexit, and received ninety-seven responses: 'And all because Leave voters can't cope with the fact that we are no longer in the 1950s' . . . 'I refuse to hear excuses for these people who have trashed my children's future' . . . 'None of them is capable of reasoned argument. Not ONE. And believe me, I've tried'.

The sealed-off silence of his flat oppressed him. He went out for a walk, wandering through streets lined with spacious Victorian houses, much like the one he grew up in. Some had their curtains drawn, with the TV flickering inside. In others, no one was in and the curtains were open so he could look into the unlit front rooms with their bookshelves, dark shapes of pictures on the walls, silent pianos just visible in the streetlight.

A fine rain began to fall. He found himself in one of the long commercial roads that laced the city. He passed laundries, halal butchers, convenience stores, a hardware shop with a display of mops and buckets in green, purple and blue. Mattress World was closed and so was Sunbed World, but electric signs glowed and flashed on either side of them: Open! Open! Open! Red, blue, white, yellow gleamed on the wet pavement. Shopkeepers sat behind their tills in caves of electric light, surrounded by their stock: practical people, Harry thought, who left it to others to speculate about the big questions, and focused on keeping going day by day. A white and purple sign shone out atop the flaking façade of a former cinema to proclaim the Sacred Waters Tabernacle. Two old men emerged from an Islamic Centre in what had once been a Nonconformist chapel.

'No one really knows what this world is,' Harry said to himself. 'We just stick to whatever story makes us feel most at home.' Flattened chewing gum pocked the shining red and blue pavement outside a Tube station. People went in, others came out, and there was a brief moment in which he saw all of them glowing with purpose, each in their own way confronting the strangeness of being alive with whatever resources their particular history had bequeathed to them.

A new message arrived with a ping. He fished the phone from his pocket and found a new text from Michelle.

I love you too, Harry. Seems mad to say that so soon, but you said it to me, and I want you to know I feel the same.

He thought about the shame he'd felt only yesterday when they'd run into Letty in the Tate, the intensity of it, the way it took over his mind and his body, a primitive, urgent, biological force whose function was to preserve a social order. It had been so completely outside his control; that was what shocked him most about it.

He felt like a dry leaf that, at any moment, a gust of wind could pick up and blow away.

Michelle dreamt that night about that huge black bird.

TWENTY-THREE

Charlie was going over to Sir Gerald's every week now. The Colonel had recruited some other ex-army men to act as trainers, and they took the group for runs in the nearby forest, or drove them across assault courses, or set them punishing training regimes involving tractor tyres. Charlie was good at all this. He was physically strong and he had stamina, and he loved the sense of purpose and the comradeship. He made friends with another young man called Ed.

At the end of a day's training, they were invited to use the plunge pool that Gerald's great-grandfather had installed in its own brick building outside the back of the house. It was white-tiled inside and functional, like a butcher's shop or a public toilet, with water so cold that it made them yelp. But they splashed around in it happily, yelling abuse at each other and flicking each other with towels. Afterwards, Gerald or one of his trainers would gather them together in the hall, where there would be beer and sandwiches and someone to give them a pep talk.

One time it was a woman that Gerald invited to the stage and Charlie, like everyone else, recognized her at once.

'Fucking hell!' he murmured to Ed. 'It's only Tiffany Flynn!'

They all cheered and hooted, still warm and glowing from their exertions and from the endorphins pumping through their veins. A tall, confident, physically fit woman in her early thirties, Tiffany had until recently presented the sports on one of the major TV channels. A scandal involving cocaine and a married football manager had got her face on the front pages of all the tabloids and led to her resignation.

Gerald laughed. 'It looks as if my wonderful great-niece needs no introduction!'

Tiffany beamed out at them. 'Great to meet you, boys!' she called out, with that same, easy, somehow masculine confidence that she deployed in conversations with football stars and premier-league managers. She was a woman who was at home in an extremely male world, or that at least was how she presented herself.

'It's really *great* to meet you!' Tiffany told them. 'I'm totally stoked about what you guys are doing and Uncle Gerald is so proud of you all. *So* proud, you wouldn't believe! You're brilliant.'

Her slightly husky voice was as posh as her uncle's and, like him, she was completely unabashed about it, and didn't even try to tone it down. Each one of the men must have known perfectly well that she was completely out of his league, and she didn't pretend otherwise, but nevertheless she conveyed to them somehow that as a group she was attracted to them, and took pleasure in their company, and relished their admiration.

'I want to tell you something about my Uncle Gerald. I've known him all my life and I love him to bits, but you need to understand that this affable, handsome, polite old buffer you see before you is only part of the story. Don't get me wrong, that's all real – you couldn't wish for a warmer, kinder uncle – but underneath it all, Colonel Sir Gerald Butler is pure steel.'

Standing in his usual place to the side of the stage, Gerald winked at them, made tiger claws and mimed a roar.

'Any history buffs here?' Tiffany asked. 'Any of you know why this part of the world is called East Anglia? You don't? Well, it's because fifteen hundred years ago, this eastern part of Britain was conquered and settled by a fighting people from Germany called the Angles. I like to think of you blokes as their heirs. Tough, fighting men with no airs or graces.'

She paused and surveyed them, arms folded, relaxed, head forward a little on her shoulders rather than stiff and straight. She looked from one face to another, smiling, holding eye contact for a second and moving on. She nodded.

'Yep. You chaps would have been right at home back then, I reckon. And Uncle Gerald would have been at home then too. In fact, I know he would have absolutely loved it. And I'll tell you what he'd have been in those days. A warlord. I don't mean what we call a lord now – the sort that's friends with Tony Blair and sits on committees about urban regeneration and promoting diversity in the arts – I mean a *real* lord, whose position comes entirely from his ability to win and hold the loyalty of a group of fighting men. I mean, look at him, guys! Can't you just picture it?'

Gerald pulled a funny face and put up his hands in imitation of the wings on the helmets of mythical Norsemen. The men in the hall clapped and cheered.

'I can *so* picture Uncle Gerald back then,' Tiffany said. 'He'd have had his own big hall, a bit like this one, but rougher and without the paintings and the windows. There'd be a big fire burning in the middle of it, with tables and benches down either side of the room. And there in his hall, he'd have had men just like you guys sitting along the benches, drinking the ale he provided and eating his meat until they'd had their fill, while he sat at his high table, up here where I am now, eating and drinking with them. You'd have been his housecarls, his warriors, and if you fought hard for him, he'd look after you, and feed you, and give you bracelets and gold rings to pass on to your women. Of course he'd be different from you, the same as an officer is different from his men. He'd wear fine things and drink from a cup made of gold or studded with gemstones. Well, if he didn't, you'd have asked yourself what kind of half-arsed lord you'd got yourself, wouldn't you? But he wouldn't be somewhere far away. He wouldn't be living a completely different life. He'd be right there among you, so that you knew him personally, and he knew every one of you.'

She beamed down at them. 'Imagine it. You'd all be down there getting pissed, and gorging on all that meat, and yelling and joking around, and Uncle Gerald would be up here, maybe proposing a toast from time to time, or challenging you to a drinking contest, or telling the odd joke, like he was your uncle too and not just mine. And then when the feasting was done, and you'd eaten and drunk your fill, you wouldn't go home, you'd just wrap up in blankets or animal furs and go to sleep right here on the benches, with all your mates around you.'

She had a way of turning half sideways to them as she asked a question, with her hands on her hips, so they could admire her strength and her athleticism. She was taller than most of the men there.

'So how does that sound?' she asked them.

'Fucking great!' Charlie shouted out. Gerald laughed at that, and twinkled across at him, and a lot of the other men cheered. And in the delicious warmth of that moment in which he was the centre of everyone's attention, an image glowed dimly in Charlie's mind. Or perhaps image is the wrong word. It was not so much an image as the tactile equivalent of an image, a kind of shape, and not exactly even that, but more a kind of bundle of feelings. He couldn't have named it or begun to describe it – no one could have done – but like an old and powerful memory, it was very rich in meaning. And it made him feel like he could have the warmth and safety of being held like a child and the fierce exhilaration of kicking the shit out of someone, both together in the same package. He could have blood and steel along with mother's breast.

'I *know* men like you,' Tiffany said, and laughed. 'Ha! You *know* I know men like you. I know what matters to you. And I know what doesn't matter to you as well. For example, do "human rights" float your boat at all?'

There was a groan, and Tiffany laughed. 'I thought not. Rights for who, eh? And how about parliamentary democracy? How about the rule of law?'

They groaned louder this time, and booed, getting the hang of the game now and beginning to enjoy it. Tiffany laughed. 'You really don't give a shit, do you?'

They all cheered. 'You *bastards*!' Tiffany told them with great affection. 'You hard bastards! You absolute brutes. Well, okay, how about culture, then? How about the arts?'

The men jeered and gave hoots of incredulous laughter.

She affected surprise. 'Oh, so you're not opera fans? You don't listen to the culture programmes on Radio 4? You don't go down to

Cambridge for the Shakespeare plays? I'm disappointed in you. It's only forty minutes from here, after all!'

They laughed raucously and she gave them that lovely tough ironic smile that they all recognized from the TV. 'Face it, lads, you're a bunch of fucking savages! What are we going to do with you? It's the twenty-first century and you're no different from what you were a thousand years ago. There's nothing civilized about you at all.'

They cheered and hooted and laughed.

'Nothing civilized about you at all,' Tiffany repeated, simultaneously beaming at them with proud affection and sadly shaking her head in a pantomime of weary resignation. 'You're a lost fucking cause.'

They cheered again. She smiled and nodded, arms crossed, standing at ease.

'But do you know why that is?' she asked them. 'Do you know *why* you give so few fucks about civilization? It's because it's not *your* civilization. It's not even meant for you. It's theirs. It belongs to the people that run things. It's *their* rights, it's *their* parliament, *their* laws, *their* culture, their paintings and opera houses. They let you have plasma TVs, and cars, and fridges, and holidays in Greece if you're lucky, or maybe even Florida. And in exchange for that, all they ask is that you keep your great clumsy clodhopping boots off their civilization and let them enjoy it in peace.'

She came right to the front of the little stage, and looked out at them, arms still crossed. They gave catcalls of admiration.

'But how about *your* civilization?' she asked them. 'How about *your* culture?'

There were more hoots of derision. 'Oh, I know it sounds ridiculous, you lot having a culture.' She looked at them sideways, scrunching her face up in an expression of incredulity. 'I mean, just look at you!' More hoots. More laughter. Tiffany laughed with them.

'But seriously, lads, *your* culture . . . what would it look like if it existed? I mean, I know you're a bunch of savages, but you do have things you believe in, don't you? Give yourself *some* credit. You've got a sense of right and wrong, haven't you? You've got a sense of honour. You've got people you care about and things that make you feel that life is good. It's just that your things are different from theirs. So really and truly, all kidding aside, what would *your* society be like if it wasn't for them? What do you think it would look like?'

They looked up at her blankly, unsure of what she meant and uncertain how to respond to her now that she was no longer either teasing them or flirting with them.

She smiled at them. 'Well, I don't *know*, of course – it's really not my call – but if you want my opinion I reckon it would be a bit like the kingdoms of the Angles all those centuries ago, when they first settled here, and before their leaders got too comfortable. Small communities, tight-knit groups, and men raised to be fighters in a tough world where you needed tough men to protect the tribe against its enemies. Tell me I'm wrong if you like, but I think that's your natural habitat. Am I right?'

The men cheered noisily, though perhaps more out of general good feeling than as an indication that they agreed in detail with her analysis. She nodded and smiled.

'Human rights, parliament, art galleries, universities, Enlightenment values . . . all that stuff has got nothing to do with you, has it? In fact, I bet a lot of you haven't even heard of that last one. But you've got a culture. Seriously, all kidding aside, you've got a strong culture. It just isn't about things like that. It's about being part of a tribe, and being loyal to it, and being willing to fight and die for it if necessary against anyone who tries to push it around. It's like the culture of sport in a way. In fact, I reckon that's why we love sport so much, because it lets us get back to those old simple values. It feels good to support your own team, doesn't it? To stick up for your lot against the others, no matter what, for no particular reason except that it's yours. And there's nothing to beat that feeling, is there, when your side scores that winning goal. It's shit for the other side, of course, but who cares? That's their problem, isn't it? They should have been better, shouldn't they? Or they should have fought harder. Either way, it's not your concern. It's not your concern at all.'

She stood with her hands on her hips, right at the front of the stage, looking down at them affectionately. 'I reckon what your culture's all about is courage and loyalty. And, most of all, I reckon it's about *belonging*. And I'll tell you what: I bloody love that about you. I wouldn't change it for the world.'

They didn't react at once. They were still taking on board the change of gear from being teased affectionately to being asked what really mattered to them.

'What do you reckon, boys?' She'd turned slightly sideways again. She had that masculine habit of constantly shifting around, planting and replanting herself on the wood beneath her, as if readying herself for some physical challenge. 'Belonging. Isn't that it? It's a tough world out there, and it's getting tougher. The people who've been running things don't get that yet. Their lives are still easy. They've noticed that the world has changed, and it bothers them, but they still imagine that they can change it back. But you know better, don't you? You know the world has changed for good. You may not know it with your heads, perhaps – men like you don't think with your heads about stuff like this – but you know it deep down in your guts. There's danger ahead, there are threats, and you're getting yourselves ready to fight for your own.'

TWENTY-FOUR

'**C**an I get you anything while you're waiting?' asked the young waiter.

Lucy shook her head. 'Thanks but I'll wait till my friend gets here. She was at King's Cross forty minutes ago so she must be close.'

'I think there's been some sort of problem on the Tube,' the waiter said. 'One of the other customers mentioned it.'

'Really? Oh crap.'

She picked up her phone, pushing her thick red hair out of the way as she searched for London transport updates. Around her young couples, about half of them Chinese, sat at the single row of tables that were laid out along the wall of a tiny, corridor-like Soho restaurant. It was all very functional. White tablecloths. White strip light. Linoleum floor. No decorations of any kind, other than the calendar behind the counter with a picture of Tiananmen Square. Lucy liked that. It felt authentic, like the food they served here, fiercely hot and brutally carnivorous.

'Lucy darling! *So* sorry to keep you!'

Her friend had made it. They hugged and kissed. They'd met at school, a progressive independent school near Hampstead

Heath, and though they disagreed about almost everything, their friendship had endured. There was a certain energy that each of them recognized in the other. 'Lovely to see you, Tiffany. It's been way too long.'

Tiffany settled into her seat and picked up the menu, chewing at her lower lip for a moment as she briefly surveyed the options, and then looking up again at Lucy with her bright lively eyes. 'I've been up at my great-uncle's place in Norfolk. The whole journey was absolutely fine until I hit London, and then there was a signal failure or something on the Northern Line. Typical, isn't it? An eighty-mile journey, and the last three miles lets you down. Anyway, what do you recommend? I'm absolutely fucking *starving*!'

Lucy signalled to the waiter, miming the act of drinking from a bottle. 'The dandan noodles are pretty amazing, but let's get some beers sorted first. Now listen, Tiffany. It's really great to see you, but let's decide while we're still sober what kind of evening we're going to have. Get thoroughly hammered and have a screaming row about Brexit? Or just get thoroughly hammered?'

The woman at the table behind Lucy twisted round in her seat to get a look at Tiffany, who her companion had recognized from the TV. Tiffany wiggled her eyebrows at her. The woman looked quickly away.

'Hmmm, tough choice,' Tiffany said. 'Tough choice. They're both pretty tempting.'

The waiter came over with two half-litre bottles of ice-cold Chinese beer.

'I think I'm probably going to need the screaming row, to be honest,' Tiffany decided as they clinked the bottles together. 'But let's not kid ourselves. It's not really about Brexit between you and me. It's not even to do with all the other nonsense we used to argue about, Labour versus Tories, Left versus Right. I was thinking about this on the train. We're so alike at one level. We've both read our Nietzsche, we both believe that only excellence redeems the world. It's just that we have different ideas about what excellence actually is. Your people were lawyers and mathematicians and you see excellence as intellectual brilliance. My people were soldiers and adventurers, and I see it as charisma and strength. Maybe we should scream at each other about that?'

'So you're still peddling that crypto-fascist mystico-chivalric cultural Viagra?'

Tiffany laughed. 'Later, Lucy, later. We've got news to catch up on first, and some serious drinking to do. Crypto-fascist chivalric Viagra is very good, but keep it for a few hours' time.'

TWENTY-FIVE

'So now two of your made-up characters meet in a restaurant and have a conversation?' Cally says. 'It's a funny kind of history book you're writing.'

We're on another of our hikes across London. A hot sticky blanket of cloud is pressing down on the city, and we're walking along a busy street south of the river, avoiding hawkers and beggars, weaving round pavement stalls where people shout out their wares and roadside preachers peddle their sundry syncretic religions.

'Lucy's not made up at all,' I tell her. 'She really was Richard's daughter and she really was a lecturer at LSE. And we know from Harry's diary that her dad and step-mum were setting up a discussion group. Okay, I don't know whether Lucy really did come along to it as a guest speaker, but you have to admit it's more than possible. And the views she expressed there really are hers. I got them from her tweets and blog posts, and the tweets and blog posts of her friends.'

'And she *really* used the phrase "Guiding Body"?'

'I've got no evidence that she used those actual words back then in 2017, but it doesn't seem so unlikely. The idea was already in the air. And it's not just Lucy. You can find lots of instances of that kind of argument in the Twitter archive of the period. And Lucy certainly uses the expression later on in her life. She wrote a book – *Toward Epistocracy* – and "Guiding Body" appears there many times.'

'And Tiffany?'

'I've taken more liberties there, I admit. Lucy did have a sports journalist friend by that name who went to school with her and was, as far as I can tell, the only friend of hers to be on the opposite side of the Brexit argument. I've studied Tiffany's social media presence in the archive and think I've been true to the way she looked and talked and her general attitude to life, but I don't really have any evidence she was involved in giving speeches like that.'

'Speeches to a non-existent prototype of the Patriotic League, at the country seat of her non-existent great-uncle. I should imagine not!'

I shrug. 'I've sort of mythologized her, I suppose; made her the embodiment of a force or an idea. You know? Like a Greek deity.'

Cally brushes flies off her face. 'So what would she be the goddess of? Martial Virtue? Ethno-Nationalism? This is some weird book you're writing, Zoe. You need to be careful. You really do.'

I laugh. 'But you're always telling me I'm *too* careful!'

We trudge on. I'm actually rather pleased that she's worried for me, because I suspect that my cautiousness is one of the main reasons that she isn't attracted to me in the way I want her to be. She's drawn to more flamboyant types.

'Seriously, Zoe,' she says, 'they won't like what you're doing. There's an agreed version of history and that's what we're paid to write.'

We're headed towards the Vauxhall Camp, which stands on the

site of Richard and Karina's riverside apartment, and also happens to be the location of one of the last major battles of the Warring Factions period. We're walking through streets that I suppose are the modern equivalent of those long commercial roads that Harry described as lacing through the whole of London. Back then this city was one of the wealthiest in the world, a global financial centre, the capital of a country rich enough to import half of its food. But after that came the period during which every window in these streets would have been smashed, and many of the buildings reduced to piles of rubble over which the militias fought with guns and rocket launchers while drone-bombs buzzed overhead like lethal wasps. The Catastrophe was well underway by this point, hundreds of millions of people across the world were fleeing floods and fire, and, if there was a time when it would have been a good idea to set aside differences in order to focus on the really important things, that would certainly have been it. But no. Those guys blasted away at each other as if nobody and nothing mattered but them and their quarrel.

But the fighting did eventually end and life returned to the streets, a bit like a forest regenerating after a fire, even if in a much more stunted form. Rubble was cleared, buildings were patched up and replaced, and back came Harry's practical people, the kind who concentrated on making a living and relied on tradition to deal with the bigger picture. Temples and shrines of sundry gods and saints were re-established along with the shops, to help them feel at home.

It's very different from Harry's day, of course. There would have been a constant procession of cars back then, while now there are almost no mechanized vehicles at all except for police carts, and, when darkness falls what lights there are will be dim and functional, and nothing like the blaze of colour that Harry describes, gleaming on the wet pavement, and on the road, and on the spray thrown up by the wheels of cars. Here and there small, ramshackle wind turbines turn above the roofs to help charge up the batteries that some storekeepers like to use when the mains supply cuts out. (Whoosh! Whoosh! Whoosh! Clink-clank, clink-clank. Each one has its own rhythm.) And the shops are of a different kind as well. There are tailors sewing shirts; workshops where they beat old metal into new utensils; small, specialist markets where traders sit behind rows of tables, buying and selling stale bread or rags or metal or bones. We even pass a place that buys dog faeces, which I've heard they use for tanning leather. But in spite of all these differences, the world as Harry would have seen it is still visible. Many of the buildings date back to the twentieth or nineteenth centuries – that row of shops there, this church tower pocked by bullets – and the layout of the roads is virtually unchanged, even if their formerly metalled surfaces are barely maintained at all.

But then we round a corner and the connection between then and now abruptly ends. There's no trace in front of us of the London that Harry lived in. There are no towers, no buildings of any substance at all for two or three kilometres, just a wire fence, two metres high, punctuated every fifty yards or so by an open gate, and beyond it a vast shanty-town, smoking and steaming in the heat, a city within a city of improvised shacks constructed from cardboard and salvaged pieces of wood and plastic and iron. It's a place where even the fossilized imprint of the past has been systematically pounded into dust, and all that remains is the future. There is a stench of sewage and rotting food waste. And three birds watch us, spaced out along the fence: a parrot, a seagull and a crow.

The Warring Factions is Cally's period. She's brought her screen with her and we work out exactly where the apartment block would have stood where Richard and Karina lived with their son Greg. There's a metalled road round the outside of the fence, built for the convenience of the security forces in the event of civil disorder and, rather than going through the camp, we follow this road to the river, and then along the top of the concrete flood barrier until we reach the right spot. The apartment block isn't even visible as a ruin, its remains broken up to make the platform on which the camp is built. There are just shanties there now, and a gate through the fence that leads to a jetty where boats come to pick up workers and take them to the flood works and the paddy fields.

People stream around us on foot and on bicycles, many of them craning their necks to look at us, as Cally shows me pictures on her screen. First we look at the glass towers as they once were, and then at what they became during the conflict when their windows and their plaster and their furnishings had all been blasted away and the apartments were just bare strata in concrete cliffs, in some cases collapsed or sheared sideways as if by some geological force, with Patriot soldiers perched here and there on their precarious ledges.

Why was the fighting so fierce in this particular spot? Some people say that it was the presence near here of the headquarters of a powerful security service, but Cally insists that this is an irrelevance and that the reasons were entirely to do with the contingencies of the battle. She says it's like the games of chess that she and I sometimes play. At certain points, everything seems to converge on a particular square, though that same square, at other stages of the game, or in other games, has no special significance at all.

The original inhabitants had long since fled. The Patriot militias had made the towers a vantage point from which to fire rockets and mortar shells across the river and at the surrounding city. The Liberal forces – the so-called Progressive Alliance – flung lead and explosives at them. But the Liberals knew the Patriotic League had prevailed in most of the rest of the country and that Patriot soldiers were already moving towards them from the north to relieve their comrades in the towers. By now, almost all of the other factions had been either defeated by or subsumed into these two. Only the Democrats, who wanted to settle the whole conflict by a free election, still clung on by their fingertips in a few redoubts. But they were a spent force and had been for a long time. Universal suffrage, as we all now know, was a wonderfully generous idea but only really worked in a time of such exceptional bounty that even the poor could be persuaded to give their support voluntarily to sensible leaders. And there was no particular class or segment of the population that saw the Democrats as their own. So it was just the Patriots and the Liberals slogging it out.

A woman comes to the door of one of the shacks next to the gate, right where Karina and Richard's apartment block would have been. She has Afro-European features like my own, but is much thinner and smaller than I am, with the skull showing through the taut yellow skin of her face. She eyes us anxiously as she empties a bucketful of dirty water into the ditch that leads from the camp into one of the culverts along the riverside track. Five or six parrots immediately arrive to investigate the refuse, screeching and squawking excitedly.

I smile at the woman reassuringly. She tightens her lips slightly in minimal acknowledgement of my attempt at friendliness, but doesn't smile back. A small girl of perhaps two or three comes out to look at us, wearing only a grubby T-shirt. Still holding her empty bucket, the mother shoos her back inside with another anxious glance in our direction. She wipes the sweat off her forehead. She looks around for something else to get on with. The neighbour on the opposite side of the ditch calls something out to her and she answers. She glances back at us again. The stench of raw sewage is almost overpowering.

TWENTY-SIX

On the way back from Gerald's, Jake dropped Charlie off at his grandmother's house. It was her seventy-fifth birthday and she was having a party.

'Hello, Charlie, my love!' she greeted him as she reached up for a kiss. 'You made it!'

The tiny little old woman held him tightly round the neck. He'd always been her favourite, since he was a baby. 'I wouldn't miss it for the world, Gran!' he told her. 'It's not every day your best grandma turns seventy-five!'

The rest of the party were already there. His mum was carrying plates of food out from the kitchen and, through the kitchen door, he could see his pretty auntie, the subject of many fantasies during his teens, sliding a tray of sausage rolls into the oven. Charlie turned into the living room to the left. It was a room he'd known all his life, and had remained almost unchanged, as if it was an exhibit in a museum. There were grey leather armchairs and a slightly worn fitted carpet in a darker grey flecked with white and pink. Dozens of family photographs covered the walls and the surfaces, interspersed with little china puppy-dogs, a Spanish bull, a gondolier music box, a coy shepherdess, a set of china cats, a doe and two fauns made of glass linked together by little chains, and a plastic Welshwoman in traditional costume bought on a coach trip to Betws-y-Coed. The back of the room had been knocked through into a small and slightly damp conservatory, in which there were more ornaments in a glass case, two cane chairs with pale blue cushions, a life-sized china dog with big brown eyes and a table on which a buffet was now being set out by the women: green salad, tomatoes, Scotch eggs, cheese on sticks, drinks. One of his cousins was out there with his little nephew and niece, looking at a picture book with them in a big wicker chair while the two of them munched on crisps.

Two women were sitting on the sofa, his uncle's girlfriend and his sister-in-law. But Charlie headed for the men, who were standing in a group with their beers, laughing in a rather forced way. His father was there, and his uncle, and his brother Gary, but with them was another man he'd not met before. The stranger was a different kind of person from the rest of them, Charlie could see that immediately. It was as if his doctor or the headmaster of his old school had turned up for a family gathering. The way the man dressed, the way he moved, the way he talked, all marked him out from everyone else in the house. He was the reason for the strained laughter, and it was obvious that the man sensed this himself because he looked very ill at ease there, being towered over by Charlie's great pear-shaped lump of a dad, and his burly uncle, and his big broad-shouldered brother Gary. The three of them looked uncomfortable too. They would have been fine together otherwise, bantering and joking away, but they were struggling to deal with the newcomer.

'Well done, Charlie, you made it!' his dad called out with unusual enthusiasm, as if relieved to have reinforcements. 'Come and meet Harry, mate. Come and meet Michelle's friend Harry.'

Charlie shook the newcomer's hand. 'All right there, mate?'

'Harry's driven up from London,' his father said.

'I suppose you came on the M11, did you?' Uncle Trevor asked.

'That's it,' Harry said.

'It's usually all right, I find,' Trevor observed.

'It can get a bit slow around Stansted,' said Charlie's pear-shaped dad. He wore a long-sleeved T-shirt emblazoned with the words, DON'T ASK ME, I ONLY WORK HERE.

Michelle carried some plates through to the conservatory and then came to stand beside Harry, slipping her arm through his. 'Harry grew up in Norwich,' she told the men. 'He supports Norwich City.'

'A Budgie, eh?' exclaimed Charlie's dad, as Michelle returned to the kitchen, his eyes lighting up with relief at the discovery of a topic that he and Harry could talk about.

'Norwich City?' Trevor shook his head. 'Well, good luck with that, mate. Good luck with that, because let's face it, you are going to need it.'

Ken, Charlie and Trevor all spoke with the same kind of south-eastern accent as Michelle, as did Michelle's mother Kath, but something Harry noticed was that the men's accent was much more pronounced than the women's. This was especially obvious with Trevor, to the point that he almost seemed to be parodying his own way of speaking, as if his deliberate intention was to come over as common and uncouth. He remembered noticing Phil and Richard's voices becoming posher when they were angry, as if, like animals facing a threat, they were trying to make themselves as big as possible. And it seemed to him that these men were doing the same kind of thing, not by making themselves posher – that wasn't on their menu of options – but by making themselves rougher and tougher instead.

Harry imagined they would have done this anyway, because it seemed to him to be a thing that certain kinds of working-class men just did, like spitting, or riding a push-bike ironically with your legs splayed open as if to make space for your enormous balls. But he felt sure all the same that they were laying it on extra thick because of his presence. They could tell he was better off and better-educated than them and higher in social rank, and they felt the need to even the balance.

The funny thing was that it actually worked. That middle-class fear of inauthenticity, that anxiety about being so refined as to have lost all contact with the solid earth, meant that he was actually quite vulnerable to these men's habitual posture of rough, blokeish masculinity. He found them very limited as company, he was quickly bored by what they had to say, but just as Michelle had seemed small in the Tate Modern, here in Kath's former council house in Breckham, Harry felt small.

'Yeah, I know,' Harry said. 'Norwich aren't doing that well at all lately, are they? But you know how it is, I was born in Norwich and I've supported the Canaries since I was a kid, so I'm kind of stuck with them, aren't I? What's your team, Trevor?'

'Me? West Ham, mate! West Ham till I die!' A kind of sweaty defiance came into Trevor's voice as he spoke, and his eyes seemed to gleam, as if (as Harry sourly puts it later) 'loyalty to a football club really was a thing to be proud of, on some sort of continuum with, say, attacking an enemy machine-gun nest'.

Harry smiled. 'West Ham? That was an amazing goal Carroll scored a couple of weeks ago.'

Trevor shook his head, not to contradict Harry but rather to convey that he hadn't spoken with anything like sufficient vehemence. 'You don't get any better than Carroll. I don't care what anyone says. He's a proper, old-fashioned centre forward. He's bloody *brilliant!*'

'You blokes not planning to eat anything?' Michelle called out and Harry gratefully hurried over to the table to pile up a plate and open another can of beer. He hoped that this would also be an opportunity to get into conversation with the women, preferably *instead* of the men, or at least *as well* as them. Jules seemed lively and bright and he knew that Michelle was especially fond of her, and though Kath and Michelle's sister Jen didn't offer very exciting conversational prospects, they would certainly be more relaxing company than Trevor.

But it seemed that Trevor had latched on to him. 'This fucking government's a joke, isn't it?' he said, moving into place in front of him. He tore off a chunk of chicken and washed it down with a swig of beer. 'They're just taking the piss.'

'I'm not a fan of them myself,' Harry offered carefully, not certain what aspect of the government's behaviour Trevor was referring to.

'The British people have spoken,' Trevor said, 'and their job is to get on and do what we fucking told them to do.'

'They're taking their time about it, aren't they?' said Charlie's dad Ken, who had piled up his plate and come to join the other men.

'We should have been out by now,' Charlie chipped in. 'It's doing my head in, to be honest.'

Oddly, and slightly menacingly, Trevor was grinning. 'They're dragging their feet on purpose. They're traitors to the British people, if you want my opinion. We ought to line them up and shoot the lot of them.'

'Too bloody right,' said Charlie.

'Well, I have to say I voted Remain,' Harry said.

Ken and Charlie glanced uneasily at one another. Trevor roared with laughter.

'You should see your face, Harry!' he guffawed, giving Harry a friendly pat on the arm. 'Don't look so worried, mate! I'm not going to shoot *you*! You're allowed to vote for whatever you want. It's a free country. And if you'd won, well, fair enough, that would be it. But your side lost, didn't they? And our side won.'

'I think the government accepts that, but the detail of it is really quite—'

'Detail!' Trevor was still grinning. 'Don't give me *detail*! That's just an excuse, mate. Just *leave*! Just fucking *leave* and get it over with. That's what people voted for.'

'I just think it's a bit more complicated than—'

Jules came to offer them the plate of chicken thighs. 'You're not going on about Brexit *again*, Dad? Sorry, Harry, he's completely obsessed with it!'

'No worries. Most of my friends are, too!'

Jules laughed. 'We'll all be glad when it's over, eh?'

And to Harry's dismay, she moved away again.

TWENTY-SEVEN

In the morning, Michelle and Harry took Pongo for a walk in the forest.

Michelle was uneasy. She'd seen the strain on Harry's face the whole of the previous evening, and she'd been forced to see her family through his eyes: Jen passive and pathetic, her brother loutish and overbearing.

'I'm sorry Trevor had a go at you about Brexit. He's like a dog with a bone once he gets going.'

Harry squeezed her hand. 'Don't worry about it. You should hear some of my friends.'

'Are they really as bad as that?'

'Just as bad but on the other side. Don't worry about it, Michelle.'

'Okay,' she said, but as she told her diary later, 'How could I *not* worry about it when I could see he was? He'd been tense in the party. He'd been tense in bed afterwards. And he was still tense in the forest the next day, even though he was trying to cover it up. It was obvious what he was thinking. He was thinking what a bunch of peasants we are, and did he really want to be a part of a family like ours.'

'Trev's heart's in the right place,' she said.

Harry smiled and nodded but didn't answer and Michelle wondered whether it was really even true, that thing about Trevor's heart that she and her mother and sister always repeated. Trevor wasn't an actively malicious person, it was true, but he was a self-centred, narcissistic man, who treated women like servants, and fell out with them when they showed signs of having an agenda of their own, a man who thought he was entitled to strong opinions about things he knew nothing about, with little self-awareness, and almost no interest in the contents of other people's heads.

A hawk soared above them, slipping sideways in the wind, under a heavy grey sky.

'He *is* really thick, though,' Michelle said.

Harry laughed. 'He's not the sharpest pencil in the box, I can see, but that's not a crime. Some people are brighter than others and an awful lot of people aren't very bright at all. That's just how it works. It doesn't have anything to do with whether you're a good or bad person. I know some very bright people who are absolute shits.'

'No, it hasn't got to do with whether you're a good or bad person. Mum isn't that bright either, but she's the kindest, gentlest person I know.'

'She does seem nice,' Harry said – but without great enthusiasm, Michelle couldn't help noticing, and she saw through his eyes an anxious downtrodden little old woman with very fragile self-esteem and almost no interests apart from her ornaments and her cats and her grandchildren.

'And who am I kidding?' she thought. 'It's not really a case of seeing her though Harry's eyes at all. It's me being forced to see things I'd see myself if I hadn't made up my mind not to notice them.'

'And Jen's nice too,' Harry said after a few seconds, perhaps realizing that if he didn't volunteer opinions of his own, he'd put Michelle into the position of having to list her family members one by one.

'Ken and Charlie seem like nice chaps too,' he added. 'Charlie seems to take after your mum. Very gentle.'

Lumbering along ahead of them, Pongo paused to sniff something and cock his leg over it.

'He *is* gentle,' she said. 'It's funny. He collects army medals and he's fascinated by war and all of that, but he wouldn't hurt a fly.'

'And of course Jules is delightful,' Harry said. 'Not least because she looks a lot like you. I gather she's starting university next September.'

They were walking past Michelle's favourite spot by that grassy clearing, where she liked to sit and think and have a smoke. She wondered whether to point her tree out to him, but decided against it. What could it possibly mean to him, after all, or to anyone else except for her? It was just one more tree like all the others, at the edge of patch of a grass. And so Harry walked by it with no inkling that he'd been in the presence of a kind of holy place.

'Mum *is* kind and gentle,' she said. 'But my dad treated her like shit. Funny thing is, she misses him horribly. It's five years since he passed and she really hasn't got over it. We all try and look after her. She'd do anything for us, absolutely anything! If you needed an outfit for school or something, she'd stay up all night. But I was horrible to her when I was a kid. All the things my dad said, I'd say to her as well. And if she asked me to do something and I didn't fancy it, I'd just ignore her. I'd walk away from her and do whatever I wanted, and bloody Dad would back me up. I must have made her life absolutely fucking miserable.'

'But that's normal,' Harry said. 'I was mean to my parents, too. Teenagers are like that.'

'I suppose so.' They'd been walking separately but she reached for his hand. 'So . . . ' she said. 'What do you think, Harry? Do you think you could cope with them?'

'Your family? Yes, of course I could. They're good people.'

She looked up at him, studying his face sceptically. She'd noticed that, throughout this conversation, he'd been putting on a cheerful voice that was slightly too bright and positive to be real.

'It was lovely to meet them, Michelle,' he repeated, turning to look at her and almost managing to rid his voice of that artificial brightness. 'I haven't got such a big family, of course, but I've spoken to Ellie about you meeting up with her and Phil and the boys. My nephew Nathan's rock group is doing a big gig in a couple of weeks and she suggested we go and see them with her and Phil, then go on and have something to eat afterwards. How does that sound? I've seen Nathan's band before and they're actually pretty good.'

She nodded. 'It sounds great. I just hope they like me more than you liked my family.'

He stopped and turned to face her. They were surrounded by birch trees and bracken laced with spider's webs.

'I *did* like them, Michelle. I wouldn't want to spend all my time with them, I admit. We haven't got enough in common. But then I wouldn't have wanted to spend all my time with Janet's family either. I *definitely* wouldn't, in fact. Her parents are really hard work and always have been. But that doesn't matter, does it? I don't have to be with your family all the time, do I? It's you I want to be with, and we get on fine, don't we?'

She slipped her arms round him under his coat. 'You know when you said you'd like us to have a baby? Did you really mean that? Or was it just a nice thought at the time?'

'I *completely* meant it, Michelle! I can't think of anything I'd like more than to make a baby with you.'

She glanced downwards for a moment, and then looked back up at him and laughed. 'You like the idea of *making* a baby with me, Harry, I can certainly tell that. But would you really want to live with me, and have my mum as your kid's gran, and Trevor as their uncle?'

He looked down at her in silence for a moment, and it seemed to Michelle that the fondness in his eyes flickered for a moment, like an electric lamp flickers when it's got a faulty connection to the mains. It struck her that most of the time when he looked at her, he clothed her in his mind with a certain idea of who she was that he felt he loved, but in those moments when the light flickered, she turned back into a stranger.

And then it happened to her as well. She saw *him* as a stranger: a slightly weak man, full of insecurities, who didn't quite have the confidence to make a decision as to who he was and then stick to it. What did they really have in common?

'We're not strangers any more,' Harry insisted, as if he could hear her thoughts. 'I know you. I don't just know what you look like and how you behave when you want me to like you. I've seen . . . I don't know how to say it . . . I've seen the challenge which life has set you. I know what shape it is and how you battle away at it and won't let it go. Of course I want to live with you. Of course I want to be your baby's dad.'

'Where would we live?'

Harry kissed her. 'We'll come up with something.'

'Do you really think so?'

'Why not?'

She studied his face. 'It's a bit mad talking like this, isn't it? I mean, it's not even two months since we went out for lunch in that pub.'

'But we're in the middle of our lives. We haven't got time to hang around. I really love you, you know. I've loved you pretty much from the first time we met.'

'But, Harry, you've said that and taken it back, and then said it again and taken it back again. I'm not calling you a liar. I know you mean it when you say it, and when you mean it, it's lovely. But I wonder if you can really see me or just an idea of me you have in your mind.'

'Well, can you really see me?'

He seemed to assume that her answer would be yes. ('It's because we can't see our own faces,' she thought. 'It's hard to believe that people can't just look straight into our heads.') In fact, she could tell he'd asked the question on that assumption, so he could say it was the same for him and then that would settle it.

But she didn't say yes. 'I don't know,' she told him. 'That's the truth. We're different, aren't we? There are loads of things about each other we don't understand. We both like that in a way –us being different, I mean – but at the same time . . . '

She removed her arms from around him to look around for Pongo, who turned out to be a few yards behind them, sniffing gloomily at the dry and flattened remains of some kind of bird. She called him away from it and they carried on walking.

'The way I see it,' Harry said, 'is that you have to make our own truth. I mean, okay, I don't know everything about you, but then I don't know everything about me either. If you had to know everything about a person first, well, no one would ever love anyone, would they?'

She didn't answer him. From behind the trees to the west of them she could hear a plane warming up its engines over at the American airbase.

'I mean, for example,' Harry persisted, 'when you have a baby, all you've got to go on at first is that little squirming, wheezing thing that can't even focus its eyes. You can't know what kind of person it will be, but you love it anyway, don't you? Not because you know it, but because it's lovable, and you'll love it no matter what. And I do know things about you, I know lots of things, but I also love you because you're lovable and that makes me want to know you better.'

He looked down at her, smiling. It all sounded a bit elaborate to her, but he seemed to have convinced himself.

From over at the base the engine sound surged up into a roar, then subsided, then surged again.

TWENTY-EIGHT

'That woman thinks we're spying on her,' I say to Cally. 'Let's talk to her and explain what we're doing.'

We walk in through the gate of the camp. We're very aware of everyone watching us. Imagine a tribe, I think, that could never have a leader of its own, because any leader it produces at once becomes part of the tribe of leaders. Of course, Cally and I don't think of ourselves as leaders at all, but that's how people here see us all the same. We might only be Level 3 Associates of the Guiding Body, but we're still part of the Guiding Body as far as they're concerned.

'I could see you looking worried,' I say to the woman. 'But there's no need. We're not checking up on you or anything. It's just that my friend and I are interested in history. I've been reading about some people who used to live here long ago in the twenty-first century, and we thought we'd try to find the spot. I apologize if we've made you uneasy.'

She relaxes a little. 'I didn't know the camp was that old!'

'It wasn't a camp back then,' Cally tells her. 'There was a tall apartment block standing right where your place is, and other blocks all around it. Look, I'll show you a picture of it.'

She passes her screen to the woman, who hesitates before taking it from her but then spends a long time looking down at it in silence.

'The people who lived here must have been very rich.'

'They were pretty rich.'

'Were they Chinese?'

'No, this was long before the Protectorate.'

The woman's little girl comes out again to look at us, insinuating herself into the space beside her mother, and slipping her small hand in hers. Her mother shows her Cally's screen. People nearby are watching us, some frowning, some with puzzled smiles, brushing the flies from their faces from time to time. An elderly man who's been leaning in the doorway of the shack next door turns and says something to whoever's inside, and out rushes a cheerful little boy of four or five. The old man looks as if his background is mainly European, but the boy has light brown skin, a round face and somewhat oriental features.

The boy stops just short of us, his expression suddenly wary, as if we had some kind of force field around us that it was dangerous to enter. He passes his hand over his face to get rid of flies. 'Who are those ladies, Auntie Jane?' he asks the woman, who's still holding Cally's screen.

Some children who've been playing further up the track come closer to listen and find out what's going on.

'They came here specially to see where we live, Georgie,' Jane says. 'They're interested in someone who used to live here a long time ago. But it wasn't a camp then, look. There were big glass towers.'

She shows the picture to the boy, who makes loud impressed noises, and then Cally offers the screen around for other people to look at – rather trustingly, I think, since one of them could easily run off with it into the camp, and there'd be no way of getting it back.

'Here's a picture of what one of those apartments looked like inside,' she says, when the screen has been returned to her. 'Oh, by the way, my name's Cally and my friend here is Zoe.'

Crowding round, adults and children digest in silence the spacious room depicted in an estate agent's brochure, the small potted tree, the elegant furnishings, and, in a shot taken at night, the shining city beyond the plate-glass window.

'Bit different from now,' Jane says.

'Would it be too nosy of me,' I say, 'to ask if I can see what it's like in your place now?'

The woman looks troubled and Cally frowns at me. *What gives us the right,* her expression says, *to barge into these people's houses just because we're curious?* But Jane consents. 'Well, you'd have to take it as you find it.'

'Oh, you should see my flat!' I tell her. 'At least your place doesn't smell of mud and eels.'

Such comparisons are hollow, of course. My flat may be damp but I have two rooms to myself in a properly constructed building. This is a single-room structure lit only by the light coming through the doorway and the cracks in the walls and it's constructed of a mixture of planks of wood and pieces of plastic of the kind that people dig up from old landfill sites. The only decoration is one of these sentimental pictures of Jesus that you sometimes see in poor homes, framed by a ring of Chinese dragons.

A very frail old man lies on a couch in one corner, staring at the ceiling with pink, watery eyes. In the opposite corner are two mattresses with blankets on them, where an old woman sits hunched against the wall. There is a sour smell of stale sweat and urine. A baby is crawling on the worn carpet that covers the middle of the floor and a younger man is sitting in an old armchair in the middle of the room with his head tipped back and his eyes closed. He looks absolutely worn-out but he jumps to his feet when he realizes that we're strangers. Jane laughs, explains who we are and tells him he should have a look at Cally's screen. He duly looks, but he really isn't interested. He says he works on the flood defences out on the estuary and that a boat comes every day to fetch him. It's obvious he just wants us to leave so he can close his eyes again.

When we go back outside, even more people have gathered. Our visit would be a novelty, after all, even if we weren't carrying pictures of the towers that used to stand here. Cally and I shake proffered hands and explain over and over who we are and why we've come. To us, of course, our presence here is the result of nothing more than a whim and it's troubling to see what a very big deal it is for them. Some of the adults, learning that we're interested in history, tell us bits and pieces they've learnt themselves about the camp in days gone by. None of it goes back more than a generation. It's almost as if they can't quite grasp how long ago it was that Harry and Michelle were alive in this world.

Cally and I are beginning to enjoy the feeling of being the centre of attention, when suddenly the mood of the people around us changes completely. They all fall silent and straighten up, looking past us at something on the riverside track. A long black car is approaching from the west, pedestrians parting to let it through. The only sound it makes is a faint crunching noise as its eight fat tyres move up and down to accommodate the many gaps and potholes in the metalled surface. The windows are tinted but, as it comes alongside us, we can see that there are three people inside: a single passenger in the spacious compartment in the back, a driver, and next to the driver a bodyguard in goggles. On the driver's door is stencilled a white nine-pointed star.

TWENTY-NINE

Nathan's band was playing in a large pub about a mile away from Richard and Karina's flat, and now just part of the rubble beneath the Vauxhall Camp. There was a kind of hall at the back that was used for performances. There were no seats and it was rather bare, not this time in the artful self-consciously industrial manner, but simply because it was functional, like a *real* industrial site. When Harry and Michelle arrived, Ellie was already there. Phil and Josh were helping with the transport for the band.

'It's lovely to finally meet you, Michelle. I gather you've got a hairdressing business in Breckham?'

'That's right. We do nails and facials as well. Doesn't seem a lot when I think about what you must have to do.'

'Actually, you'd be surprised how routine most of a GP's work is,' Ellie told her. 'The same half-dozen things over and over, most of the time. To be honest, a lot of the people who come to me don't really need medical help at all. They're often just lonely, or sad, or worried, and want to talk to someone.'

'It's the same with us!' Michelle felt herself relaxing just a little. 'Loads of our ladies come in to have their nails done or refresh their highlights, when all they really want is a chat. My partner Cheryl has a moan about it sometimes. "This isn't a counselling service!" she says when she thinks I've given someone too much time. She likes to think she's this hard businesswoman, but really she does it too. Truth is it would be a pretty boring job otherwise. Plus we'd lose half of our customers.'

'Well, what could be nicer than talking things over with someone while they stroke your head or your hands?'

'It *is* relaxing. We've got one lady who always falls asleep in the middle of a treatment. Bless her. It happens every single time! She's *so* full of worries, I reckon she must be absolutely exhausted most of the time. But she always leaves us with a smile.'

Michelle asked Ellie about her sons.

'And Harry tells me you had a little girl,' Ellie said, after she'd talked a bit about Nathan and Josh, 'but you lost her, just like he lost his Danny.'

'Yeah. I think it was what brought us together in a way.'

'What was Caitlin like?'

Michelle writes later about how touched she was that Ellie thought to ask her about Caitlin in just the same way as she would have asked about a child who was still alive. It meant she could be a mother again for a little while and talk about her daughter, not as a calamity, but just as a person. 'She was lovely, but I suppose every mum says that. She was kind and funny and really smart. I used to think she might end up as a doctor like you. Playing hospitals with her dolls was one of her favourite games. You should have heard the way she bossed them around.'

'So how are you getting on with my dozy brother?' Ellie asked when they'd talked about Caitlin for a while.

Michelle slipped an arm round Harry's waist. 'Well, he overthinks every single bloody thing, but apart from that . . . '

'God yes, tell me about it! Every single thing! Oh, by the way, I should mention, there's a change of plan, I hope that's okay. Instead of going out for a meal after, we're going back to Richard and Karina's to eat. They're the parents of one of the other boys in the band. Richard's daughter's going to come along as well.'

Having begun to relax a little, Michelle felt her anxieties soar. More people. More people to feel outnumbered by.

'The food will be brilliant, anyway,' Harry said, squeezing her hand. 'Karina writes about food for a living.'

'Oh fuck, not Karina Stoke?'

'Yeah, that's right. Have you heard of her?'

'Well, she was on *MasterChef*, wasn't she? It's my sister's favourite programme.'

MasterChef was a TV cookery contest that took place, like the dance show *Strictly*, over a number of weeks, with contestants eliminated in each episode. In the later stages of one of the show's several formats, the surviving competitors had to prepare three-course meals which they served up, as if to customers in a restaurant, to a group of three food writers. When the anxious contestant had left them, the writers would be shown tasting the various dishes. They would wave their forks around expressively while their mouths were still full, as if trying to semaphore their verdict in advance, and then, when it was decorous to do so, they'd comment in an articulate and amusing way on the merits or otherwise of the food. Part of their role (or so it seems to me) was to model a certain kind of urbane sophistication to which their viewers might aspire, for, as well as being food experts, the participants were accomplished social performers, able to marry rather elaborate manners and prestige language with acerbic wit and taste.

'*MasterChef*?' Ellie, like her brother, watched very little TV. 'Do you know what, I believe she was?'

'Oh my God, Jen will go *mental*. She loves that show! I can't believe you didn't tell me you knew someone who'd been on it, Harry!'

'I didn't know to be honest,' Harry said. 'I knew about her column in the *Guardian* and her cookery books, but I honestly didn't realize she'd been on TV.'

Michelle was filled with dread now. She was with people who were so comfortable with the idea of having a friend on the TV that they didn't even mention it, barely even knew about it even, and now she was going to have to spend the evening with the beautiful TV celebrity herself. They would all see through her, she was certain. They would see her smallness, her ordinariness. It would be like one of those dreams when everyone can see you're naked but pretend they don't notice, and there's nowhere you can go to get away from them to pull on some clothes. She rummaged in her bag. She sometimes had a cigarette in there because she occasionally mixed tobacco in her spliffs, and she thought it would calm her nerves. But there was no cigarette, only the little packet of cannabis, which would very definitely make things worse.

Phil arrived then with Nathan and Josh. Polite middle-class boys, they shook hands and said, 'Nice to meet you, Michelle,' to their uncle's surprisingly attractive girlfriend, before Nathan headed off to join his bandmates and Josh found the friends he would spend the evening with. Phil was a little stiff and shy with Michelle, and started to talk to Ellie about Josh's plans for the evening.

As the place filled out, conversation became difficult in any case and the four adults, clutching their drinks, couldn't share much more than short, simple sentences, while the voices of the animated young people all around them merged into that strange loud babble that human speech becomes in aggregate – restless and yet steady, smooth and yet agitated, meaningless and yet unmistakably charged with purpose. As time went on there were regular interruptions in the form of crackly and almost incomprehensible announcements from the stage from various excited young men and women who were rather obviously enjoying their position of prominence. Michelle had finished her glass of white wine, and Phil went to fetch another round.

Richard arrived, radiating intelligence and energy, along with Greg and Richard's tall and beautiful daughter Lucy with her red hair and her fierce appraising eyes. Karina was with them too, also tall, also beautiful, and looking just like she did on TV, with the same dauntingly posh voice and the same patrician confidence.

'Lovely to meet you, Michelle!' Karina's eyes narrowed as she regarded the small hairdresser from Breckham, or so, at least, Michelle imagined.

'It's amazing to meet you, Karina,' she gabbled. 'My sister Jen loves *MasterChef*. I'll have to do a selfie of us to prove I really met you or she won't believe me.'

She knew at once that she'd said the wrong thing because Karina's smile became strained and weary.

'Well, I was only on the show a few times,' Karina said, 'so I doubt your sister will be that impressed!' And she turned to Ellie to say hello and speak about something else.

Phil arrived with the drinks. Michelle downed her second glass of white wine in a few gulps.

After various technical problems had been resolved, the band – it was called Dark Matter – assembled on the stage. Nathan was on guitar at the front, Greg was on keyboards, and there was another boy on drums and a girl who played bass, saxophone, electric violin and sometimes a second keyboard. They were rather nervous, and, in place of his earlier attentive politeness, Nathan was now affecting a nonchalance so extreme that when he thrashed out the smudgy chords that began the first song through the pub's ageing speakers, it was as if he could hardly be bothered to play at all.

It wasn't great music for dancing, but people tried. Ellie went at it with enthusiasm, and drew Michelle in with her. Michelle liked dancing and was good at it, and the two glasses of wine had helped her to relax a bit. Karina just undulated elegantly, Richard did his own peculiar dance on the spot, like a steam engine under power, Harry performed what he liked to think were stylishly understated moves, and Lucy danced gracefully, but very inwardly, with no eye contact with anyone at all.

When the song ended, Ellie and Michelle cheered and whooped. They were both working hard at building some kind of connection.

'They were three middle-class boys and a middle-class girl,' Harry writes later. 'The girl, Ellie told me, is the daughter of a composer and has a place next year at the Royal College of Music. Nathan and Greg shared the frontman role, which they performed in a kind of home-made proletarian argot, loosely based on an Estuary accent, in the time-honoured tradition going back to the Stones, and even before that for all I know, laden with glottal stops and smudged Ls and Rs. I wondered what Michelle thought about this. She'd heard

Nathan before he went on stage, after all, talking in his polite RP, yet now he'd slipped into a kind of pastiche of her own dialect. How did she feel about this act of cultural appropriation, this class equivalent of blackface? But if it bothered her, she showed no sign of it. She was slightly pissed already – it never took a lot – and she was concentrating with Ellie on loudly performing a shared good time.'

'Hello, Baker's Arms! How yer doing? All right?' Nathan yelled out, the T of 'all right' silent, the L and the R merged into a sort of W. Nathan had got over his original nerves, it seemed, and was now at home in his rock-star persona.

Greg began to play gentle arpeggios, having selected an almost harpsichord-like timbre for his instrument, and, as Nathan launched into a tender love song, his singing voice shifted into another accent again, American-tinged this time, mid-Atlantic, but still full of glottal stops so as to give it a rough, untutored vulnerability that was reinforced by a repeated double negative in the concluding line of each verse which he would never have used in everyday speech: 'There ain't nothing in my head but you!' he sang with a glottal stop for the final T in but. This kind of music was meant to be vernacular and unrefined. It just wouldn't work if you stood there sounding like your mother was a GP and your father was a professor of medieval history.

They played another song then, harsher and more political, about a popular uprising against the super-rich. 'You cut our money but you don't cut yours,' sang Greg at the keyboards. 'You send us off to fight in your endless wars,' screamed Nathan, pushing his guitar aside so he could contain the microphone with both hands, 'but we ain't gonna stand for it no more.' And again, Harry noticed the double negative which Nathan would never use in any other context, and the Ts lopped off from 'cut' and 'fight'. But Michelle didn't seem bothered at all.

Karina left early to go home and get the food ready. Richard and Lucy went to help Greg load his keyboard into the car and then drop him off somewhere where the band were going to spend the rest of the evening. Phil and Ellie had to do likewise for Nathan. So it was agreed that Harry and Michelle would make their own way to Karina and Richard's apartment.

'I'm too fucking pissed for this,' Michelle said.

'You're fine, dear. No more pissed than the rest of us.'

She took his arm.

'I wondered what you thought about Nathan switching out of his posh accent when he was on stage?' Harry said.

Michelle laughed. 'What do you mean, switch? He talked posh all the time. Just like you do. I can't believe Karina's been on *MasterChef* and you didn't even warn me!'

'Honestly, I didn't know. I've never seen *MasterChef* in my life.'

'I can't wait to tell Jen. She will be so—'

'Don't go on about it, though, Michelle. Karina knows she's been on TV. She doesn't need you to keep telling her.'

Michelle stopped dead. 'Oh God, Harry. It's happening again, isn't it? It's like in that art museum. You're ashamed of me.'

He put his arms around her. 'You know that's not true. You know I love you like you are.'

She was unyielding, as stiff in his arms as if she was a tailor's dummy. 'I shouldn't be here. I shouldn't have come.'

'Don't be silly, Michelle! Relax! Really and truly, you'll be absolutely fine.'

'That's not what you just told me, Harry. What you told me is that I can't relax, I've got to be careful what I say, because if I put one foot wrong, those people will look down on me. You might as well ask me to have a nice relaxing swim through a pool of crocodiles.'

'It's not like that at all. Listen, you know you drew that picture and I said how good it was and how that was a talent you could make something of? You had a go at me, remember? You told me that whether or not you had a talent for drawing made no difference to who you were. And you were quite right. What you said really made me think about how shallow it was to look at life as if it was all a big competition to notch up achievements and be as important as possible. All I'm saying now, Michelle, is that if you go over the top about Karina being on the telly, you'll be doing exactly what you told me off for. Do you see what I mean? I'm saying that if you think achievements aren't all that important, then act like they aren't! Hold your head up! Don't abase yourself. Be proud of being who you are.'

'I won't drink any more,' she decided. 'I've already had too much.'

'I'm sure you—'

'I wish I'd never come here. Ellie's lovely, but the rest of them . . . Well, I don't think Phil even likes me. And—'

'Oh, don't worry about Phil, Michelle. He's a typical boarding-school boy, that's all. He's a little bit afraid of pretty women until he gets to know them.'

'And as for Karina and Richard and Lucy. They looked right through me, like I was so thin and empty there was nothing here for their eyes to see. I feel absolutely fucking terrified.'

'Don't be. Ignore what I said. I can see I've made things worse and I'm really sorry, but I honestly didn't mean to. You're worth ten of them, dear one. You're worth a hundred of them. Just be yourself. Don't take any notice of my crap.'

She was still completely stiff in his arms. 'I won't ask her about being on TV.'

'No, *do* ask her! It's something to talk about, isn't it, and I'm sure she'll enjoy telling you. It must have been quite a big thing for her, I would have thought. It's not like she does it all the time.'

'But I thought you said —'

'I didn't mean you shouldn't ask. I just meant there was no need to get all excited about it.'

'So I can ask, but I have to pretend not to be impressed? Even though it was a big thing even for—'

'It doesn't matter, Michelle. It really doesn't matter. Just be yourself. Be proud of being yourself.'

THIRTY

One of the features of early twenty-first-century television food shows is the recurring trope of what might be called the fantasy dinner party. I've already mentioned the segment of *MasterChef* in which prominent food writers are served dishes by contestants as if in a restaurant, but there was another genre of cookery programme in which a celebrity chef was the star of the show and would cook a whole meal for the instruction and entertainment of the viewers. In such programmes the chef is often shown serving up the dishes that she or he has just prepared to a group of friends who are sitting round what is apparently the dining table in the chef's own home.

These scenes were in fact constructed in TV studios, but they were presented in such a way that viewers could imagine themselves to have been given a glimpse into the lifestyle of the successful and famous. So the setting, like the food itself, would be designed to suggest a combination of good taste with homely comfort, high status with ease and relaxation, the cosiness of the old with the sharpness of the fashionable and new. And, as with the food, there is about the whole package a certain kind of carefully constructed informality which appears casual but nevertheless manages to get everything just right. Each detail is very artfully placed to achieve a heightened carelessness that actual carelessness could not hope to reach.

The guests, often celebrities themselves, laugh and chat in this milieu of good food and fine wine served up in gracious surroundings. They're completely at home in the company of one of the nation's best-known chefs who, after all, is not to them a dauntingly famous person, but simply their friend and social equal. What is being offered to the viewers in these scenes and images is, in part, vicarious pleasure – they can enjoy imagining what it would be like to feel at ease at that mythical table, bantering elegantly with the assembled celebrities – but they are also being provided with a role model, something which, at least to some degree and insofar as their resources allow it, they can imitate, in the belief that what they're being taught is one of the elements of the refinement that separates the higher classes from the lower ones.

When she and Harry entered that glass apartment block beside the river, to be let through the security gate by the concierge and carried upwards in the glass lift with its views of the river and the city lights, it seemed to Michelle that she was actually being taken to one of those imaginary dinner parties. And when Richard opened the door of the flat, and she saw the amount of space in there, the elegant furnishings, the carefully chosen and understated colours, the tree in its pot in the little garden high above the world, and the enormous plate-glass windows with their views of the shining metropolis, these things only confirmed her feeling that she had entered a world that to her was almost mythical. Once they'd all gathered together in the dining room, all the essential features of the fantasy dinner party were in place: (1) Someone beautiful from the TV, (2) Confident and wealthy hosts with top-of-the-range accents, (3) A selection of confident and well-spoken guests who were familiar with the host and completely at ease in her company, (4) A large and beautiful dining room whose decor combined order with charming informality, (5) The food itself, which also combined artfulness with the particular kind of informality that is in fact a higher level of artfulness, like the apparently effortless brushstrokes of a great painter.

Of course, given time, she'd get used to it (as I'd get used to it if I was suddenly and unexpectedly elevated to full membership of the Guiding Body). Given time, she'd find out that, after all, a meal is still just a meal, and TV people are just people. But she wasn't used to it now. It was still magical. And it was impossible to relax and enjoy the experience because of her sense that she didn't belong here and that, in her nervousness and excitement, she'd make a fool of herself.

Over the starter, Richard and Karina, as hosts, engaged Michelle in polite conversation, asking her about her hairdressing business, and about the town of Breckham (which Richard somehow seemed to know a great deal more about than Michelle herself, having looked it up on his phone on his way home). Both of them, it seemed to her, were polite but distant. Trying to generate a less stilted conversation which they all could share in, Harry began to talk about the evening's performance, which kept things going for a while. And then Ellie said something to Michelle about wanting advice on her hair, at which point Richard disengaged immediately from the general conversation and began talking directly to Phil, Lucy and Harry about football, politics and the news.

Michelle, at least outwardly, had overcome her earlier panic. She asked Karina what it was actually like behind the scenes on

MasterChef and what the show's main judges were like as people, and was pleased to hear in her own voice a genuine grown-up curiosity rather than the giggly star-struck excitement that Harry had cautioned her about. And Karina, as Harry had said, was not a regular performer on television, and so was interested in her questions and seemed to enjoy talking about just how different a show like that was in real life to how it appeared on the camera. She explained that the room in which she and her fellow food writers had been served was not really a room at all. She said there were long waits while lighting or sound was adjusted, with the participants frequently being asked to repeat things they'd said until they came out sounding right, sometimes many times over, to the point that, on one occasion, they had ended up pretending to taste food that had gone almost completely cold. The end result was, Karina said, that what viewers imagined to be a continuous scene was in fact a collage assembled by the programme's editors from different moments in a constantly interrupted process: 'If you watch it on TV, it seems like a single conversation, but when you're actually there you realize you're just generating the raw material from which a sort of idealized conversation is going to be constructed by the editors.'

Ellie said something to Karina about how she and Michelle had discovered their jobs were actually much more similar than most people realized. Richard picked up on this somehow, and briefly paused in the middle of saying something to Phil about the rise of China as a global power to observe that, of course, surgeons and barbers had once been one and the same profession. But then he returned to China, while Karina asked polite questions about Shear Perfection and listened with such a show of interest that Michelle increasingly experienced it as a *performance* of interestedness, such as you saw when a politician or a member of the royal family was shown on TV listening to a member of the general public.

Richard gathered up plates and Karina went to fetch the main course. Michelle remembered a funny moment from the pub earlier and mentioned it to Ellie, which made them both laugh and then, emboldened by how well things seemed to be going, she leant across the table to ask Lucy what work she did. She hadn't stopped drinking after all.

THIRTY-ONE

The eight-wheeled car pulls up. The front doors open and the driver and the bodyguard climb out into the sticky grey heat of the London summer. Out over the river, seagulls shriek. The driver opens the rear door for the passenger, while the bodyguard keeps watch. She is a woman of about my age (and so a little older than Cally). Tall, lean and with curly hair cropped short, she's wearing one of those grey Mao suits that, with their connotations of thrift and seriousness of purpose, have recently come into fashion in the upper echelons of the Guiding Body. In terms of facial type, she has quite fair skin and Mediterranean, or perhaps South Asian, features. She takes a white cloth from her pocket and wipes it over her brow.

'Good evening, everyone!' she calls out to the inhabitants of the shacks as she approaches the gate. She wrinkles her nose and waves her hand in front of her face to drive away the flies. Behind her the bodyguard scans the scene with his goggled eyes, like a radar sweeping the sky.

'Evening, madam,' mutters the little group that has gathered round myself and Cally.

'I hope you've all had a good day?' asks the woman in the Mao suit.

Yes, they say, they have, and their hands sweep away the flies.

'Excellent. I've been having a look at the flood defences along here. All very impressive. I expect some of you work on them, don't you?'

'Yes, madam, I do,' says Jane's husband, who has come out of the shack holding the baby.

'You're doing a fine job,' says the woman in the Mao suit, 'and we're very grateful to you.'

Jane's husband bows his head very slightly in minimal acknowledgement of the compliment. From inside the shack comes the sound of the old woman wailing. 'Jane? Where are you? Jane? Jane?' Two parrots fight noisily in the ditch.

'Why's that car got a star on it?' asks Jane's little bare-bottomed girl.

Her father shushes her, but the woman in the Mao suit laughs cheerfully. 'Well, I wonder if we can figure it out together. How many points does that star have, my dear?'

The girl hides her face in her father's grubby trouser leg and won't say, but the little boy from next door counts out the points out with gusto. '*Nine!*' he shouts triumphantly.

'Jane!' wails the old woman inside the shack. 'Jane? Jane? Where are you?'

'Nine indeed,' the woman from the car says, 'and do you know why it's nine?'

'No!' Georgie shouts with the same vigour as before, apparently every bit as pleased about his ignorance of the Guiding Body's emblem, as he is about his ability to count.

'It's to remind us of the Nine Principles, dear,' the woman says, brushing a fly from her face, which is now beginning to shine with sweat. 'I wonder if you can tell me what they are.'

The boy looks round at his grandfather in bewilderment and I sense all the adults shifting uneasily as it occurs to each of them that the woman may turn to one of them to list the nine wise, humane and rational principles that Hu Shuang distilled for us from the history of human thought.

The woman ruffles the little boy's hair. 'Never mind, dear. Time enough to learn. They *are* very important, though. They show us all how to live happier lives and free ourselves from ignorance and superstition.' Her eyes narrow slightly as they alight on myself and Cally – no doubt she's wondering who we are and what exactly we're doing here – but she doesn't linger on us for more than a second. Her bodyguard's goggles will have identified us and recorded our presence, so she can check us out later on at her leisure if she feels like doing so. She could even look into our screens and see what we're working on.

'I won't keep you,' the woman says to the little crowd. 'I'm sure you all have lots to do. I just wanted to thank you for the work you're doing along the Thames here in London and down at the estuary to protect us all from floods, and to increase food production. We do notice, I promise you, and we really are all very grateful!'

She glances for a moment in our direction – what *are* women like me and Cally doing among folk like these? – and then turns back to her car.

THIRTY-TWO

Eight storeys up from Jane's shack, and 250 years earlier, Richard, Lucy and Phil started on Brexit. The three of them had pretty much abandoned any attempt at general conversation and Harry had turned his attention to Michelle, Karina and Ellie. But during a brief lull, when Harry and the three women had finished one topic and were casting about for the next, Lucy happened to raise her voice at the other end of the table.

'The vote is irrelevant,' she was saying very firmly. 'Most people are economically illiterate and the decision was simply *wrong*. We need to stop beating about the bush and just say it. A vote doesn't make something true if the evidence shows it to be false. The referendum result should be set aside.'

To her own surprise Michelle responded. 'So votes only count if you agree with them, do they?'

Lucy looked across at her with her fierce, confident, intelligent eyes. Her father chewed on his lip.

'I read somewhere,' Lucy said, 'it may be apocryphal, that the state of Indiana once tried to make a law setting the value of pi at 3, in order to simplify mathematical—'

Michelle scrunched up her face. 'The value of pie?'

Lucy glanced at her father and, just barely perceptibly, she sighed, as if, just by asking the question, Michelle had made her point for her. 'Well, okay, let's use another example. Suppose someone wanted to make a law to say that a circle was the same thing as a square, and suppose they won a referendum in support of that. Would that make it true?'

'Oh, come on, Lucy,' Harry said. 'That's not a fair comparison at all. Even if some of the claims made by the Leave side were untrue that doesn't mean that wanting to leave the EU isn't valid. There are loads of imponderables. How large and how porous can a community be before it stops being a community at all? How wide is it possible to make a pyramid before the top loses all sight of the bottom? There's no incontrovertible answer to these things! People are—'

But Michelle interrupted him. 'So you lot should make the laws about the important stuff, is that right? And just leave the easy stuff for us chavs?'

Lucy shrugged. 'I'm sorry, Michelle, but that's just silly. It's not a question of "our lot" or "your lot". It's a question of what is factually correct.'

'And who decides that, then?'

'I think anyone can, can't they?' Phil suggested. 'But they need to look at the evidence.'

'We were lied to in the referendum, Michelle,' Karina said very gently. 'We really were. We were told it would be easy. We were told we'd get back three hundred and fifty million pounds to spend on the—'

'Oh, for fuck's sake!' Michelle interrupted her. She had preferred Lucy's contempt to this. 'What do you think we are, Karina? *Babies?*

Of *course* people lie in elections. They all promise everything's going to be different and it never is. Everyone knows that.'

'That's true,' Harry said. 'I mean, we all love Obama, don't we, but he promised he'd shut down Guantanamo Bay, and eight years later it's still—'

Michelle dismissed him with a wave of her hand. 'What *really* pisses me off is that you lot seem to think none of us had any opinions before all this. Do you actually think we were just sitting there thinking about nothing at all until that red fucking bus came around?'

'I work in the City,' Richard said. 'My job is looking at risk. I make a lot of money because I'm very good at it. And I'm telling you that leaving the EU will be a disaster. That's not an opinion, it's a fact.'

'How do you know until you've tried?' Michelle said.

'How do we know we'll get wet if we go out in a rainstorm?' Phil said.

Lucy sighed. 'Well, okay, let's start with supply chains. We've been part of the EU for forty years and our economy is closely integrated with Europe's. A large proportion of British manufacturers have factories all over the Continent, and they depend on frictionless borders to be able to shift components back and forth between one factory and another precisely when they're needed. Put in tariff barriers and customs checks, and their costs will go up. And since they have to compete against the rest of the world, those additional costs will make it harder, and in many cases impossible, to stay ahead of the game. So they'll have no choice but to close down the parts of their operation that are now in the UK and move them across the Channel, which means that people will be put out of work. It really isn't rocket science.'

Lucy shrugged. Those were the facts and Michelle could take them or leave them. She'd be perfectly happy to go back to talking to Phil and Richard if Michelle preferred not to engage with them.

But Michelle's bloodstream was full of adrenalin and ethanol, and she had no intention of leaving it there. 'We've got through worse, haven't we?' she persisted.

Richard and Phil exchanged glances. ('We've got through worse' was an emerging theme on the Leave side which the Remain side found particularly exasperating.)

'You mean, like the Blitz?' Lucy said, glancing round the rest of the company with a small knowing smile. 'Or Dunkirk, or the Great Depression? Sure. But nobody voted for those things to happen, did they? It's not as if the Germans said, "We're thinking of firebombing London, how do you feel about that?" and we held a referendum and told them it was fine and they should go ahead.' Again she shrugged. 'Look, we probably won't starve after Brexit, I'll give you that. But so what? Why would anyone choose to do something that will manifestly make things worse?'

'Because they don't agree it will make things worse,' Michelle suggested.

Lucy made an exasperated noise and turned away.

'It *will* make things worse,' Richard said. 'It will make things worse, period.' Presumably unconsciously, he had dialled up his voice to the poshest register available to him. 'I'm sorry if you don't like it but it's just a fact. Like the fact that you'll get burned if you put your hand in a flame.' He shrugged. 'I mean, if you want to run after unicorns, be my guest. But there's no point in even talking about this if we can't base our discussion on some kind of—'

'Michelle *is* your guest, Richard,' Harry told him. 'How about you treat her that way?'

'Harry's quite right,' Karina said. 'You need to apologize.'

Richard chewed on his lip for a second, then nodded. 'I apologize, Michelle,' he said, though he was barely managing to suppress a shrug. 'I have strong feelings about this as you can tell, but I shouldn't have made it personal.'

'Don't worry about it,' Michelle said and Harry was surprised by how calm she seemed. 'I'm used to it. You should see my brother when he gets going.'

Karina laughed. 'Maybe we should put your brother and Richard together and leave them to it! Why don't you clear the plates, Richard? I'm just going to check the dessert and we can perhaps have it in about ten minutes.'

Richard stood to stack the crockery with his big red paws. Lucy got up to help him and they both withdrew to the kitchen with Karina. Harry squeezed Michelle's hand. 'You did really well there.'

'You certainly did,' Ellie said. 'I never even *try* to argue with Richard.'

Michelle shrugged. She actually wasn't calm at all. She was just intensely focused, like a tightrope walker on a high wire. 'It wasn't a problem,' she said. 'When you're the baby of the family you get used to standing up for yourself.' She didn't remove her hand from Harry, but she didn't squeeze him back either, just let her hand lie limply in his until he chose to let it go. She could feel herself trembling, just like Kath used to tremble in the aftermath of one of her husband's blasts of sarcasm.

'Richard was out of order,' Harry said. 'And Lucy was too.'

'Don't worry about it,' Michelle said. 'I mean, I was pretty harsh with Karina, wasn't I?'

But she knew they could all see her trembling.

'I'm just going out for a minute,' she said.

'I feel badly about this,' Phil said when she'd left the room. 'Poor Michelle. It was wrong to gang up on her. We need to keep right off politics for the rest of tonight.'

'She actually has a point,' Harry said. 'People like us do tend to assume that, just because we know a lot, what we happen to want must be what's right for everyone.'

Phil smiled and gave the little sideways tip of the head that means, *I don't agree with you, but there may possibly be something in what you say.*

He asked Harry about his work, and whether he still wanted to have a change of career.

'No, not really,' Harry said. 'I think it was just that I was just aware of a hole in my life, and now . . . I wonder if Michelle's okay. I'll just go and check.'

Michelle had put on her coat and left the flat. She was waiting on the landing by the lift. The river glowed beneath them.

'Oh Michelle, don't go! Richard and Lucy were totally out of order, but they won't do that again, they really won't!'

She frowned at the button that summoned the lift, wondering if she'd pushed it correctly. 'They don't like me, Harry. You know that. They think I'm thick and ignorant and boring. Maybe they're right. But there's no point in my being here, is there?'

The lift arrived with a ping. The door slid open. She stepped inside and pushed the button for the ground floor.

'Please, Michelle!' He put his arm in the door and followed her into the lift. The brilliant city shone all round them as they descended.

'This isn't going to work, Harry,' she said as they passed the concierge's station. 'We need to end it now. You're a nice man but, like you said yourself, we haven't got time to keep on trying if we can see it's not really going to happen.'

'Michelle, I love you! I want to marry you! I want to have babies with you!'

'You like the idea of it, Harry, but you know I won't fit into your world.'

'*Fuck* my world!' he told her. 'Fuck them all. I don't even fucking *like* Richard and Karina and their ghastly stuck-up daughter! I don't even like my own tribe. If you don't want to live in London, that's fine. *I* don't want to live in fucking London. I'll come and live in Breckham instead!'

They were outside the building now at the top of a short flight of marble steps. The city hummed all around them. An emergency vehicle rushed along the north side of the river, its siren sounding, its light casting brilliant splashes of blue across the water, so that a solitary seagull flying just above the surface turned from shadowy silhouette to neon blue, and back to shadow again.

Michelle smiled and shook her head. 'Oh come on, Harry. You wouldn't last a week in Breckham. I saw how you were at my mum's. You looked like you were being very good and brave and grown-up while someone pulled your teeth out one by one. It's like you've always said: we come from two different tribes.'

*

Michelle started down the steps. She badly wanted to be alone so she could find somewhere dark and quiet to sit down and work out what to do next. She was full of tears, but she was determined not to let them out until there was no one there to see them.

There were late trains, she supposed. If she got a move on, she could be back home by the early hours.

'Please don't do this, Michelle,' Harry begged her. 'It really is completely crazy! We get on well together, you know we do.'

'You'll be all right, Harry,' she told him. 'I guarantee that in six months' time you'll be wondering what the fuck this was all about.'

THIRTY-THREE

The woman in the Mao suit climbs back into her eight-wheeled car and, having settled into her seat, she turns to the window to wave goodbye. Then her driver releases the brake and the vehicle begins to move off towards London, soundless but for the soft crunch of its tyres.

The people around us look at each other but remain oddly silent, glancing uneasily at Cally and me. There are things they'd be saying to each other, I realize, if there weren't two strangers present whose role they're unsure of, but whose allegiances are almost certainly different to their own.

'Chinky!' the little boy calls out after the car in his loud cheerful voice. Which seems a little ironic, given that his own features are quite definitely more Chinese than those of the woman in the back seat. But of course these days the word is not so much a racial epithet as a general-purpose term for members of the regime that our Chinese liberators helped to put in place.

The little boy's grandfather reproaches him, sharply, but a little theatrically, with an uneasy glance in our direction: not so much telling off the child, as performing the act of telling him off for our benefit. 'That's a bad word, Arnie. Your mother will be very angry with you.'

I shrug and smile to show that I'm not in the least troubled, and, thanking them for their time, Cally and I pass back out through the gate and on to the road along the riverbank.

We continue our walk along the edge of the camp. Parrots screech above our head. Boats pass by on the water. As we brush away the flies from our sweaty faces, Cally talks about the final stage of the battle, when the Liberal besiegers suddenly found themselves hemmed in by new Patriot fighters, and realized they were very close to defeat.

It was at this point that they struck the historic bargain under which Chinese forces would invade, establish a Protectorate, and then help them put in place the self-perpetuating Guiding Body of qualified, able and scientifically minded people that the Liberals now regarded as the correct way to govern a country. You can see why the Chinese found the idea congenial. The Guiding Body as an idea was really quite similar to what China's ruling Party had become, and it fitted well with Confucian notions of order and hierarchy that had been reintroduced in Shuang Hu's Great Synthesis.

After striking the agreement, the Liberal leadership withdrew all their forces from the area. Imagining that that they'd won, the Patriots celebrated in their towers, hanging out St George's flags and their own Three Lion emblem, until Chinese jets came in from the east, wave after wave of them, to pound the towers and their garrison into the expanse of rubble that formed the base of the huge refugee camp beside us.

'I suppose China was always going to back the Liberals in the end,' I say.

Cally's not so sure. 'They did have talks with the Patriots as well, you know. I wonder what things would have been like now if they'd taken the Patriot side?'

I'm about to answer when two armed militiamen stride out from the warren of the camp, so suddenly and unexpectedly that we both gasp. Their goggle eyes linger on us for a moment. They can see your heartrate if they want to. They can see where you've been over the past month, or year, or decade. They can call up a list of all the people you know. And they don't just see; they record as well. They're part of a unified system that, whenever you come to its attention, notes down where you are, who you're with, and all the various metrics that indicate your current emotional state, so that the next time a pair of goggles looks in your direction, or someone in authority chooses to look up your name, that new information will have been added to your file. It was the Chinese authorities' parting gift when they finally handed over to the Guiding Body.

The militiamen head east along the river. In subdued silence, we walk another kilometre in the opposite direction until we reach the first building to the west that wasn't destroyed by the Chinese onslaught. The paintwork is fading and most of the faces are barely visible, but on its east-facing wall is the faint remnant of one of those old stencilled murals from the days of the Protectorate. Charles Darwin, Marie Curie and Isaac Newton can just be made out looking down with wise serenity at the sprawling shanty town stretching away in front of them to the east and the south.

'Support the work of our Guiding Body!' they are saying. 'Study and apply the Nine Principles!'

'In answer to your question,' I say, 'it would have been absolutely awful if the Patriots won. They didn't really care for the poor; they just cynically exploited their tribal instincts for their own ends. So there'd be a ruling class living in comfort in gated areas, with the poor left to fend for themselves, and some sort of Chinese surveillance system watching over them to be sure of keeping them in their place. It really is too painful to contemplate.'

Cally laughs at this, and then she stops and takes my hand. Her eyes search my face for a moment, and then suddenly she pulls me against her and kisses me on the mouth.

ACKNOWLEDGEMENTS

particularly want to thank Sara O'Keeffe, who has been my editor since *Mother of Eden* but is now moving on to other things. She is very good at what she does and I will miss her.

I would also like to thank:

The copyeditor, Alison Tulett, for so skilfully decluttering my prose.

My friends Tony Ballantyne and Sarah Brown for reading and commenting on an early draft of this book.

My daughter Poppy who helped me think about Michelle's clothes.

My old schoolfriend Jonathan Charteris-Black – and his friend Paul Harley – for football advice.

John Jarrold for being my agent, and Kate Straker for working so hard on getting me and my books out there.

My friends Ian Pinchen, Peter Scourfield, Clive Seale, Pam Toussaint, David Howe, Rowlie Wymer and Alison Warlow for indulging me in long conversations about some of the topics of this book. Also my son Dom, for the same, as well as my daughter Nancy and my dear wife Maggie.

Chris Beckett, Cambridge, 2019

Read on for an extract from

TOMORROW

1 THE RIVER

Tomorrow I'm going to begin my novel. That's what I came here for. That's why I gave up my job and my apartment in the city. I was going to make up a story. There were going to be lots of imaginary people in it, and a beautiful wide green river – this river that's in front of me now, with its soft, cool, almost oily skin – and people would come in boats, like new cards dealt from a pack. It was going to be . . . But why am I saying 'was'? It *is* going to be like life, a microcosm of life, but more alive than actual life, so that people can read it and think to themselves, 'Of course, *this* is what life really is, and how wonderful this author must be to be able to see all that and communicate it to us.'

Tomorrow, then. Or if not tomorrow, then next week or, at the very latest, before the end of the month. I ought to get on with it, if only to avoid looking foolish when I return to the city empty-handed, but I have to admit that right now I find it hard to care about the opinion of my family and friends.

That's for another me to deal with. (The barriers we build between our present and future selves are important, I feel, just like the barriers we build between ourselves and others. Infinite empathy would be as bleak as no empathy at all.) And as to those imagined readers who are going to admire me . . . well . . . the truth is, isn't it, that I'm a fraud? What do *I* know about what life really is? What purpose is served by seeking the endorsement of people who don't know me, for an idea of myself that I know to be unreal?

But still. Tomorrow. Or next week, or certainly the week after, I'll make a start.

As the afternoon begins to cool and the swallows start to hunt over the water, I like to take a dip. It invigorates me. On my second day here I swam across to the opposite bank but the river is nearly half a kilometre wide, the current is challenging out in the middle and there were a few minutes there on the way back where I felt I'd lost control. So this evening I swim upriver. I watch the swallows on the way out and the bats in the dusk as the current carries me back. I turn round at a spot where a side channel flows in from a hot spring and there's a warm and steamy patch in the water.

When I return, I haul myself out by the big tree that grows right next to the cabin. Its leaves are the size of dinner plates, and its roots divide and divide again until they become strands as fine as human hair, bright red in colour, and spread out in the water to feed. I take a bottle of beer from the plastic crate I keep suspended in the river and sit on my veranda to watch the yellow moon as it rises from behind the trees on the far bank.

I have spent many hours on that veranda with its pleasant smell of river and sun-warmed wood. In fact, I've sometimes passed entire days there, just watching the water go by, the little dents and gradations on its surface, the bits of branch that drift down, the birds that cross from one side to the other, carrying nest materials or food. A few times a day, local people pass in their small boats, staring in at me, waiting for me to greet them before allowing themselves to wave or smile. Sometimes I smoke some weed – there's a plentiful supply in the overgrown plot behind my cabin – and from time to time I drink a beer, but most of the time I'm happy just to sit.

Because I *do* feel alive. This *is* what life is really like. This is what I so badly wanted to experience, even just in that extraordinarily remote, vicarious and fetishistic kind of way that consists of evoking it in my novel and then being told by others that I have created a vivid world for them. So why would I want to turn away from experiencing it directly, in order to stare at a white page and try to cover it with heavy, clumsy words? I imagine some gaunt starving man – why a man, though, and not a woman? – I imagine some gaunt starving woman laboriously writing out a fantasy for other people about a feast that would satisfy her hunger and theirs, while ignoring the large and delicious meal that's been laid out right in front of her.

That image makes me laugh.

There is no road to my wooden cabin. In these parts the river is the road. Today, Friday, as I do every Friday, I start up the outboard motor on my little boat and set off on the twelve-kilometre trip downriver to the modest-sized provincial seat. There's a kind of beach there where you can drag your boat out of the water. A tough-looking woman called Dido presides over the place with her three sons. She has one blind eye like a boiled egg. The other eye darts about, ensuring that nothing, however small, happens on her beach without her consent. She and her boys will watch over your boat for you for a small fee. I bought mine from her when I first arrived, fresh off the plane, unloading my cases and my box of provisions from the taxi, looking forward to seeing, for the very first time, my writing retreat up the river.

The town's main business is the onward shipment of products from the surrounding forest: latex, timber and certain minerals. Just downstream from Dido's beach the river turns sharply right to head east towards the sea, and there are docks with cranes to load and unload the barges that come up from the coast. The town has four banks, a produce market, a supermarket of sorts and (surprisingly) a fine, if modest-sized, cathedral in the Manueline style that would grace a much larger and more important city, and which makes me think, when I go inside, of a kind of coral, as if all of these elaborate columns and arches were the secretions of some sort of highly specialized polyp whose particular characteristic is that it quite naturally forms representations of . . . well . . . of something I vaguely feel I remember, as if from another life, or from that early period of childhood that everyone says they can't recall. (I think myself the truth is quite the opposite: we remember our experience of that time *so* well and *so* thoroughly that we just don't recognize it as a memory at all, but rather as the surface on to which all our subsequent experience is projected.)

A few streets from the cathedral there is a rather pleasant colonnaded promenade built more than two centuries later in the same pinkish, coral-like stone. Arranged in an elongated circuit like a Roman hippodrome, around a row of five fountains, the promenade was bequeathed to the city by a rubber millionaire who, having made himself rich by forcing indentured labourers to harvest latex for him for almost no pay at all, wished in his later years to be thought of as a good man, and so, along with a hospital and an orphanage, built this central meeting place that brings the whole town together. Some are inclined to sneer at the motives of a man like that. I am more cautious. We're all hypocrites. A common way of dealing with that is to loudly denounce the hypocrisy of others to distract attention from one's own, but isn't that hypocrisy squared?

In the middle of the central fountain stands a twice life-sized statue, not of the rubber millionaire, but of his friend, hunting partner and hero, the novelist Mago Barca, wearing what purports to be 'Carthaginian' armour, and staring boldly into the distance. The inscription below it comes from his novel, *Atlantis Rises*:

> *The Upper River is our nation's heart.*
> *Master it, and we will master the world.*

Large numbers of townspeople like to parade around this promenade in the cool of the evening wearing their best clothes. Others sit outside cafés watching them while small bats swoop and dive around the streetlamps. I have a friend called Amanda I sometimes meet here – we have a drink together, spend the night in her small apartment just up the road and return to the promenade in the morning to have breakfast in our favourite café – but today I buy what I need and, stopping only for a coffee and a pastry, return upriver at the end of the afternoon.

It's dark by the time I get back, but I keep a small blue light on the veranda to guide me to my mooring, its battery charged by sunlight during the day. When, after travelling for some while among dark, silent trees, I see it on the right-hand bank in the distance, a kind of happiness rises inside my heart that I feel I never experienced before I came here. This is what it feels like to come home.

It's only in the middle of the night that I worry about the precarity of my situation. Sometimes – and this was particularly the case in the first week or two – the thought that haunts me is that I'm all alone, and that at any point robbers, or guerrillas from any one of the dozen ragtag armies of the insurrection, or just impoverished locals with every reason to resent someone who has enough spare cash to take six months away from work, could arrive and do what they wanted with me. I lie and listen to the creaks and groans of my wooden cabin and the sound of the water, imagining small changes and odd silences, and piecing these together into very precise and specific images of enemies creeping towards me.

These days what haunts me more often when I wake at 2 a.m. is the thought that soon I'll have spent all my money, and then my time by the river will be over, and I'll have to return to the city and my old life, having not only failed to do anything constructive about building a new one, but having blown all the savings that I set aside for that purpose – and all of this will just be a small and shrinking memory, which, after a time, I will have to stop talking about to avoid boring people, but which I will idealize and fetishize for the rest of my life until nothing of the real experience is left, only a sense of a door, now beyond my reach, that I could have opened once but didn't. I'm already thirty-four, after all.

I can sometimes lie awake like this for several hours, appalled by my own lack of responsibility, yet in the morning

I shrug it all off without the slightest effort. For surely the matter is quite straightforward. If you have a choice between writing a novel and being a character in a novel, you've got to choose the latter, haven't you?

A character in a novel. That's exactly what I feel like. Smiling to myself, I make a pot of coffee and carry it out to the veranda.

DON'T MISS THE EDEN TRILOGY FROM CHRIS BECKETT

WINNER OF THE ARTHUR C. CLARKE AWARD

Chris Beckett is a former university lecturer and social worker. He is the winner of the Edge Hill Short Fiction Award, 2009, for *The Turing Test,* the prestigious Arthur C. Clarke Award, 2013, for *Dark Eden*, and was shortlisted for the British Science Fiction Association best novel award for *Mother of Eden* in 2015 and for *Daughter of Eden* in 2016. *Two Tribes* is his eighth novel.